Paul Turner returns. In ⸺⸺⸺ this gay Chicago detective and father of two sons gets caught in a tangle of intrigue and corruption. A brutal Chicago cop is found murdered at a gay leather festival. Turner, plus his police department partner, Buck Fenwick are assigned the case. Through a rising tide of danger, they need to find the truth among police corruption and cover ups. Some top cops and A-list leather queens are among those whose lies and fears drive the web of desperation and deceit that Turner and his partner must unravel.

MLR Press Authors

Featuring a roll call of some of the best writers of gay erotica and mysteries today!

Derek Adams	Z. Allora	Maura Anderson
Victor J. Banis	Jeanne Barrack	Laura Baumbach
Ally Blue	J.P. Bowie	Barry Brennessel
Michael Breyette	Nowell Briscoe	Jade Buchanan
James Buchanan	Charlie Cochrane	Karenna Colcroft
Jamie Craig	Kirby Crow	Ethan Day
Diana DeRicci	Jason Edding	Theo Fenraven
Angela Fiddler	S.J. Frost	Kimberly Gardner
Michael Gouda	Roland Graeme	Storm Grant
Amber Green	LB Gregg	Kaje Harper
Jan Irving	David Juhren	Kiernan Kelly
M. King	Matthew Lang	J.L. Langley
Josh Lanyon	Anna Lee	Elizabeth Lister
Clare London	William Maltese	Z.A. Maxfield
Timothy McGivney	Lloyd A. Meeker	Patric Michael
AKM Miles	Reiko Morgan	Jet Mykles
William Neale	Cherie Noel	Willa Okati
Neil S. Plakcy	Jordan Castillo Price	Luisa Prieto
Rick R. Reed	A.M. Riley	AJ Rose
Rob Rosen	George Seaton	Jardonn Smith
Caro Soles	JoAnne Soper-Cook	DH Starr
Richard Stevenson	Liz Strange	Marshall Thornton
Lex Valentine	Maggie Veness	Haley Walsh
Missy Welsh	Stevie Woods	Lance Zarimba
Mark Zubro		

Check out titles, both available and forthcoming, at
www.mlrpress.com

BLACK AND BLUE AND PRETTY DEAD, TOO

A Paul Turner Mystery

MARK ZUBRO

mlrpress

www.mlrpress.com

Copyright 2011 by Mark Zubro

Published by
MLR Press, LLC
3052 Gaines Waterport Rd.
Albion, NY 14411

Visit ManLoveRomance Press, LLC on the Internet:
www.mlrpress.com

Cover Art by Deana Jamroz
Editing by Neil Plakcy

Print ISBN#978-1-60820-467-0
Ebook ISBN#978-1-60820-468-7
Issued 2011

Fenwick sweated. Summer in Chicago. Dampness formed sticky pools on the overweight detective's desk where he rested his forearms. Heavy, dark splotches under his armpits, patches of wet in the middle of his back aiming for the crack of his ass. The six-foot-high pole fan next to his desk thrummed on high speed, clanking and whirling as loudly as the semi-trailer trucks rumbling along on the Dan Ryan Expressway half-a-mile away. Secured to the floor nearby, two low-rise fans swiveled and gurgled. The combined blasts of air barely caused a ripple in the fountain of sweat that was Fenwick.

Buck Fenwick and Paul Turner had all their papers on their desks anchored from long familiarity with the lack of air-conditioning in Area Ten headquarters, scheduled for renovation sometime in the next decade. Nobody was holding their breath for work to start while crime still lasted in Chicago.

Fenwick flung his pencil onto his paperwork. He said, "I'm going to shoot the next person who commits a crime in Chicago."

Turner said, "If you could shoot them before they committed the crime, it would save us all a lot of hassle."

"I'd need a timetable," Fenwick said. He drummed his fingers two inches from one of the damp patches. "Or I could consult my personal goddess for inside information."

"You have your own one-man psychic network? I would hope you'd keep that to yourself."

"Goddess, not psychic network."

"There's a difference?"

"If you're nice to me, maybe I'll share."

"A dream come true. Although I'm curious about how that goddess shit works. Do people have to line up to chat with yours, or do they have to get their own?"

"She calls and I listen."

Turner said, "What if she calls while you're traveling eighty miles an hour on the interstate?"

"I never go eighty on an interstate."

Turner said, "I remember last week…"

Fenwick said, "That was Clark Street, and we were in a hurry."

"To get you to an air-conditioned diner."

"You have your kinds of emergencies. I have mine."

"Tell the goddess not to call me. I'm not picking up."

"She doesn't like you anyway."

"Hell of a thing," Turner said. His cell phone rang.

Fenwick said, "If that's the goddess, tell her I'm busy."

Turner noted it was just before nine o'clock, pressed the button to answer, listened for a moment then said, "He's busy. Can I take a message?"

Fenwick smiled. He said, "One for you."

It was Ben, Paul's partner. Ben said, "Do I want to know what that was all about?"

"Fenwick's waiting for a call from his goddess."

"Again?" Ben asked. An in joke for Paul and Ben. They both loved the old Rocky and Bullwinkle shows.

"How's the camp planning going?"

"Brian has been drumming a basketball in the driveway since the beginning of time. I'm going to hear it in my dreams."

"In this heat?"

"He slathered on a million layers of sun block, level ten gazillion. He has several gallons of specially purified water that he guzzles at regular intervals." Their oldest son was a health nut and insisted on organic everything. Probably dribbling an organic basketball covered in sun block. Paul had told the boy if he could afford it, he could be as organic as he liked. "He's been packed and ready to go since dawn. Which I think is when the basketball dribbling actually started."

Paul repeated their parental mantra, "Better than drugs and alcohol."

Ben said, "Let's not vote on that until after he leaves."

"Jeff?"

"Wants to talk to you."

A few moments silence ensued. Paul pictured Ben bringing the phone to Jeff. Paul knew exactly what their youngest son was doing, sitting in his wheelchair in his room in the middle of a horrendous mess. The boy could dither about packing with the best of them.

Jeff said, "Dad, Ben says I can't take…"

Paul interrupted. "You're not trying to pit one of us against the other?"

"I'm not… Well, he won't…"

"Stop," Paul said. "What's the rule?"

"Parents always agree on everything."

"We talk and discuss before decisions. Did you talk and discuss?"

"Yes."

"And the decision?"

"But Dad."

"Son?"

"Okay." With just a hint of the soon to be teenager's whine in his voice. Paul didn't comment on it. He didn't need to take a victory lap on his son's compliance.

"See you later, Jeff. Love you. Put Ben back on."

"Love you," Jeff said. Then shouted, "Dad, Dad wants to talk to you."

Moments later Ben returned. Paul asked, "He's going to be packed?"

"He always has been before. I asked him why there was always Chess Camp drama. That's when he wanted to talk to you."

"Good question."

"Mrs. Talucci will stop over whenever you get home."

"Excellent." Mrs. Talucci was their ninety-something next door neighbor. She was planning one of her exotic trips, this time to the Amazon.

Ben lowered his voice. "They'll be gone soon."

Paul loved the low thrum of his partner's voice. He and Ben had been looking forward to the boys being gone; hot sexual escapades in a house to themselves. They exchanged endearments and hung up.

Fenwick said, "That wasn't the goddess. You lied."

"That's what she told me to say."

Commander Drew Molton tapped the top of Fenwick's desk with a rolled up piece of paper. They hadn't heard him approach because of the noise from the fans.

Molton said, "I hate to interrupt, but the criminals of Chicago have struck this evening."

"Shoot them," Fenwick said. "Shoot them all."

Molton said, "I think that's against regulations. I'll try to get the laws changed. Just for you. Meanwhile, the call came in. We've got a problem at the old Prairie Street train station."

Fenwick said, "Isn't that abandoned?"

"Obviously not abandoned enough," Turner said.

Molton said, "Just go. And try not to sweat on the corpse."

"Who's dead?" Fenwick asked.

"One of ours," Molton said.

Fenwick said, "But we aren't all rushing around madly rounding up the usual suspects? Solidarity forever and all that bullshit. What's the problem?"

Molton said, "The dead guy is Trent Belger."

Fenwick said, "Fuck-a-doodle-do."

Turner said, "I agree."

Every cop in the city knew the story. Two months ago, Trent Belger had been in a bar with another cop, Barry Callaghan, his partner for eleven years in the department. Callaghan began beating the hell out of the female bartender. Belger had stepped in, put a stop to it. When uniformed cops, detectives, lieutenants, captains, and commanders showed up, Belger backed up the bartender's story. Video from a patron's cell phone confirmed Belger's and the bartender's version of events. Since that day Belger had been vilified throughout the department. For interfering. For turning on one of his own. For disloyalty. For breaking the blue code of silence. Didn't matter if logic and the recording proved the offending cop committed a felony.

Within hours of the event, even before reporters splashed the video all over the news, everything in Belger's locker in the Ninth District had been stolen or destroyed, his car keyed, his tires slashed.

Molton said, "I want a real investigation. Our guys are the obvious suspects. Be careful. Follow all the rules."

"Don't we always?" Fenwick asked.

"Depressingly so," Turner said.

"This is going to be complex and maybe dangerous," Molton said.

"Dangerous?" Fenwick asked.

Molton raised an eyebrow. "You don't think so? Cops investigating cops?"

"I think so," Fenwick said, "I just can't imagine someone trying to mess with us." He flexed the mounds of fat on his right arm. Turner knew that Fenwick's heft included a great deal of muscle and toughness.

Molton said, "They won't have the balls to confront you. It'll be sneaky and nasty. Behind your back. Be careful."

"Got it," Turner said.

Molton added, "I'll send over pictures of Belger and Callaghan. That's the least you'll need. I'll try and think of any kind of paperwork that would help. I can tell you that neither one was scheduled to be on duty tonight. I'll have Barb put a packet of data together for you." He left.

His secretary, Barb Dams, was possibly the most efficient in the CPD.

When Molton was out of earshot, Fenwick said, "Fuck-a-doodle-do up the ass."

Turner said, "That doesn't sound at all pleasant."

"Not for the chicken," Fenwick said.

Over the past few years Fenwick had weaned himself from his triple-fuck system of categorizing people, places, things, and ideas he didn't like. He'd replaced it with the fuck-a-doodle system. Turner wasn't sure it was much of an improvement. The lowest rungs in Fenwick's fuckdom were reserved, as always, for Bears quarterbacks who threw game-losing interceptions, or Cubs pitchers who walked in winning runs. Turner didn't disagree.

Fenwick said, "This case is a no-win, ball-buster."

Turner said, "Aren't they all?"

"Sometimes we catch bad guys and bad things happen to them."

Turner said, "And sometimes we don't."

They grabbed blank forms and sport coats and got ready to leave. When the dew point in the city soared past seventy degrees, as it had today, Fenwick evinced a different set of oddities. Turner had learned to ignore most of these no matter what the weather. His practiced aversion of his eyes allowed him to take no notice of Fenwick's ostentatious grabbing, through his pants, of his underwear out of his ass crack as he stood up.

Two

The first thing Fenwick did after starting the car was lower all the windows. The air-conditioning barely worked on their standard-issue CPD wreck. Turner and Fenwick were taking their turn on rotation for night duty. Both wore short-sleeve shirts. They'd dumped their sport coats in the back seat. Fenwick said, "I hope wherever this corpse is, it's air-conditioned."

Turner nodded agreement.

Area Ten encompassed Chicago's First, Eighteenth, Twelfth, and Twenty-first police districts. The districts handled minor crime, crowd control, and parking tickets. Chicago hadn't had precincts since O. W. Wilson came in during the early sixties and attempted to clean up the department. The Areas handled major crimes. Area Ten's boundaries included the Loop, north Michigan Avenue, the wealthy North Side, the resurgent South and West sides, and the slums farther south, ending with the university community in Hyde Park.

It was a short drive from Area Ten headquarters to the old train station at Prairie Avenue and Roosevelt Road. In the past few years this part of the city had thrived with wildly expensive new condos replacing many of the old slums. Parking could be a nightmare and traffic a hellacious mess. From several blocks away they could see the still prominent clock tower. Lights glowed from the top windows.

Unlike other train stations in the city, the Prairie Avenue one had been built of Joliet limestone. The original owners, The Quincy, Quad Cities, and Chicago Railroad had wanted to outshine all the others. It turned out to be smaller than Union Station and dingier than all the others. The limestone had weathered to a drab gray.

Police cruisers littered the streets around the station jamming traffic worse than usual.

Fenwick sighed, "Lots of help on this one. I wonder if this

guy is worth it."

Even at this hour all the illegal parking spaces for blocks around the station were taken.

"Somebody having a party?" Fenwick asked.

"And we weren't invited," Turner said.

They spotted a clump of uniformed officers on Indiana Avenue. A blue light shone over a side entrance. Two spot-lit flags flew from staffs above the door. They were both the same. Each had nine horizontal stripes: a white bar in the middle with four alternating blue and black stripes above and below. In the upper left corner was a red heart. Turner recognized these as Leather Pride Flags. He'd seen the original when he and Ben visited the gay historical mecca in Chicago, the Leather Archives and Museum. Several heavily muscled men in leather pants and chain harnesses guarded the door.

Fenwick double-parked next to the cars illegally mushed bumper to bumper at a bus stop.

The uniformed cops stepped back while the two men at the door eyed the approaching detectives warily. One was tall, one short, but both were heavily muscled with a bulk that suggested steroids and strength. As Turner reached for his ID, the shorter of the two men held up his hand and took a step toward them. He spoke in a high-pitched whine. "You two can't come in. You don't meet the dress code." The detective's attire didn't match either of these men's.

The taller man said, "We've got permits for being here. This has all been cleared with the city."

Turner didn't ask how the taller one knew they were cops.

Fenwick showed his star and said, "I'm Detective Fenwick…"

The guy was already talking into a walkie-talkie. After a few moments of static a short, fat man burst from the door. "I'll handle this, Harold. I'll take care of it. I know what to do." He had a cell phone, flashlight, set of keys, and walkie-talkie clipped to a belt cinched tight against the extra weight.

A tall, skinny beat cop, Mike Sanchez, emerged behind the man. Turner and Fenwick had worked with Sanchez before. The beat cop saw the two detectives and sauntered over. He said, "I told him not to rush out here."

Fenwick asked, "Where's the problem?"

The short guy said, "I'm Denver Slade. I'm in charge. We have to be discreet. We can't have any publicity. This is awful. You have to do something. You have to be careful. Follow me."

Fenwick said, "Just a moment." They walked out of hearing range with Sanchez.

"What's the story?" Fenwick asked.

Sanchez said, "You'll see it. This place is jammed, but the body is way the hell away from all the activity."

"What's going on?" Fenwick asked.

"You'll have to ask the short, fat guy. He seems to be in charge. I left my partner down with the body. It's Trent Belger all right."

Turner said, "We'll go with Mr. Slade. If you would try and find out where Barry Callaghan is right now, I'd appreciate it. And Molton said he'd be sending us some data. Have it sent down to us as soon as it arrives." He glanced at the loitering uniformed cops. "We can get those guys to monitor the entrances and exits. We may even have enough to surround the place. Unless they discover they have real work to do."

THREE

The station's old Grand Concourse with its vaulted ceiling had deteriorated nearly to the point of ruin. Then the train station had been renovated into a mall in the sixties. That retail dream had gone broke in the eighties. None of the store fronts remained as businesses. Tonight, however, music that sounded to Turner like heavy metal rock mixed with a disco beat thundered continuously as they strode down the old main concourse of the building. A crowd of mostly men, but a few women, crammed the interior. All wore leather garments running the gamut from skimpy thongs to heat-defying leather pants and jackets.

"What is this?" Fenwick asked.

"The annual Black and Blue Party," Slade said.

Turner could have explained to Fenwick about leather fairs and how they worked, but it was better to have Slade go over it.

Dressed in sports coats and ties, the detectives drew stares. Slade quickly led them to a side door to avoid having them walk through any more of the party. Turner caught enough of a glimpse of the outfits and activities to recognize the resemblance of this area of the Black and Blue Party to the Folsom Street Fair in San Francisco and the dealer's room at the International Mr. Leather weekend in Chicago. Lots of butch-looking men and their hangers-on swarmed booths of vendors hawking an immense variety of leather wares and porn.

They entered a dimly-lit corridor with water-stained cement block for walls. Slade spoke. "I'm sure the party had nothing to do with this. I'm sure no one at the party would engage in this behavior. I'm sure there's some kind of mix-up."

The small elevator they entered needed to be operated with an old-fashioned hand crank. Slade had to close the wooden slatted doors from the top and bottom. He worked the old-fashioned lever and sent the elevator down.

Fenwick asked, "What's the Black and Blue Party?"

Slade said, "A leather party. A gay leather party. Are you going to be assholes about that?"

Fenwick asked, "What exactly happens at a Black and Blue Party, and why does it need this much space?"

"Gay people and leather go back decades," Slade explained. "This is just a chance for those who like it to be together, see each other, attend seminars, hook up, buy some specialty items. We've been doing this in Chicago now for four years. This is more refined and less commercial than other leather events around the country. It's more... intimate." All the while he talked, Slade twisted his hands together, or rubbed them on his leather pants, or ran them through his ill-arranged comb over.

The elevator rocked slowly down. "How far below the surface is this?" Turner asked.

Slade said, "Several floors at least. We're going down to some of the earliest parts of the station." The elevator clanked, rumbled, and jerked as it moved. "This elevator is an antique."

"Is this the only entrance?" Turner asked.

"This place is a maze," Slade said. "The original was built before the Great Chicago Fire in 1871. It burned. A lot of the Loop has been raised over the years over the original swamp. You can still find houses with stairs leading up to front doors built above sidewalk level. They didn't dig this place that far underground, it's just that the city kept being built up and up and over it. The original building sometimes gets lost in all the additions and renovations. When this was part of the levee district, supposedly there was prostitution going on down here. And then during Prohibition, it's rumored Al Capone had a speakeasy or one of his headquarters down here."

"Is any of that true?" Fenwick asked.

"That's what I read." Slade shrugged. "I have no idea if it's true."

The elevator bumped to a rocky stop. Once they were outside

of it, the three of them entered a long hallway. The light came from sconces high on the walls. An immense mural covered one wall. It was done in black and white and featured rough-looking, masculine men. Turner vaguely recognized it.

They passed portals through which they caught glimpses of wavering light and writhing bodies and the continuous thump of more heavy metal music.

"You own this place?" Fenwick asked.

"We rent it for the party every year."

"Who owns it?"

"I can give you the name and address of the man we deal with. It'll be with my things in the temporary office we have."

"How much of the party is down here?" Turner asked.

"We have some specialty rooms on this level, but nothing as far below as the... problem."

They continued down a long corridor, came upon three switchbacks, followed them. As they moved, the noise from the party above and behind them slowly abated. After the switchbacks, they descended several sets of stairs.

"What's a specialty room?" Fenwick asked.

Slade faced them from the bottom of a set of steps. He put his hands on his hips. He wore leather pants and a leather vest. The logo of a dragon chomping on a snake caught in its massive jaws adorned his left shoulder. "Look," Slade said. His hands finally stopped moving. "Let's get this straight. I'll tell you anything you want about leather and this party, but I'm sure it has nothing to do with what's happened."

Fenwick and Turner exchanged looks. Turned nodded at his partner. Suspects' fears wouldn't hinder the investigation in the slightest.

Slade saw the exchange of looks and said, "I've put in a call to my lawyer. And there are several attorneys I know, who, I believe, are upstairs now. If I need to, I'll get them."

Turner said, "We're not out to ruin the party or to cause you undue trouble, but we've got a corpse to deal with. We'll cooperate with you, but we'll need even more cooperation from you."

"What does that mean?" Slade asked.

Fenwick said, "We may need all the names of all the people attending the party."

"You're not going to get the name of everyone who's at the party. That's over three thousand people. We can't have their names in the paper. We can't have them bothered by the police. This is private property. We were doing nothing wrong. You can't arrest me."

"Sure I can," Fenwick said. "Our dead body trumps any problems you might have."

Slade turned pale.

Turner soothed, "Mr. Slade, we'll do what we can to minimize any inconvenience to you." He also knew that there were very likely to be people in attendance who wouldn't want it to be known they were at a gay leather fair. This he understood very well.

Slade led them down three more corridors and shallow flights of stairs each less well-lit than the last. The air smelled dank, mixing with an odor of rot. At the end of the last flight of stairs they descended a steep ramp. At the bottom of this the ground flattened out. Slade said, "This is one of the original platforms trains stopped at when the station was built."

The lighting here was much dimmer than above. They could see perhaps as far as ten feet in front of them. Turner flicked on his flashlight. Hefting his own flashlight, Slade led them farther along. "Nobody from the party is supposed to come down here," he said. "Hell, I don't think anybody knows about this area except me and a few of my security people. Plus, I read up on the place. I'm kind of a train buff."

They strode along the platform. The humidity down there was as stifling as it had been on the street.

"There must be outside openings," Fenwick said.

The smell became more noxious and with each step grew exponentially. It soon became nearly as oppressive as the humidity. Turner and Fenwick knew what it was: unwashed human mixed with rotting garbage and dead animals. Turner suspected homeless people would know about these areas. He presumed garbage and dead critters of all kinds must have been accumulating for decades. And it wouldn't take long in the heat and humidity for a corpse to deteriorate.

They turned a corner. A beat cop, Perry Deveneaux, shone his flashlight on their faces.

Deveneaux said, "The dead body is down there."

Fenwick added the glow of his flashlight to Turner's. They stepped gingerly forward. Down a short flight of stairs, they could see the corpse. They stopped. They'd wait for the Crime Scene Investigation team to arrive before proceeding.

"Who found the body?" Turner asked.

Slade said, "I did." His hands began their wandering again rubbing over various bits of his costume and flesh.

FOUR

The detectives shone their lights on the floor, walls, and ceilings. Slade kept himself on the far side of the detectives, away from the body. They did a cursory examination. The search for details would come later. They turned to Slade.

"How'd you happen to find the body?" Turner asked.

"We patrol down here. There are about a million entrances and exits to this place. The ones above are all secured, but down here, who knows? I and several of my security people come down here periodically. We get people trying to sneak in. It's a hassle. Maybe an hour ago now, maybe a little less, I was down in that direction."

He waved his flashlight toward the darkness on the far side of the corpse. "I heard somebody. Nobody is supposed to be down here. I commanded him to stop. He ran. I ran after him. He stumbled. I thought I'd catch up to him, but I'm not as young as I used to be. But then I came to here, and I saw..."

He gulped and turned paler. He whispered. "I was in such a rush, I almost fell on the body. It was awful. I got out my cell phone, but it won't work down here. I used my walkie-talkie and got one of my security guards. I had them get help. I had to direct them. This place is a warren built by a succession of mad men. The time I had to be alone with the corpse wasn't long. The two beat cops came, and they recognized the body. Seemed kind of odd to me."

"Did you get a look at who you were chasing?"

"A little. Thin. Blond. White. That's all I could really say. Wearing leather short pants. That's all I know. Really. Can I go now? I hate standing near...that."

Turner saw the crime scene investigators toting their heavy gear down the last ramp toward them. He said to Slade, "Thanks for your help. We'll need to talk more later so don't leave."

"I can tend to my work?"

"Just don't leave the premises."

FIVE

Turner and Fenwick took the time to make sketches of what they could see from this vantage point.

Turner said, "No signs of a struggle up here or on the way we came down."

Fenwick said, "No sign of a body being dragged. Although there are a lot of footprints. For a section that was supposedly unused, they might have been herding buffalo down here."

Turner shone his light on the edges of the platform. "We better get the forensic guys to go over the floors of all the halls and platforms, but especially along the edges on the way down here. There might be a lot of traffic in the middle, but maybe checking the edges will give us something." Turner knew it wasn't likely. Then again, a lot of the cop stuff they did was unlikely to lead directly to the killer. But they always did all the basics because you never knew which one of those bits of information might lead to a criminal and a conviction.

They sent Deveneaux to round up several other beat cops so they could begin examining all the possible exits and entrances to this area of the old station. Turner knew the plethora of beat cops available to them would be nearly limitless. This was the death of a Chicago cop, and people would want answers fast and results faster. Or hushed up. Depended on how powerful the person was whose ox was being gored and which side he or she was on.

While they waited for the techs to finish, Fenwick asked, "How much do you know about this leather shit?"

"Enough to have a good time. Probably not enough to solve the murder."

"Cryptic and enigmatic," Fenwick said.

Turner said, "Don't you have to pay a fee to use polysyllabic words?"

"I get grammar points for them."

Half an hour later, after getting the okay from the techs and donning plastic booties, Turner and Fenwick approached the corpse. Arc lights now lit the scene. Turner said, "No drag marks or signs of a struggle down here either." They checked a ten-foot radius around the body.

Fenwick said, "Lot of unclear marks. Nothing obvious. We'll have to wait and see what they find with the ultra-violet light."

The body lay on its side. His leather pants were down around his ankles. Belger still wore black boxer briefs which bulged several inches at the back. Tit clamps encased his protruding nipples. Flecks of blood dotted his torso.

Fenwick pointed to the bulge in the back of the briefs.

"What's that?" he asked.

The ME, a gray skinned functionary, said, "The bottom end of a large dildo."

"He's gay?" Fenwick asked.

Turner said, "Enjoying having your butt played with is not limited to gay guys. Not as far as I know."

"It's not the butt play, per se," Fenwick said.

The ME groaned. He, and anyone else who had the slightest acquaintance with Fenwick, was used to the detective's attempts at puns and word play.

Fenwick continued, "It's the size of the dildo."

Turner said, "My comment remains the same. Although I could add, I sure get suspicious when a guy is at a gay leather event, and he's found dead with a dildo up his butt. Not saying it proves anything. Gay or straight, he's pretty damn dead, and I'm not sure yet whether the gay or straight part had anything to do with it." Turner pointed to the corpse's left hand. "He's wearing a wedding ring."

"Kind of odd," Fenwick said.

"Wearing a wedding ring is odd?" Turner asked.

Fenwick said, "Being at a gay party dressed in serious leather, with evidence of S+M, plus the wedding ring, and being dead. That's odd."

"Depends," Turner said. "This day and age, wearing a wedding ring doesn't definitively mean he's straight. He and his partner, male or female, could both be into S+M. It might be a turn-on for a gay guy who knew he was whipping a straight guy, or for a straight guy to get whipped by a gay guy. Or a straight guy to whip a gay guy. Which part of that, if any, means he was gay, I have no idea. Nor does it tell us who killed him. We've got to try to find out what he was into."

"I like weird," Fenwick said. "It adds zest to an investigation."

"That's my goal in life," Turner said, "to make sure you have zesty investigations."

The ME gave Turner and Fenwick his observations and conclusions. "He's been dead for at least a couple hours. I'll work on trying to be exact. I don't know how accurate I'm going to be able to be with this humidity. Guy was an asshole."

"You knew him?" Fenwick asked.

"I never saw his fifteen minutes of fame. Not interested. I don't watch the news. I did meet him on a few cases. He was an asshole. So was his partner."

"You kill him?" Fenwick asked.

"I wish I'd had the chance. He could fuck up an investigation like few others and his partner Callaghan was just as bad. Even I knew about their reputation. They'd bully witnesses and scare suspects. We had more people ask for attorneys when they were around than any other half a dozen cops. They were incompetent boobs."

Fenwick said, "Tell us how you really feel."

The ME snorted.

Turner leaned over to get a closer look at the body.

The ME pointed with the tip of his pen. "We've got fresh whip marks here and here. They happened within the last six hours certainly."

"Did the whipping kill him?" Turner asked.

"I doubt it."

Fenwick said, "But the killer whipped him?"

The ME said, "I have no idea. Whether or not he knew his murderer and something just went wrong with an S+M scene this time around is something for you guys to figure out. He may have been whipped before he died, while he was dying, or even after he died. Whether or not it was the killer tearing up his body, I have no idea."

Fenwick said, "I like definitive. The killer may or may not have whipped him."

The ME said, "You're welcome."

Turner said, "I wonder if the whip marks may or may not have happened at the leather thing upstairs. There aren't any old scars." This didn't surprise Turner. He knew that people into the whipping scene were often very careful, and the action was often mostly show, without actual blood being shed, and usually involving a minimum of real pain.

"Would these cuts have left scars?" Turner asked.

The ME peered at the wounds closely. "Yes. Some of these are pretty deep. Somebody beat the hell out of him. I very much doubt if he did them himself."

"Why not?" Fenwick asked.

"Angle and direction. If he was doing it himself, I'd expect deeper impressions here and here with the angle either from the side or from the top. These look to me like they came from someone standing directly behind him."

Fenwick said, "The question is by whom?"

The ME said, "I love when you use the correct interrogative pronoun."

Fenwick said, "Corpses inspire me, and I need to build up grammar points."

Turner said, "That's the second time you mentioned points. We having some kind of contest tonight or you just in another rut?"

Fenwick said, "Ruts to the left of me, ruts to the right of me."

Turner knew it was best to ignore Fenwick when he started mixing misquoted poetry with an investigation. Turner said, "Another question is, was it voluntary?"

The ME said, "You'd think his wife would have noticed when he got home. She'd have to notice, and if he wasn't telling her the truth, I can't imagine an explanation that would make sense." He paused then added, "We didn't find a whip."

Fenwick said, "The killer is undoubtedly at Area Ten headquarters even as we speak, and he is calmly placing the whip into evidence."

The ME asked, "You fantasizing again?"

"His personal goddess calls him," Turner said. "He claims she fills his every need."

"Hate when that happens," the ME said.

"Him and his personal goddess are having a thing," Turner said.

The ME said, "Don't tell Madge."

Madge was Fenwick's wife and one of Turner's favorite people.

Fenwick asked, "Who would win in a wrestling match between my personal goddess and a psychic?"

The ME said, "You mean like between Batman and Spiderman."

Turner said, "Which Batman? A wrestling match between Christian Bale and Toby McGuire? I'd pay to see that."

"Well," Fenwick said, "that's not the same thing."

"Depends on your perspective, doesn't it?" the ME asked.

"We're just encouraging him," Turner said. "As for whips,

plenty of them at the party upstairs."

Fenwick said, "We going to have to interview everybody who owns a whip or who has scars on his back? I am not in the mood for that crap."

The ME said, "Is there anybody ever really in the mood for the crap we do?"

Fenwick said, "Not many. This will take forever. I'm not in the mood for forever. Not tonight. Not with this heat."

"What actually killed him?" Turner asked.

The ME said, "He wasn't conscious when he was down here. Once the body got plunked here, it didn't move of its own volition. Probably brought here wrapped in something that is not currently visible. You've noticed the lack of pools of blood?"

Fenwick growled. He hated when people stated the obvious.

The ME said, "The growl thing is getting a little old."

Fenwick said, "Sometimes it works."

"And sometimes not," Turner said.

The ME said, "I'm not sure he was dead when he got here, but he might have been. I'm not sure when he died. Certainly, it was in the last twenty-four hours. Not longer. I'm actually not sure how he died. He's got that huge dildo stuck up his butt, and it caused bleeding. He's also got a large orgasm ball in his mouth."

"Orgasm what?" Fenwick asked.

Turner said, "Weighted balls in the butt, or vagina for that matter. Often plastic, sometimes in graduated sizes linked together with heavy duty string or some such. Used to add sexual pleasure. Or so I've heard."

"Oh," Fenwick said. He asked, "How can you tell it's an orgasm ball? With smaller ones below it?"

The ME said, "I looked."

Fenwick said, "Cheater."

Turner examined the closed mouth with smears of blood around the lips. With his pointer the ME lifted the upper lip slightly. Turner glimpsed a flash of pale blue.

"He has a graduated series of them down his throat. I don't know if the loss of blood killed him, or he choked to death or he got stuck on the dildo of death. I'll know more when I get him to the lab."

The three of them squatted down. The ME lowered the black boxer briefs. Turner saw the bottom end of a dildo protruding from the corpse's asshole. Belger's ass was blood-smeared, the underwear blood-soaked.

Fenwick asked, "Was he having a good time or was he being fucked to death?"

"Or both," the ME said. "I can at least let you know about one of those options."

"Lot of bruises all over his ass," Turner said.

Fenwick said, "Black and blue and pretty dead, too."

The ME said, "Keep that up and you may be next."

Fenwick said, "I was having a gritty and insightful moment."

Turner said, "I never thought I'd say this, but maybe you should stick with ghastly puns. Gritty and insightful doesn't look good on you."

Fenwick said, "Everybody's a critic."

Wearing his plastic gloves, Fenwick began removing items from the victim's pockets. He found change, car keys, wallet, and a pass to the leather party. In the wallet he found about fifty dollars in mixed bills. In a back pocket he found nine one hundred dollar bills. He showed them to his partner.

Fenwick said, "Wasn't a robbery. Was he going to pay somebody for a good time, or did they pay him?"

Turner said, "If it was this much money, either way it was likely supposed to be a very good time."

After examining each item, he bagged it carefully.

When they were finished, Fenwick nodded at the pass, "He was attending the party?"

Turner said, "We'll see if we can find out if it was his or may have been planted on him. Although he could probably have gotten whipped at the party, which would be logical. Still we need to be sure it isn't just proximity, but actual fact that it happened above. We'll have to be very careful about cause and effect."

The ME said, "Fenwick's grammatical precision is rubbing off on you."

Turner said, "Yeah, but I could never eat as much chocolate as him."

Fenwick said, "No one can eat as much chocolate as I can."

"Spare me," the ME said.

Turner said, "Another possibility is Belger could have been killed by someone who set it up here at the party with all these accoutrements of sex and leather to make it look like a killing connected to the gay community or done by a gay person. Maybe trying to divert suspicion from the real killer. Someone who knew his kinks and his peccadilloes. Even a wife or girlfriend, although how they'd get in to the party above might be a little tough."

Fenwick said, "Depends a little on how he got in and then down here."

Turner said, "With luck, we'll know more when we get the report from our people as they double-check all the corridors, ramps, hallways, whatever. With this blood, he's got to have left smears somewhere."

The ME said, "There's no blood around except in the immediate vicinity of the body. Not enough to show he bled to death, but still."

Fenwick said, "Logic would dictate the killer is an angry cop who didn't like him ratting on a friend. That's the place to look for suspects. He could have been whipped off-site and dragged here."

Turner said, "Off-site or on-site, he wound up here. We didn't find any signs of a body being dragged on our way in. With all this debris and even this small amount of blood, you'd think we'd find something. He must have been wrapped in something and carried here."

At that moment Deveneaux and Sanchez returned to report. Sanchez handed Turner an envelope. Turner glanced inside. He found pictures, background sheets for Belger and Callaghan, and other bits of data Molton had promised.

Deveneaux glanced at his notes as he said, "There are only a few ways down here to where the body is, but there are a lot of ways to get to those few ways down here. From this spot you can cross these tracks and climb the cement barriers on either side to the next sets of tracks."

They all looked. Pillars marched in both directions into the gloom on both sides of the tracks. The rows of pillars continued in each direction. Three-foot-high concrete barriers extended between the pillars.

Turner said, "Dragging him over those barriers and over these tracks and carrying a dead body? Looks tough."

Deveneaux said, "Several guys checked for bloodstains in each direction. Toward the north, the pillars end in about a hundred feet. It's the old wall of the station where a waiting room used to be. It's boarded up and looks like it has been for years. The other way goes on for half a mile. It eventually narrows, the tracks merge and dwindle down and become four elevated tracks but those peter out in empty fields south of here. No blood anyone could see. It's dark. We used flashlights, but it was tough. I'm not sure there'd be much more to see in daylight. There's very little lighting down here. The guys with luminol can spray for hours down here."

Turner said, "Doesn't rule out that direction. Or he was brought down from above?"

Sanchez said, "We found all kinds of entrances and exits above that lead to the ramps that eventually get to this platform. The guys are still checking them. We did the ones closest to here first. No traces of blood anyone can see."

Turner said, "Let me get this straight. Someone could start from far away, from outdoors, along those deserted train yards just south of the Loop and drag or carry the body here?"

"Right."

"And is there an entrance from above in that direction as well?"

"Sure, you could go down steps from overpasses."

Fenwick said, "Either way, it is still a long way to tote a body."

Turner said, "Might have been in something, a wheelbarrow, a two-wheel cart."

The ME said, "Or the killer was very strong."

Sanchez said, "We talked to all the guys who worked the door and all the registration people. Commander Molton sent over extra pictures of Belger and Callaghan. Nobody recognized either of them, but we're not sure we got all of the employees and volunteers. Slade said some might have gone home."

People who just happened not to be around; a typical loose end of police work that ate up more of their time than they liked to contemplate.

"Did the door guards or bouncers or whatever the hell they are, notice anything unusual?" Fenwick asked.

"Unusual? Here?" Sanchez asked.

Fenwick said, "I do the cryptic semi-humor in this relationship."

"Could have fooled me," Sanchez said.

Fenwick grumbled but said nothing. He liked Sanchez.

Sanchez said, "They claimed no one got in without proper ID."

Fenwick said, "Let's put a little pressure on Slade."

SIX

They found Slade fussing at a couple of beat cops, his hands in almost continuous motion. He was saying, "I've got to be able to get around. I've got to manage things. I've got to be sure everything is perfect."

Fenwick nodded to the beat cops. They left. Before Slade could resume, Fenwick asked, "Could anybody get in here who didn't belong?"

"No way. Everyone was checked for ID and registration badge. Who was he? Who died? I only took a brief look...before."

"You checked all the registrants yourself?" Turner asked.

"I trained all the people who worked the door and the registration booths myself. They knew better than to let anyone in without properly checking them. And we patrolled down here. Maybe whoever I saw was legitimately down here. I don't know why he ran. That's what was suspicious."

Fenwick asked, "You know anything about people being whipped?"

"Sure," Slade said. "For the larger demonstration rooms, we used all the old storefronts from when this was a mall. Plus, we converted a bunch of the old baggage storage areas down below for people into particular scenes. You saw some of those as we walked down here. For whipping we had separate rooms for beginners, intermediate, and advanced."

"Oh," Fenwick said.

Turner said, "We'll need to interview the people involved with the whipping booths."

"Right now? It's just after eleven. The festivities are at their height."

Turner said, "We'll start with the owners or people who are in charge of the whipping. We'll need to see if this guy was at their booth."

"Why do you think he was with them?"

Turner said, "He has whip marks on his back."

"But who was he?"

Turner said, "He was wearing leather pants. He had a pass for the party in his wallet." He wasn't about to give him all the details. If Slade were the killer, most likely he would know them. If he weren't, the police didn't want him spreading them around. The more details the cops told the public, the more difficult it would be to weed out the loons who came out of the woodwork. People confessing were often a problem in a high-profile case. It did no good to provide the resident loonies with ammunition. With luck, the case would be solved before too many of these emerged.

Slade said, "I can check to make sure whether or not he was here officially. I can't imagine someone who was supposed to be here being killed."

Turner didn't have time to disabuse him of any notions about who might or might not be motivated to commit murder.

Fenwick said, "We'll have some officers go over the registration lists with you."

"But they're private."

Turner was reasonably sympathetic on the privacy issue. For more years than anyone cared to count being gay in public had been the cause for police harassment. The Stonewall riots had been the beginning of the end of that, but to this day there were problems between the police and the gay community. Turner had heard of a recent case in Atlanta where a gay bar had been raided. So far all the court cases in that incident were going in favor of the gay community. In Chicago, especially with the gay friendly mayor and gay aldermen, things had gotten better. Still, Turner understood. He knew no one outside the investigation would get any names from him or Fenwick. He and Fenwick were exceptionally good at keeping their mouths shut.

"It's a murder investigation," Fenwick said. And they didn't want him pulling Belger's registration to try to hide his official presence at the party.

Loud voices from beyond the last turn they'd come down drew their attention. Moments later Sanchez appeared. He and Deveneaux each had a hand clamped onto a willowy-thin young man who didn't look old enough to be shaving. His tight, black-leather shorts clung to very narrow hips. Turner thought if the kid had an erection while wearing them, he might injure himself. He had a badge for the convention clipped to the side of his pants. The only other things he wore were a stainless steel, metal-link choker chain around his neck and motorcycle boots, with chains attached to them that matched the one around his neck. Delicate blond hair feathered gently around his head.

The kid stopped struggling and snarling and cursing only when Sanchez and Deveneaux stopped in front of the detectives.

Sanchez pointed at the young guy. "Beat cops found him lurking around in the lower depths way the hell around the other side from here. When they told him to stop, he ran. They chased him down. Found him trying to get out where there wasn't an official exit. And the beat cops thought he looked too young to be admitted to the thing going on up above."

Fenwick said, "What's your name, kid?"

"Fuck you." He yanked himself out of the uniformed cops' grip, and took two steps of an attempted sprint.

Fenwick reached out a paw and grabbed the kid by the elbow. The kid came to an abrupt halt. Fenwick flipped the name tag over. He laughed. The kid turned red. "His name is Peter Hardon."

Sanchez and Deveneaux smirked.

Turner said, "We need to see some kind of identification."

With a flick, Fenwick pulled the ID from the kid's shorts. From a side pocket of the plastic packet he pulled a Grover Cleveland High School ID that said the kid's name was Peter Scanlan. There was also a small brass key with a number on it.

Turner showed the ID to Slade, "How did he get in?"

Slade looked discomfited. "He must be of age."

Scanlan said, "I'm of age."

"And pigs fly," Turner said.

Fenwick asked, "What's this key to?"

From Scanlan, "Screw you."

From Slade, "We have lockers where people who want to change can leave their things."

Fenwick said to Slade, "Your security is not as perfect as you claim it to be."

"I trained them myself."

Fenwick said, "We'll have someone talk to the registration people and the door guards." They gave Sanchez instructions on what to ask the guards and registration people. He left.

Turner said, "Kid, you're not under arrest. We don't want to get you for being out after curfew or for being here. We just need to know what you saw."

Scanlan rolled his eyes, rocked on his heels, flitted his eyes from adult to adult. He gave a final gulp, then said, "I met a guy upstairs. We got about halfway down here together then he said he had to pick up a few toys, and I was to go where he said and wait. He gave me directions, but I kind of got lost. I got down to this level, and it's pretty dark. So I was kind of groping around. And the guy didn't come."

"What time was this?" Fenwick asked.

"I don't have a watch."

"About what time?"

"I don't know. I got here about five. I guess I was at the party for a few hours. There was lots to do and see. It was cool. So I waited and kind of wandered around. Then I heard someone shouting at me about being security, and I didn't know who he was, and I didn't want to get caught so I ran. And I tripped over…" He looked around. "Hey, are we back near, where…?

Hey. I don't want to be here. What happened to the guy I tripped over? I didn't do anything wrong."

Fenwick said, "He's dead."

The kid said, "Bullshit."

Fenwick said, "Have I ever lied to you before?"

The kid said, "Bullshit."

Fenwick said, "Repetitious and unimaginative."

"I didn't kill him."

"Neither did I," Fenwick said. "But you could be next."

"You can't threaten me."

"I did and I may again."

The kid tried to yank away.

Turner pointed toward Belger."Is that the same guy you were supposed to meet?"

The kid slid-hopped as Fenwick dragged him near the corpse. For several moments the kid's eyes stayed riveted on the body. He turned very pale. "I don't know who the fuck he is." Not fear, maybe annoyance. More as if adults were disturbing him and they'd better back off. Fenwick gave the kid a gentle shake.

"He's dead?" the kid asked.

Fenwick said, "He's really, really, really dead. And you're our number one suspect."

"I didn't kill anybody. This is bullshit. I didn't do nothing."

"So why'd you run?" Turner asked. Something in Scanlan's reaction wasn't right. He might be attempting bravado, but there was something beneath the surface.

Scanlan said, "This place is spooky. I got lost coming down here. When I ran, I got lost again. I didn't know the guy was dead. They should light this place better. I knew there was an entrance near where they grabbed me."

"Which you've used to sneak in by before," Turner said.

For the first time, the kid met Turner's eyes, then quickly

glanced away.

"What did the man look like who you were supposed to meet down here?" Turner asked.

"Big guy. Heavy set. Lots of hair on his chest. He had on jeans and a rubber head piece. I could see his eyes. He had this deep, gruff voice. I kinda liked it."

Fenwick asked, "How much did he offer to pay you?"

Scanlan said, "I'm not a prostitute."

Fenwick said, "How many kids your age willingly go with older, hairy, heavy-set men?"

Scanlan said, "It's not my fault I got in. They should have inspected better. It's not hard to sneak in. They should have better security."

"How did you sneak in?" Turner asked.

"Fuck this bullshit," Scanlan said. "I've been coming for a couple years. It's expensive."

"And you don't have proper ID," Fenwick added.

Scanlan said, "A few of us knew where there were openings. This place is falling apart. That's where I was heading when I got caught, but I didn't have to sneak in this year. I came with a friend I met here last year."

"What's his name?" Turner asked.

Scanlan smirked, "Daddy."

"Come on, kid," Fenwick said.

"That's what he told me, all he told me. I met him at a water sports booth two years ago. Since then I've partied with him a few times. I don't know where he is now. I don't know where he lives. We always met in motels. Sometimes he liked having me around. Sometimes I guess he got fed up with me. So, tonight I met this other guy. He offered to…"

"Pay," Turner said.

Scanlan nodded.

"How much?" Turner asked.

"Who cares? Does it really matter?"

Turner and Fenwick watched the kid in silence. Scanlan seemed prepared to attempt to bolt again, although Fenwick kept his left hand a few inches from Scanlan's right elbow. Turner was willing to bet that a great deal of what he had just told them was lies.

Scanlan said, "Are you going to call my parents?"

Turner said, "We need to know as much as you can tell us."

"Five hundred bucks."

"Did he give you the money up front?" Fenwick asked.

"No. He told me he'd pay down here."

"Kid," Fenwick said, "always get your money first."

"How did you get in touch with your leather daddy?" Turner asked.

"Slaves don't call masters. He'd call me on my cell phone so my parents wouldn't... so no one would know."

Fenwick asked, "How old were you when you started coming here?"

"Fuck."

Turner said, "Peter, at the least we could call your school. They'd identify you. We'll find out eventually how old you are. When did you start?"

"When I was thirteen."

Fenwick said, "Whoever you were with could get in serious trouble."

"I don't know anyone's name, and if I did I wouldn't give them to you."

"How the hell did you fool your parents?" Fenwick asked.

"I told them I was sleeping over at a friend's. They never called or checked."

"How'd you get here?"

"At first, I'd take the train. Then as I made friends, I'd go with them."

"Friends?" Fenwick let his tone ask the question.

"I chose who I wanted to have sex with. No one forced me."

Turner hated when Fenwick debated with suspects or witnesses, but he kept quiet. Once in a while, it led to a clue. Usually, it was a fruitless exercise in trying to convince the unwary that they'd been stupid or used. In this case, he figured both. Turner wasn't shocked by the kid's story. No detective was shocked by what people did. He'd seen heterosexual and homosexual abuse. If he was going to begin railing against the horrors of every crime they saw, he'd never do anything else.

The kid claimed he knew no more.

SEVEN

Sanchez and Deveneaux found Slade, and the three of them joined Turner, Fenwick, and Scanlan who led them down corridors they hadn't seen before to sections of the station that hadn't been renovated. The detectives had their flashlights out. Concrete floors were chipped, ceiling tiles were ripped and torn when they weren't missing entirely, walls had paint flaking off and blotches of mold, and Turner heard the soft pattering of unseen critters skittering away and saw a large cockroach sauntering away from the light.

Slade said, "This is an old, old section."

They crawled through an opening in a two-foot-thick wall. Slade said, "I think this was part of the original wall." In places where the wall had chipped or weathered away, Turner could see the original color of the limestone. They passed through a series of buildings that were little more than sheds and finally came out at a boarded-up alcove.

Scanlan pushed at several boards. They came away in the form of a sort of door for a kid's fort built unhampered by adult help.

Turner and Fenwick shone their lights out the opening. They were on the opposite side of the station from where they'd first entered, this street parallel to that one. Turner thought they were maybe fifty feet farther south down this street. They were about ten feet above ground level. No streetlights. The glow of the city barely penetrated the gloom.

Sanchez crowded next to them. He pointed down. "You climb up there and there. Can't be that hard." The detectives saw various protuberances that could be used for hand and footholds. It wasn't that far to the pavement.

Turner used the light to examine the ground around them inside and out. "Get the forensics people in here," he said. He didn't know what the smudges he saw were. The dust and dim light made observation difficult, but he would need the crime team's expertise to know if these smudges were blood, and if they had anything to do with their murder. He also ordered crime scene tape to link this area to the first opening they entered from and also for where the body was found.

They made their way back to the original murder scene. Turner and Fenwick let all the others go on ahead. Once they were out of earshot, Fenwick said, "If the kid can find and use a secret entrance, then anybody could. And there could be more than one secret entrance with cops, criminals, people crashing the party."

Turner said. "It could have been like a train station. So to speak."

"I'm the humor guy in this relationship."

"Just taking lessons from the master."

"The kid kill him?"

Turner shrugged. "He seemed more pissed off than frightened. I don't know. There was something odd in his reaction. He's lying. About what, I'm not sure. He's been attending at least one rough leather event, probably since he was thirteen. He might be fifteen or sixteen. That's at least two years of sexual activity of possibly an unusual or dangerous kind. Doing all that might make the kid think he was tough and invulnerable."

"And stupid," Fenwick said.

"Lot of that going around," Turner said.

Fenwick said, "He described the guy who talked to him about coming down here as being in jeans. That's not Belger."

"Or he's lying."

Fenwick said, "Belger had enough money in his pants to pay what the kid said he offered."

"Gives some credence to the kid's story, but doesn't give me a notion about the murder. The kid is hiding something. No kid is that confident. Can't be. Gotta be something else."

Fenwick said, "I agree."

EIGHT

They caught up with the others. Fenwick said to Slade, "Right now, we'll want to talk to the people in charge of the whipping booths, perhaps later all of the employees."

Slade looked put out, but said, "One was sponsored by a porn site. That was more a series of training sessions. A beer company sponsored another. The Leather Forever Club sponsored a third. We don't like to upset our sponsors. It took a lot of work to get some of them. I don't want to scare them away."

"Sooner makes it easier," Fenwick said.

After escorting the managers of each booth to their position, Slade left. The beer booth and Club guys didn't recognize the pictures of either Belger or Callaghan. The owner of the porn site, Frank Jordan, took one look at the body and said, "Sure, I know him. Jack Rammer."

Crossed bandoliers were draped over Jordan's mass of chest hair. When he turned around and bent down to identify the body, Turner saw his back was equally furry. He guessed Jordan was in his late thirties or early forties. His leather pants and boots gleamed in the bright lights. Turner thought the tightness of the pants showed off the guy's butt to great advantage.

Fenwick said, "You ever check his ID?"

"I knew him as Jack Rammer. I only check the paperwork if there's a problem. He was obviously over eighteen. As long as my assistant said he filled out all the required disclaimer forms, I was fine with it."

"Disclaimer forms?" Fenwick asked.

"Before they appear on my site or at the booth, they've got to fill out consent forms, proof of age forms. The usual shit that proves we're not trying to sell them into white slavery, that they're doing this willingly."

"He appeared on your web site?" Turner asked.

"Four or five times."

"And what does your web site contain?" Turner asked.

"It's for guys into more mature men or into uniforms: military, cops, that kind of stuff. And into rougher sex." Turner wrote down the URL so he could check it later.

"How long has he been doing this?" Turner asked.

"For me? About a year."

"Are you saying he did it for others?"

"Claimed he did. I never checked."

"Did the whip marks come from what he was doing connected with your site?"

"Not all of them, that's for sure. We rarely really draw blood. People don't like scars. Or most of them don't. He never had any I noticed, but he was into it. He was part of several of the demonstrations we did. We have them every hour. He was on yesterday, Thursday, at three in the morning and seven the same night. The last time I saw him was around six, tonight. He seemed to be having a great time."

"Great time?" Fenwick asked.

"Laughing and joking with people who came in to the booth. Talking to the other performers. Giving tips to everyone."

"When did you miss him?"

"I didn't. He wasn't scheduled to perform again until one this morning, so I didn't think about him."

"Perform?" Fenwick said. Turner noted that Fenwick was scratching his head. From many years of contact with his partner, Turner was fairly used to the heavy-set man's body language. Rearranging his dick and balls meant he was horny or hungry. Scratching at his arm pits meant he was frustrated. Head scratching, confused with the possibility of escalating to annoyance if it was an uncooperative witness or suspect.

"Yeah. A guy whips him with different techniques, different styles, dressed in different outfits."

Fenwick said, "Doesn't it hurt?"

Jordan said, "I believe that's part of the point."

Fenwick said, "Oh."

"Who whipped him?" Turner asked.

"Whoever paid the fee, ten bucks a hit."

Fenwick said, "That sounds kind of expensive."

"You don't want some amateur doing damage inadvertently."

Turner said, "But couldn't 'whoever' be some amateur?"

"Well, we figure if they pay, they know."

Turner didn't think this would pass anybody's logic test, except for someone eager to make money and turn a blind eye to the obvious.

"Isn't there the possibility of real damage to real human beings?" Fenwick asked.

"We're very careful. We're well trained. Everyone who gets whipped is a consenting adult. I have all the paperwork on file. We have medical personnel on standby in case something goes wrong."

Turner said, "Who else knew him? Did he have any friends or enemies?"

"I knew him a little. He was pretty cooperative. Kind of quiet. Never caused trouble. He would let himself get used, but like, he wouldn't kiss guys. Wouldn't even touch them, but he loved to get hurt by them. The last porn scene he did was the first time he let a guy blow him."

"That normal?" Fenwick asked.

"I don't know what normal means in this world," Jordan said.

"Anybody he have fights with?" Turner asked. "Anybody eager to be the one doing the whipping?"

Jordan shook his head. "Nothing out of the ordinary."

"You see him with anybody in particular? Somebody who stood out?"

"No."

"You know about this area down here?"

"Nope."

"Did you recognize him as Trent Belger?"

"The guy who was in the news for something, right?"

"The cop in the bar."

"He beat up that bartender. I thought that guy was named Callaghan."

"This was his partner."

"Oh, yeah, Belger was the guy who stood up for the woman. He wasn't on the TV as much as the Callaghan guy. Sorry, I didn't recognize him from that."

Turner said, "We'll need to talk to all the people who work at your booth."

"All?"

"Yeah. What time would it be most convenient to have them all around?"

"The convention starts at noon every day, but we're busiest after ten at night. That's when the most staff is around."

"Then we'll be here at ten tonight."

He looked like he was about to object, but he let it go. He left.

Turner asked, "Belger was gay for pay?"

Fenwick did the head scratch again. "Let's slow this down. Let's pretend I don't know any of this shit."

"You need Gay 101?"

"No, I got that from you years ago, and I can read. I think what we've got here is graduate level and I need to be brought up to speed."

"Okay."

Fenwick asked, "How can he have assumed no one would notice him being on a gay website?"

"He was daring? He was stupid? He didn't care? Stop me when I get to a reason that works for you."

"Gay for pay," Fenwick said. "He was a whore?"

"Depends on how you want to look at it. Does letting guys whip you but not have sex with you, qualify for you being a whore?"

Fenwick used the end of his flashlight to scratch his nose. Patted the flashlight against his open palm for a few moments.

Fenwick asked, "And he didn't let guys do more than whip him until today?"

"That's what we know so far. The truth might take a while."

Fenwick said, "I'm not as convinced as I used to be that the truth is all it's made out to be."

Turner smiled at his partner. "Are you satisfied with your advanced knowledge so far?"

"This isn't graduate level anything. This is just kinky." He gave his head another scratch.

Turner said, "The key is we don't know what, if any part of this, had to do with murder. We need more information."

Fenwick said, "We can't interview everybody at the party. Let's get in touch with Slade. We've got to find out who's behind this whole thing."

"I'm a little concerned about this, "oh", response to what these guys say. Does that mean you're stunned beyond belief? Curious? Upset?"

"I'm never upset."

"Except when you are."

"Oh, means how fascinating, tell me more."

"Not that you're a little surprised and overwhelmed by what they're telling us?"

Fenwick said, "If you know all this shit, you could just explain it."

"It's more fun to hear you say *oh.*"

"Huh?" Fenwick said,

"Precisely," Turner said.

They checked with Sanchez. He told them that no one among the people they'd talked to so far recognized Scanlan or Belger. Sanchez and a beat cop went with Turner and Fenwick to the area Slade said had the lockers.

They found the one that matched the number on Scanlan's key. Both detectives donned plastic gloves. Fenwick inserted the key, turned it. They gazed at what was inside.

Fenwick poked at the small mound. Held up a T-shirt with a Led Zeppelin logo on it and a pair of jeans that said size twenty-eight waist on the patch on the back.

"This is it?" Fenwick asked.

They checked the pockets. They checked the locker. That was it. Fenwick handed them to the beat cop and said, "Get these to the crime lab people. Have them check for any traces of blood, the usual. They'll know what to look for." The beat cop left. Fenwick said, "That was useless."

Turner said, "If we got paid for useless, we'd be rich."

Sanchez directed them to the base of the old tower and then left. The registration/control room was at the top. The walls here continued the decorating scheme of many of the halls they'd been through: flaking paint, blotches of mold. They trod heavy black wrought-iron see-through stairs up.

Fenwick paused at the second level. He always claimed his ever increasing bulk did not mean he was out of shape. Turner knew not to contradict this. Normally, reality and Fenwick got on pretty well. However, Fenwick, reality, and his weight, not so much. Turner knew to stand and wait without comment while his partner drew heavy breaths.

"Climbing," Fenwick said. "Heat."

They arrived at the top of the tower in the front of the station. A deeply rutted, scarred, and scored wooden door was open.

Slade stood in front of a metal desk. The carpet the cops stepped onto was metallic gray and as thin as a child's blanket. An air conditioner clanked in a window. Turner felt neither puffs of wind from it nor did he notice it was having any effect on the temperature and humidity. Opaque and dusty windows pushed back at the night.

Slade turned at the cops' entrance. The man behind the desk said, "This is a private conversation. Get out."

NINE

Turner thought it took Fenwick a full two minutes to stop laughing. When he did, Slade said, "These are the two detectives I was talking to you about. This is Matthew Bryner. He runs the Black and Blue Party."

Bryner said, "I'll be ready to talk to you when I'm done talking to Mr. Slade. You'll need to wait outside."

No laughter from Fenwick this time. The detective walked to the front of the desk. He looked at Bryner. He looked at Slade. In his gruffest rumble he said, "Mr. Slade, get out. Now."

Muttering apologies to the cops and Bryner, Slade scuttled out the door.

Matthew Bryner's bald pate gleamed in the orange and red glow of the lights in the Black and Blue party's offices. He wore black leather pants and a black motorcycle jacket. Turner saw tendrils of tattoos escaping from the neck of his black T-shirt. Bryner drew a lungful of smoke from a fat cigar. It stank of burning rubber and refuse. He tapped a few bits of ash into a pink ceramic ashtray in the form of a hand with the middle finger extended. Bryner said, "You can't just barge in here."

Fenwick said, "This is a murder investigation. That takes priority. Including shutting you down if we feel like it."

Bryner took a puff on his cigar. "You can't shut me down. I have friends in high places."

"And you've got a dead body in the basement," Fenwick said. "You've got a problem."

"I didn't kill him."

"Where were you tonight?"

"Taking a well-deserved break."

"Any witnesses?"

"Do I need them?"

"Yes."

"Ah, then, I have them."

Smug son of a bitch, Turner thought. Maybe he really did have connections, which wouldn't stop their investigation, but it could complicate it.

Turner pulled up two metal folding chairs. He and Fenwick sat.

"Is this going to take long?" Bryner asked.

Fenwick said, "It'll take as long as it takes."

Bryner said, "You can't just shove people around."

Turner said, "I thought that was part of the point of the Black and Blue party."

Bryner rubbed one hand over his shaved head while twirling the cigar in his other. Turner wondered if the guy could chew gum at the same time. He thought the addition of a handlebar mustache would add the right note of absurd menace. Bryner stopped the head rubbing and cigar twirling and said, "I don't know what you want of me. I'm sure I can't help you in any way. I'm sure no one at the party would have anything to do with murder."

Fenwick said, "A party that's dedicated to violence?"

Bryner said, "Look up your own statistics. Gay events from hundreds of thousands at the Pride Parades to these kinds of parties have stunningly low incidences of crimes. If you don't know that, you should."

Turner did. He nodded. He said, "Mr. Bryner, it would help us if we could get some background on how the party works. How it's set up, who works here, who comes to this kind of event."

"Why?"

"We need background," Turner said. "We don't mean to bring trouble to you. As far as we know right now, the party will be allowed to continue. Obviously your having contacts in the city could help you, but if we could solve the crime, and you were helpful, we could guarantee you wouldn't have any problems. And I'm sure, contacts or not, you don't want adverse news stories trumpeted in the media. A quick solution would help that not happen."

"Are you threatening to go to the media?"

Turner felt Fenwick stirring with annoyance. Before his partner could begin to bluster, Turner said, "No. If I wanted to threaten you, I would. I'd much rather work with you. And remember, even you can't control all the people connected with this. Things could slip. The faster we work, the better for you." Turner knew the majority of what he was saying was mostly true, but what was important was that Bryner think it was all true, or at least take it seriously enough not to be an asshole about cooperating.

Bryner thought for a minute then nodded. He seemed mollified for the moment. He said, "Putting together a leather party is a nightmare. I'm almost sorry I started this thing four years ago."

"Why did you?" Turner asked.

"I got sick of all the prima donnas at every other leather event in this country. You ever tried to organize members of the leather community into doing something? You've got as many mad leather queens as you have ditzy drag queens or politically correct assholes at any other gay event. They are supercilious, condescending, and nasty and that's on a good day."

"Why?" Fenwick asked.

"Why what?" Bryner asked.

"Why are they all those things? Why doesn't everybody just have a good time?"

Bryner sighed, let bushels of air escape his lungs. Then he sucked them back in. He said, "Because they're morons and Looney Tunes and queens desperate for a little attention for themselves. It's madness. I wanted a place where real leather people could go for some real connections with real men who didn't need to preen and play-act. But some prefer to wreck things and tear down what others have tried hard to put together."

Turner said, "But isn't that what a lot of leather is all about, play acting? I mean, come on, if somebody is being led around by a harness and treated like a slave…"

"Because they are slaves."

"Because they chose to act that way," Turner said. As soon as he'd said it, Turner realized he'd fallen into a debate.

Bryner said, "You just don't understand. Most people don't. Leather is supposed to be different."

Fenwick said, "Kinky is as kinky does."

Bryner gave him a quizzical look.

Turner said, "So what happened to turn this sour?"

"I thought it would be perfect. We didn't have those stupid beauty contests and 'talent' contests. Beauty pageant. Pah. And talent! Nonsense. I knew I could make this perfect. This party has everything a real leather man could want. And sure, I've got connections, but murder! Even I know that could destroy everything."

Turner said, "It wouldn't destroy the party. Not unless the party was the direct cause of the murder."

Fenwick added, "Or you go back to your original attitude when we walked in here."

Bryner sent Fenwick a nasty glare. Turner wondered if they taught that particular glare at one of the more dangerous leather booths, or if Bryner came by it naturally.

Fenwick said, "What if the leather event people from around the country wanted to sabotage you? A dead body could do that. You'd be shut down. And if not shut down, the bad publicity could drive people away. You said it yourself, a lot of these people want to wreck and tear down."

Bryner said, "They wouldn't dare."

"Why not?" Fenwick said.

"They just…they…I don't know. I didn't see any of their names on the registration list. I…they wouldn't."

"You know all of them?" Fenwick asked.

"All the important ones."

"Did you know Belger?" Turner asked. They showed him a picture.

Bryner barely glanced at it. "We don't ask for a person's autobiography when they sign up. They just have to prove their age." He pushed some papers toward them from the top of his desk. "Slade said you wanted that man's registration. There it is. I glanced at it before you came in. I don't know this man. When I heard his name, I didn't associate him with that bar incident. The other guy did the beating. Everybody's heard of him. But I don't know either man. I don't care that this one died, except in so far as it affects me. That may be heartless, but I don't know him, and I do know how many thousands I have invested in this event."

Turner and Fenwick examined the registration. The date was three months prior. It was one page of basic facts: name and age, but with a number of extra items such as leather preferences, as well as lines to fill in that showed he consented to participate. It listed his home address and credit card number, and Belger had checked the box that claimed he was over twenty-one.

Bryner said, "We have that, and we check them once again when they enter the party. We're very careful. He was a consenting adult. He paid to be here."

Fenwick asked, "And you didn't know Barry Callaghan?"

Bryner said, "I know of him. Everybody on the planet must have seen that video a hundred times. It got what, ten zillion hits on the Internet? And wasn't it on half the newscasts for weeks? He beat up that poor woman. He's a pig. He had no entry pass for the party. His name is not on any list."

"People have gotten in without passes and whose names were not on lists. We were shown one way."

"Slade will be fired. I can't have that. But your dead person had an entry pass. So did a few thousand other people."

Fenwick said, "Peter Hardon, real name Scanlan, the guy who found the body, wasn't old enough to shave."

"People can bring guests but we monitor them closely. Some people try to cheat. Obviously somebody did and got in."

Fenwick said, "We had uniformed officers talk to the men posted at the door and the men at the registration desks. No one remembers Belger or Scanlan. That strikes me as convenient."

"We have thousands of people here. How can they be expected to remember one or two out of all those people?"

Turner asked, "I saw a mural down below. Black figures with a white background."

"You really don't know what that is?"

"If I knew, I wouldn't have asked."

"It's a reproduction of a famous mural painted by Chuck Arnett. The original used to be in the basement of The Tool Box bar in San Francisco. We like to replicate any of the good things from the old, glory days of leather."

"Where were you tonight?"

"I needed a break from the tension for a few hours. I can't be here every minute. I've got to trust some things to other people. Most of them don't know I'm in charge and that I fund this."

"Why's that?" Fenwick asked.

"I own a family company in Des Moines. I can't have my name in the papers. The family name would be ruined."

Turner said, "Isn't that kind of sixties thinking?"

Bryner said, "You live in Des Moines? Obviously, there are a lot of nice people. There are also a lot of assholes. The religious right will make a hassle for anyone. I come to Chicago to indulge my tastes. I have this fair in Chicago because it suits the leather community and me."

Fenwick said, "We still need to talk to a lot of people. We'll have to come back later today."

"If you're going to talk to a lot of people, and if you want to get answers, you might want to try to blend in. As it is now when people see you, they'll know you don't belong. Even someone with average intelligence will think you're cops. People are either going to be intimidated at the least or start leaving in droves at the worst."

Fenwick said, "We'll consider it."

While walking back to the murder scene, Turner said, "We're coming back in disguise?"

"How hard can it be?" Fenwick asked.

Turner said, "I can handle it. Can you?"

Fenwick said, "I've been giving butch lessons for years. I can handle it."

Turner said, "He's got friends in high places."

Fenwick said, "We've got friends in high places."

Turner said, "We do?"

Fenwick said, "I've got a direct line to the goddess."

"I'm not sure she's more powerful than the Commander of a Chicago police district or an alderman for that matter."

"For district commanders we better have Molton make the initial contacts. Commanders are a weird bunch, and Aldermen can be a danger to themselves and others. Bryner sure does have a strong sense of his own suffering."

"He's putting something together with the gay community. He should have known there would be petty, nonsensical crap to deal with."

"Why is that?" Fenwick asked.

"Simple explanation? Everybody wants to be a chief. Nobody wants to do basic work. Complex explanation? They're egotistical morons making up for every slight they ever endured in the school yard."

"Really?"

"Would I lie to you?"

Fenwick said, "Never ask a man who has a direct line to a goddess that question."

"Why not?"

"I might be forced to answer honestly."

Turner said, "Honesty doesn't seem to be something you're hesitant about."

Fenwick said, "Finding a body seems to have sent some of these leather people into a tizzy."

"Do you mean they'd be better equipped to handle a dead body, or you'd expect them to be tougher? Maybe it's just the difference between fantasy and reality."

"Just seemed odd to me."

"And if being odd was our criteria for judging, one of the two of us would be in deep shit. And I don't think it would be me. And by the way, I would never say 'tizzy' to a leather queen."

"Now who's being judgmental?" Fenwick asked. They returned to the entrance to the station where they first entered. The flags still hung unmoving in the humid-dense air.

Sanchez hurried up to them. "I found out where Callaghan is. He hangs out at the Raving Dragon, the cop bar where the bartender incident happened."

Fenwick said, "I know it."

Turner said, "He still goes there? That's a hell of a nerve."

Sanchez said, "I don't have an actual sighting, but supposedly he hangs out there every night until it closes. It's got a four A.M. license."

Fenwick said, "We've got a lot of people to talk to here. We go after Callaghan or we worry about these guys?"

"Both," Turner said, "but I gave up bilocating years ago. I think we go talk to Callaghan. He's the prime suspect."

"He'll lie," Fenwick said.

Turner repeated the great cop truism. "They all lie." Then continued, "Callaghan has got to realize we're not going to be intimidated just because he's a cop. I think we need to pressure him. He's the logical suspect. He's gotta know that."

"Then he comes first."

Turner said, "I'd like to be the first to tell him the news."

Fenwick said, "Every CPD employee breathing at this hour knows the news. It's worse than a small town in East Nowhere, and I like East Nowhere."

"That's so like you," Turner said.

Fenwick turned to Sanchez. "If you would, please, get the name and address of everyone working all three whipping booths. If they're not local, get their motel or hotel and their home addresses. Check driver's licenses. Remind them we need to talk to everyone tonight between ten and eleven. We'll meet them here. Get the Scanlan kid down to Area Ten headquarters. Have them get in touch with his parents. He's under age for being here and for being out this late. Don't let him out of your sight. He may not be a suspect, but he's the closest thing to a witness we have."

Turner said, "And let's see if we can't find him something to wear."

"No," Fenwick said. "No change of clothes. I want to see the look on his parents' faces when they see him in that outfit. If they let him go out dressed like that, they should be liable for some kind of prosecution. If they don't know anything about it..." He shook his head.

Turner wanted to meet the parents as well. He thought Fenwick might want to take a picture of them and add it to his rogues gallery of criminally negligent parents. Turner wanted to meet them to see if they were as clueless as he guessed them to be.

TEN

Outside, after the car started moving, Fenwick said, "I have a technical question. Did I really see a big burly guy strutting around? Said burly guy was leading another burly guy around by a leash. Guy on other end of leash was on all fours."

"Yes," Turner said.

Fenwick glanced at Turner. "To whom is that a turn on?"

"Probably the same people who get goose bumps when you use the correct interrogative pronoun."

"I talk correctly," Fenwick said, "and I have the soul of a poet."

"I can't help that," Turner said.

"It turns you on?" Fenwick asked.

"You being a poet? No. The leather stuff? Some of it does sometimes. Just like I'm sure you're turned on by things that I'm not turned on by."

"Like what?" Fenwick asked.

"Tell you what, I'll make a list for you, right after you make a list for me."

"Oh," Fenwick said.

"Precisely," Turner replied.

Fenwick dropped it.

After a few minutes fiddling with the air conditioning, Fenwick said, "We've got to figure out how the kid fits into all this. One option, he's totally innocent. A second is that he did it. Another is that he's being set up by the killer. A killer might think that just because the kid's young, we wouldn't believe him. Maybe make him a suspect."

"If that was true, wouldn't there be more evidence linking him to the murder?"

Fenwick said, "We don't know yet if there isn't any."

"He claimed he got lost. What if he had stayed lost and never found the body?"

Fenwick said, "Kind of fucks up a murder plot if your fall guy is a screw-up. Or they were improvising. They didn't know if it would work, but if it did, they've got a fairly dumb kid with no explanation."

As they drove, Turner scanned the materials Barb Dams had prepared. Turner found a stack of photos that included Belger, Callaghan, and any other police personnel connected with the case, as well as Stephanie Preston, the bartender from the notorious incident at the Raving Dragon. There was an Incident Summary Packet of what different witnesses said happened at the bar. A one-page background summary of every cop who had been at the bar. Included on that page was the current contact information for everyone involved. Barb had included a Post-It note that promised more if they needed it. She also added a memo that she'd called Stephanie Preston.

Turner agreed with the call. Despite the hour, he thought she deserved some warning. The press might decide to camp outside her door. They might ignore her. She might be in danger. Turner also knew that Barb was the perfect one to make such a call. She was fabulous at soothing and calming especially with possibly upsetting news. Turner added the bartender to the list of people they'd try to get to before returning to Area Ten.

No sign identified the Raving Dragon bar near Western Avenue and Irving Park Road. As Fenwick parked in an illegal parking space half a block away from the bar, he said, "The goddess watches over my good parking karma."

Turner said, "My goddess doesn't like your goddess."

"There's more than one?" Fenwick asked.

"If you can have one goddess, I can have two. Or ten."

As the detectives entered, they saw a couple of uniformed cops clustered around the pool table in the back. The city's no indoor smoking ordinance could barely be read because of the smog-choked haze. It was a cop bar. No inspectors from the city would show unless the mayor himself planned an appearance. A few neon lights around the mirror behind the bar tried to give enough light so you could make out the face of the person next to you. The bartender's tattoos all merged into one massive blur even at this short distance. A newish-looking, hand-lettered sign on the bar said in wide-point magic marker, CELL PHONE USE STRICTLY FORBIDDEN. Below it was a jar with the smashed remnants of a cell phone. Nobody was going to be taking any more pictures or doing any videotaping if the management could help it. It was just after midnight. At least the bar's air-conditioning was working.

Fenwick lumbered down the narrow aisle between the barstools and the booths to the right. In the occupied booths he glanced at the denizens scrunched over their drinks. A few of them muttered sounds of recognition. Turner followed.

Alone in the last booth, Barry Callaghan gripped a cigarette in one hand and a shot glass of bourbon in the other. A half bottle of beer kept his pack of cigarettes company on the table top. Turner eased into the booth first. Fenwick and his bulk would be more comfortable on the end of the maroon, ripped and torn cushioned bench.

Callaghan stank. He was more overweight than Fenwick. Turner guessed from the beard stubble that Callaghan might have last shaved a week ago. The odor he emanated indicated no baths or showers or applications of deodorant in the interim, either.

Callaghan glared at them. His words slurred as he said, "What the fuck do you want?"

Fenwick said, "Trent Belger is dead."

Callaghan said, "Party at my place."

Turner had seen the video of Callaghan's beating of the young, female bartender. Turner hated the creepy bully who thought he would get away with spreading his bulk in any manner he wished and be damned to the rest of the world. Someone had said, 'no' to him and he attacked, as he probably always did, but this time he'd gotten caught. At the same time Turner didn't want to get swept away in the maelstrom that was now Callaghan's life. The guy was an asshole, a caught asshole, but an asshole many in the rank and file were rallying around.

Fenwick asked, "What do you see when you see yourself on that videotape?"

Callaghan said, "The fucking bitch deserved it."

Turner wasn't in the mood for a moral debate. Getting Callaghan to acknowledge and accept reality was not part of his job description. He doubted if it was remotely possible for any amount of conversation to bring Callaghan and reality to any kind of working agreement, although Fenwick did enjoy the occasional pointless debate.

"When did you last see Belger?" Turner asked.

"Fuck him. The dumb shit could have helped me. Instead he fucked me over. I almost got banned from my favorite bar. I'm lucky I still get to hang out in this dump. I could've been thrown out permanently. Bullshit."

Fenwick said, "Where were you tonight?"

"Wherever I wanted to be."

Fenwick leaned over the table, lowered his voice to its most menacing grumble, and said, "We want answers. If you want, we'll take you into the alley behind this place, and I will personally beat the shit out of you. No one will stop us. Even though they've rallied around you, anybody with sense, and there are more cops with sense than you'd care to believe, wants you to go away. You're an embarrassment."

"I'm bigger than you are," Callaghan said.

"Let's try it," Fenwick said.

Callaghan didn't move.

There was no doubt in Turner's mind that Fenwick would be able to overcome Callaghan, and he would certainly be willing to help. But Turner didn't believe in torture, and he knew it didn't work, and they really did need answers.

Fenwick asked, "When did you last see him?"

"The day he turned on me."

"You weren't still partners?" Fenwick asked.

Callaghan quoted the official department statement. "Detective Callaghan is on paid administrative leave pending an investigation. Bullshit."

"Where have you been all night?" Turner asked.

"Here. I been here all night."

A hulk of uniformed cop flesh loomed at the entrance to the booth. "If he says he was here all night, he was here all night." Turner and Fenwick gazed at the intruder.

"Who the fuck are you?" Fenwick asked.

"A loyal cop who doesn't try to stick it to his own." The stranger's hand hovered near his gun. Echoing the action of Gene Hackman's character in *Mississippi Burning*, with a lightning quick movement, Fenwick grabbed the guy's dick and balls through the front of the guy's pants with one hand. Fenwick added a twist different from the movie when he used his free hand to pull the interloper forward by his uniform tie. The stranger's nose wound up an inch from Fenwick's.

He tried to struggle, but Fenwick's dual grip was firm. In his very lowest and most menacing grumble, Fenwick said, "Never put your hand near your gun while you are anywhere close to me. Never. Stay the fuck away from here or I will hurt you." The uniformed cop gasped for air.

Holding a baseball bat in one hand and tapping it against the other, the bartender appeared behind the new guy. Fenwick let the stranger go. Released from Fenwick's grip, he leaned over and gasped.

"No problems in here," the bartender said. Up close Turner could see that his tattoos had masses of different colors and swirls. Still he couldn't make out if there were specific designs or just one massive dye job of an artist gone nuts.

Callaghan said, "They don't believe I was here all night."

The bartender said, "He was here all night." He tapped the stranger on the shoulder with the bat and said, "Claude, go back and sit down."

Trying to retain what little dignity he had left, Claude said, "I'm sitting close enough to keep listening." But he kept himself out of Fenwick's reach.

The bartender watched him hobble a few feet then said to the three in the booth, "You need anything?"

"Another shot and a beer," Callaghan said.

"You guys?"

Turner and Fenwick shook their heads. The bartender left.

Turner asked, "Before the incident, did you and Belger get along?"

"We were never buddies."

"But you were partners," Fenwick said.

"Not my choice."

"You could have asked for a transfer," Turner said.

"Fuck the police bureaucracy."

"Ever have a physical fight?" Fenwick asked.

"I wouldn't touch the fucking twerp."

"Ever have words?" Fenwick asked.

"Nope."

"Ever beat the hell out of suspects?" Turner asked.

"No."

"We'll find out," Turner said. "We'll look through your files."

"You won't find anything."

"How about Belger? He get rough?" Turner asked.

"He was an asshole. Okay, at first when we started, he seemed like a decent guy. You know, somebody you could depend on, who'd back you up."

Turner knew this was the universal and highest praise a cop

could give one's partner, that he or she could be depended on. Turner trusted Fenwick implicitly.

The bartender delivered Callaghan's refills and left.

"So what went wrong?" Turner asked.

Callaghan downed the shot then gulped a third of his beer, then answered, "The motherfucker turned on me."

Fenwick said, "But a partner you can depend on doesn't turn on a partner."

"He was a wimp. A pussy. He was willing to sell me out."

"Why?" Turner asked.

"You'd have to ask him."

Fenwick said, "He's dead. We're asking you."

"How the fuck should I know? Maybe his mother beat him when he was little. Maybe he got a bribe. I don't know, and I don't care. I hate him — alive or dead."

Turner asked, "Who else hated him?"

"Like I'm going to give you names."

"Who else?" Fenwick repeated.

"Everybody," Callaghan said.

"Anybody who hated both of you?" Turner asked.

Callaghan paused this time. "No," he finally muttered.

A chink in the armor? Turner switched tacks. He asked, "What happened in here that night?"

"Nothing. I got nothing to say about that. Nothing."

Turner gazed around the room. Most of the others turned their heads away when he glanced in their direction. A few didn't. Claude and several buddies hunched over in quiet conversation.

Turner needed to piss. He told Fenwick that he'd be back.

The washroom was small. The one stall's door hung askew. A florid, elderly cop sat on the toilet with his pants around his ankles and his head leaning against the partition. He snored.

The sink hadn't been cleaned this century. The mirror had dots of pimple residue, water spots, and smears of liquid of unknown origins. The urinal was a six foot trough against the far wall.

Turner stepped to the trough and began to piss. He shut his eyes and thought. They weren't going to get answers out of Callaghan, and they weren't likely to get cooperation from any other cops. And he doubted anybody would come forward from the leather party. He sighed. They had hours to go before the end of their shift.

"Hey ya," a deep voice next to Turner brought him out of his reverie. A tall, lanky cop who'd been playing pool stood next to Turner. He unzipped and began to piss. The guy in the stall continued snoring.

"He wasn't here all night," said the young cop.

"Where was he?"

"I don't know."

"When did he get here?"

"A few minutes before you did."

Turner finished and zipped up. He turned to the sink. The filth-encrusted soap holder was empty.

The bathroom door banged open. A baritone voice said, "The fag detective in here?"

A hulking, middle-aged cop who'd also been playing pool, leaned insolently against the wall. He propped his back against the gritty tile, put his right foot flat on the wall, and grabbed his crotch. He said, "Suck this, bitch." He pulled at the front of his pants covering his dick and balls.

The lanky young guy scuttled out. The cop sidled along the wall so that he blocked Turner's exit.

The detective tensed, ready for a fight. All he said, very quietly, was, "No."

The newcomer said, "Maybe you can give all of us blowjobs.

I hear all you fags prefer giving head in johns."

Turner had an impulse to attack the oaf confronting him, but he waited. The guy would make a mistake. Turner's muscles tensed. His mind rushed on high alert. He didn't ask if the guy was making an assumption or actually knew Turner's sexual orientation. Not only didn't he care, he wasn't about to explain, beg, plead, or lie.

A second later, the guy lunged at Turner. Prepared as Turner was, the guy had at least seventy-five pounds on him. The man was drunk, but that was not necessarily a plus for Turner, especially in such a small place. Being drunk could also make the guy more willing to take a stupid chance or make a stupid mistake. Turner staggered back into the stall partition. Braced as he'd been, still his head thunked hard on the dented and cheap metal. His collision with it caused the askew door to slip even further off its remaining hinge.

The stall occupant snorted, snuffled, and resumed snoring.

The initial lunge had unbalanced Turner's attacker who tried to right himself. The drunk hulk was halfway up when he launched himself at Turner again. Turner twisted, grabbed the man by collar and back of the pants, and heaved. The man's momentum propelled him into the partition, which came loose from its mooring. The young cop and the slab of now loose metal landed on the no longer snoring inhabitant. Turner thought the noise from the banging and breaking might get the attention of Fenwick and the others.

Turner's attacker scrambled to his feet, shook his head, cursed, and flung himself toward the detective. Turner let the man come in close then brought his knee up into the uniformed cop's exposed crotch. The guy bent halfway over. Turner took him by the back of the neck and rammed his head into the urinal trough.

The cop muttered, "Mother fucker," and, face down, slipped to the floor. Turner noted that the trough was now cracked. The man groaned. Turner touched the back of his own head. He felt a lump growing.

The inhabitant of the crushed stall staggered out grabbing at his zipper and belt buckle. He tried to focus bleary eyes on Turner, failed. He muttered, "What the fuck?" He tripped on the leg of Turner's fallen attacker. He staggered toward the door. As he arrived, it opened. He banged his head on the edge. He swore again and shuffled unsteadily out.

Fenwick entered. The bartender, baseball bat in hand, followed him. Fenwick saw the guy on the floor, glanced at Turner and said, "You giving lessons to cops again?"

Turner said, "He wanted to be introduced to the floor." Turner breathed heavily. He examined himself in the mirror, touched the back of his head, looked at his hand. He wasn't bleeding.

The bartender said, "Somebody's gotta pay for this."

Fenwick looked at the dingy interior. "Hire a decorator and send the Chicago Police Department the bill."

Fenwick and Turner walked out.

Turner glanced around for the thin young cop. Gone. Had the guy been trying to set him up or give him real information? If the information was accurate, he wanted to thank him. If he was part of the set up, he wanted to at least talk to him. If he'd been telling the truth, Turner wouldn't thank him in front of the others. It might destroy the young guy's career. The drunk old guy who'd been asleep was gone. Callaghan had vanished.

Turner and Fenwick walked out. Outdoors. One in the morning. Waves of heat radiated from the pavement. The atmosphere was as oppressive as if it were mid-day.

Fenwick asked, "You okay?"

Turner said, "I don't get to beat up assholes often enough. I should try it more often."

"I could give you lessons."

"I don't think Claude with his crushed balls is going to be your new best friend."

"He didn't seem to be enjoying himself. I was."

Turner said, "Or I can wait until the adrenaline wears off and stop trembling. It shouldn't be necessary to pound the shit out of your own."

"From the results I saw, I think you did a great job," Fenwick said.

"And I'm glad I did. I'm a little surprised at how good it feels."

Fenwick glanced at his friend. "What happened in there?"

Turner said, "A young guy who wasn't kissing the floor when you entered, told me Callaghan came in just before we did. He left before the action started." He told him what his attacker said.

Fenwick said, "I think more cops are disgusted by Callaghan's behavior than approve, but ain't nobody gonna go against him publicly."

Turner had seen the same thing over and over again. A cop did something stupid, but peer pressure, fear for their own screw-ups, whatever it was, drew the people on the job together in solidarity behind the screw-up. Turner would never be able to change that attitude among his colleagues and wasn't interested in trying to. He'd be supportive and rally around, when appropriate. He wanted no part in any cover-ups.

ELEVEN

They walked to the car. A figure in a blue short-sleeve shirt, khaki pants, and a slouch fedora leaned his butt against the passenger side door of their unmarked vehicle.

Only Ian Hume would be wearing his trademark outfit complete with hat on one of the most humid nights of the year. Ian was a reporter for the *Gay Tribune*, the largest gay newspaper in Chicago. Many years ago he had been Turner's first partner on the police force and his first lover.

Ian gazed carefully at Turner. "You okay?" he asked. "You look upset."

"I'm fine."

Fenwick said, "My buddy here beat the crap out of some homophobic pig."

Ian raised an eyebrow. "That's not usually your style."

"Today it was."

Fenwick told the story.

Ian said, "Guy had it coming."

"Yes, I know," Turner said. The adrenalin rush was gone and his reluctance to use violence was reasserting itself. He said, "The other guy was drunk and stupid. It wasn't a big deal. Fenwick did his bit in the bar for peace and understanding."

"He yanked somebody's chain?" Ian asked.

"In a manner of speaking." He told about Claude, the guy in the bar who wanted to back up Callaghan's story.

Ian said, "We'll have to give both of you medals for making assholes suffer."

"Is that a category for the Olympics?" Turner asked.

"If it's not, it should be," Fenwick said.

Turner said, "The odder question of the moment is how the

hell did you find us?"

Ian said, "Sources."

Fenwick said, "Bullshit."

Ian said, "Bullshit sources? I kind of like the notion."

Turner said, "It's too hot for pointless repartee, and we haven't been lovers in enough years to justify an argument."

Ian said, "I heard there was a problem at the Black and Blue party. I got word that Belger was dead. I knew you'd have to talk to the former partner. I know enough about cop bars in this city, and I still know people in the department. I didn't want to go into the bar. People might know me in my incarnation as gay reporter. Remotely possible, but still possible. I knew somebody who gave me the license plate number of your car. All I had to do was check the nearest illegal parking spaces. I decided to lurk out here. Good thing I did. Your car would have had its tires flattened and the sides keyed."

Fenwick said, "Good news travels quickly."

Ian said, "It's not like it's your personal car."

Fenwick said, "It's the principle of the thing."

"Who tried it?" Turner asked.

"Older cop, heavy set, big jowls, hat pulled down low, no visible ID, beat cop outfit. Didn't know him. He took off when I looked obstinate. He didn't want to call back-up for an attack on the vehicle of one of his own. I might have been half his age and in better shape so I don't think he wanted a fight."

Fenwick said, "Why didn't he just arrest you?"

"I was charming."

Rare, but Turner had seen Ian charm some odd characters in his time.

Fenwick said, "I need to be fed."

Ian said, "It's only a few blocks to a Dunkin' Donuts. We can just walk."

"A few blocks," Fenwick said. "In this heat? You must be mad."

Turner thumped the trunk of the car. "After what you said, wreck though it is, we shouldn't really leave this thing unattended."

They piled into the car and drove three blocks to the restaurant. They parked in a lighted spot in the lot where they could view it from a table inside.

Ian had coffee. Fenwick had an order of donut holes and a large diet soda. Turner, who had long since learned not to question Fenwick's dietary habits, had ice water.

Turner wasn't averse to talking a case over with Ian. Their friendship triumphed over Ian's need to be a reporter. He knew Ian would keep anything they said confidential. Turner gave him the details they had so far.

When Turner finished, Ian said, "He was whipped?"

Turner nodded.

"And he had a dildo up his butt?"

Another nod.

"But we don't know if he was gay?"

"I don't," Turner said. "The ME will give us the official word on what killed him. I'm not sure who can give us the official word if he liked being fucked. Or if either of those options would lead to a murderer."

"Was he dumped at the Black and Blue party or was he attending?" Ian asked.

Turner said, "Supposedly he'd been doing demonstrations at the whipping booth. He could have left. He was scheduled to come back and do another performance."

"Doesn't mean he's gay," Ian said.

"Doesn't mean he isn't," Turner said.

"What does it mean?" Fenwick asked. "You guys need to explain this whole gay leather thing to me."

Ian said, "Some people like to get beat up and pissed on."

"Those are the romantics," Turner said.

Ian said, "And some don't. It's just a kink. Kind of like kinks for straight people but different."

Turner said, "I know about International Mr. Leather. That's usually around Memorial Day, and the Folsom Street Fair in San Francisco, but I've never heard of this one."

"You wouldn't," Ian said. "The Black and Blue party goes out of its way to be mysterious and fly under the radar. They do not advertise themselves in the gay press. There are no cutesy articles in magazines desperate to be trendy. You have to have someone give you the secret password just to get on their website."

"Why?" Fenwick asked.

"A wise woman once said that if your specialty was making enough money to support a magazine then maybe it wasn't so special. These guys were making a ton of money."

"Define ton," Fenwick said.

"I heard it costs two thousand dollars just to register for the convention. That doesn't include costs for hotel room, transportation, or meals." He tore a piece of paper from his reporter's notebook and handed it to Turner. "This is the secret password for the website."

"You know these things?" Fenwick asked. He'd managed to scarf down half of his donuts and a third of his diet drink.

"I know everything."

"When will the Cubs win a World Series?"

"Not this decade."

Turner said, "Focus, boys. The party. The section we saw was mobbed."

"Money isn't the problem. They like to think they're extremely exclusive. Of course, if you're so exclusive nobody shows up, there's not much point in the whole operation. As you know the leather scene takes itself very seriously."

Fenwick asked, "These are all gay guys?"

Ian said, "This party is certainly pitched to gay men, but lesbians and straight people show up."

"You've been?" Turner asked.

"Of course. I attended the first one. I have to make sacrifices for my journalistic integrity. I haven't been since."

"Blow your integrity out your ass," Fenwick said.

"Paul can do that any time the need arises."

"Not this decade," Turner said.

"Did you wear your slouch fedora?" Fenwick asked.

"No."

Turner stifled his curiosity because he and Ian were no longer lovers. Fenwick, however, had no such restraint. "You into this scene?" he asked.

"I can be. How about you?"

Turner said, "This is way more information than any of us needs."

Fenwick grinned.

Ian said, "Some of these guys talk about the 'leather community' as if it was this awesome monolith of masculinity. I think it's just a bunch of dizzy queens over-compensating."

Fenwick said, "But why the secrecy? It's not really necessary, is it? I mean who cares what somebody does in private or do these guys get hassled?"

Ian said, "I've done enough research to know that everything they do meets the exact letter of the law. It is very private. No one from the public can get in. There's no chance some random tourist family from Nebraska will 'see' something so the party organizers don't have to worry about intrusions."

"We met at least one guy who snuck in."

"No system is perfect. But the secrecy and the exclusivity are draws in and of themselves."

Turner said, "Secrecy can also be a turn on. Or maybe they just like it. I like men, not because I'm feminine, but because I'm attracted to their masculinity."

Fenwick said, "I'm open to debating the nature of sexuality, gay or straight. I think I've got it. They let Belger in, but that doesn't mean he was gay." He finished the last donut and gulped the entire rest of his drink. Among the many things Turner had learned to not mention was the rate at which and quantity of food Fenwick was able to consume. Turner sipped from his ice water.

Ian said, "Right. I'm sure they don't discriminate. As long as the straight person behaved themselves, I'm sure they'd let them in, and if they paid their exorbitant fee."

"Did you?" Fenwick asked.

"It was a legitimate journalistic expense."

"Bullshit," Fenwick said.

Turner said, "Was Belger gay or straight and does it make any difference to the investigation?"

Ian drank some coffee. He said, "I've started to snoop around. My sources among the attendees of the party are pretty good. And I still know a few cops. I've got no clue about his sexual orientation, and I've got evidence of Belger being on camera for pay but no evidence that he was hiring himself out as an actual prostitute. I haven't been able to find any kind of profile for him on gay male escort web sites, but I haven't had a lot of time to dig through all of them. Plus I'm still looking for more information."

Fenwick said, "He didn't strike me as hot enough to be a hooker."

"Hot in the leather world can mean many things. If he was into being beaten and whipped, then among a certain set, he might have been very popular."

"How do we find these guys?" Fenwick asked.

Ian said, "The whole party is anonymous. You get your ID badge, but it doesn't have your name on the front. It's on the back along with your personal code which supposedly means you paid. They don't let just anybody into that thing. They're afraid of reporters sneaking in and trying to take pictures and all kinds of stuff."

"Who runs it?"

"Who did you talk to?" Ian asked.

"Denver Slade and Matthew Bryner."

Ian said, "Slade is kind of the manager. Matty Bryner is a piece of work."

"Matty?" Turner asked.

"We're best friends."

Fenwick said, "In a pig's ass."

"I'm sure we could get a booth for that at the party," Ian said.

Turner said, "Gentlemen. Focus."

"The real people behind the party are a consortium of wealthy gay men. I was told it started a few years ago when someone had a snit fit about a contest during a leather event in, I think, Los Angeles. I'm not sure. The main point is the person vowed to get revenge. Who was getting revenge on whom, I'm not sure. I've also been given to understand that they think the other leather fairs around the country are too commercial and too tame. These people claim to be the real thing."

"I don't get it," Turner asked. "Real thing? Once you've pissed on somebody, what else is there? Do they mean they chained people up, killed them?"

"No snuff films I've heard about," Ian said. "These are wealthy people, but they aren't nuts."

"You know them?" Fenwick asked.

"I know a few things about some of them. I do know Matty Bryner. As it happens. I made it my business to look into the party that first year. It all turned out to be remarkably prosaic until I got to ol' Matty. The deeper I looked into him the murkier it got."

"How murky can you be if you're from Des Moines?" Fenwick asked.

Ian said, "I got rumors, and only rumors. Problems with police. Bryner and a boyfriend in an S+M scene gone very, very wrong."

Turner said, "If the police were involved, there'd have to be some kind of record."

"But there isn't," Ian said. "Either it's not true, or he's got a hell of a lot of power in Iowa. The same seems to be true here. He may be from Des Moines, but he's got some kind of pull in this town."

"Who's behind him here?"

"That I don't know. Finding out didn't seem worth the effort at the time. No crime, as far as I knew, had been committed in Chicago. I could find no records of any crime in Des Moines. Sometimes rumors are just rumors. People who involve themselves in the inner workings of the gay community are subject to being viciously attacked. Same as any group. I don't know if these guys being a complicated and secretive group makes it worse or not."

"Why be complicated and secretive?" Fenwick asked.

"Sometimes it's hard to tell. Maybe it's as simple as why not or because they can. Or maybe it's because they're silly twits? They do work hard for the tough leather-man mystique."

Turner said, "Do people in this day and age really care if someone's running around in a motorcycle jacket and leather pants? It can be sexy, and that's nice if it is, but who cares?"

Fenwick said, "It must make somebody feel better."

Ian said, "For a lonely gay man from Podunk, Nebraska, who wants to be masculine and gay, it might be vital, but other than that," Ian shrugged, "I can work on my sources in the department. I think that's where your answer is to this thing."

Turner said, "I agree. Certainly putting the body at that party could easily have been a way to divert suspicion from the real murderer."

Fenwick said, "If there's this much animosity among these leather people, maybe some of the others are trying to get even with Bryner. Or maybe this party was taking business away from theirs. Maybe they were pissed about that."

Ian said, "And they committed murder and dumped a body at the party all in hopes of getting Bryner bad publicity?"

Turner said, "It's possible, but I don't know who those people are or if they were there."

Ian said, "That I can check. The more prominent fairs and festivals have publicity people. I can nose my way into it."

"Thanks," Turner said.

"What did you find out in the bar?" Ian asked.

"That cops lie," Turner said. "Stop the presses."

Ian said, "Speaking of guys in bars."

"And we were," Fenwick said.

"You interviewed the reporter who broke the original Callaghan story yet?"

They shook their heads. "I've got a rumor, very unconfirmed, that he is very closeted and very gay."

Turner said, "Are you saying there's a connection between him, Belger, and Callaghan that goes beyond what was reported on the news?"

Ian said, "My money is on the killer being someone from the department, but there's obviously a gay angle to this somewhere. Right now, it's only a rumor."

Fenwick said, "My money is on it being one of ours."

Ian said, "You have no group loyalty."

Fenwick said, "Loyalty? Sure. But this isn't some mafia omerta where people take a blood oath of silence. This is real people getting killed."

Ian said, "Mafia people aren't real people?"

Fenwick grumbled.

Ian grinned. He was one of the few people who did not get intimidated by Fenwick's grumbles.

Fenwick resumed, "Belger may have been an asshole. He may have deserved to die. I've met a lot of people who deserved to die and didn't. I've met a lot who deserved to live, but they died. I can't change any of that. None of it involves loyalty."

Turner recognized the echoes of Tolkien's famous quote in Fenwick's statement. He knew his partner loved the *Lord of the Rings* books and movies. He did too.

Turner said, "We'll have to talk to the reporter."

Ian said, "Remember, the reporter didn't make the tape."

Fenwick said, "Gotta talk to that guy, too."

Ian said, "And find out how the hell that recording made it into the press. Somebody pulled a smart, fast one there, too."

"I wondered about that," Turner said.

Ian said, "It was just too damn quick. Remember, it wasn't a bar that had security cameras."

Fenwick said, "What the hell for? It was a cop bar."

"Exactly," Ian said. "The incident happened just after three in the morning, but it was on the earliest newscasts and even made it national before eight A.M. Somebody knew somebody or something odd was going on."

"Somebody planned it?" Turner asked.

Fenwick said, "How do you plan a fight between cops?"

Ian said, "Very carefully. I've got lots of sources in the news business in this town. Some of them owe me. The guy who actually recorded it just faded into the background."

"We'll have to get to him," Turner said.

Ian said, "I know enough not to taint a witness although he wouldn't be a witness to your murder. I hope. But if the gay angle turned out to be true, maybe I can kind of chat with one or both of them."

"Do what you can," Turner said. "Anything you find out, we appreciate."

Fenwick said, "We should go see the family." He used a finger on his now empty plate to dab up bits of sugar and fried dough that had escaped his earlier inhalation.

Ian said, "You ate all those yourself."

Turner said, "He considers them fusion cooking."

Fenwick said, "It's got sugar and grease. That's as much fusion as I need."

They got up to leave. Ian tapped each of them on the arm. They turned to him. He said, "You guys should be very careful. What happened in the Raving Dragon this morning is not because one random isolated asshole was out of control. This could be lots of assholes acting randomly, or it could be a conspiracy to murder gone wild, and you guys are the ones on the case. Until this is solved, I'd be very worried and very careful."

"We know," Turner said.

TWELVE

It was nearly half past one in the morning. They had Trent Belger's address from his identification and the papers Molton's secretary had sent. Belger had four children, two with each wife. He and his first wife had joint custody. They'd been married four years. He lived with his second wife and her mother. He'd been married to the second wife for five years. They would start with her.

The least favorite part of the job, Turner always thought, was taking bad news to the victim's relatives. Had to be done. Didn't get easier with time. And sometimes you got a bonanza of unexpected information. He knew one young detective on his first murder case who had been out canvassing the neighborhood for the first time. At the second house he went to a man answered. The young detective had asked the man if he knew the murdered guy, who'd been found half a block away. The man who answered turned out to be the brother of the victim. The man said, yes, and I killed him. A few of Turner's cases came close to being that easy, but none ever matched it.

Belger had lived on the northwest side in Wicker Park on the way to O'Hare Airport. Ringing the bell produced no results. They knocked on the door for some minutes before lights began to go on in the house. They didn't want to wait for the morning to tell the family. They might hear it on the news, and they should hear such news from a person, not an impersonal broadcast.

An elderly woman in a pink-flowered housecoat answered the door.

Turner and Fenwick identified themselves. Then Turner said, "We're looking for Mrs. Belger."

"I'm her mother, Belinda Smith. She's not here. She works the night shift. She gets home around seven. What's wrong?"

Turner said, "May we come in? We have news."

"My daughter's all right?"

"Yes. We'd like to talk."

She glanced at their badges again, eyed them warily for several moments, then nodded. They followed her to the kitchen where she pressed a button on the automatic coffee maker. No dishes in the sink, a first grader's drawings on the refrigerator, plastic place mats on the table, a pink-plastic paper-napkin holder. She plunked mugs in front of them without asking. She plopped her frame onto a chair with a sigh Fenwick would envy. She lit a cigarette, then asked, "What's going on?"

"Your son-in-law died this evening."

Her shoulders visibly relaxed. "Was the worthless fool in an accident?"

Turner said, "No, ma'am, he was murdered."

Her eyes flicked from one detective to the other. "I can't say that's a surprise. Ever since that incident in the bar, I knew something would happen. My husband was a cop. I know how things work. Our house has been spray-painted, trash strewn on the lawn, all for some silly bimbo."

Fenwick said, "The woman on the tape looked like she needed help."

Mrs. Jones said, "My son-in-law didn't give a shit about that woman, or anyone else except himself."

Turner knew that a bonus in any investigation is finding someone who didn't like the deceased. Friends and lovers tend to say only positive things about the dead one and seldom led to suspects, clues, or solutions. Enemies were gold.

Fenwick said, "He was found underground at the Prairie Street Train Station. They were having a leather event at the time. He say anything about going there?"

"Where?"

Fenwick repeated the name of the station and the location.

"What's a leather event?" Mrs. Smith asked.

Turner said, "A place where mostly gay men who like leather as part of their sexual expression get together. This one was called the Black and Blue party. He ever talk about anything like that?"

"Not a word. Never. But he didn't have to."

The detectives waited using one of their most potent weapons in an interrogation, silence.

She stubbed out her cigarette, got up, took the coffee pot, filled her mug, and, without asking, filled theirs. She didn't offer cream or sugar. She sipped hers black.

She said, "I'm not a snoop. I respect my daughter."

"You found something," Fenwick prompted.

"You bet. He was a pervert. Was he gay?"

"We don't know," Turner said.

"I found all these whips and things. Disgusting things. I didn't say a word to my daughter. It wasn't my business. I know sometimes a man needs to make sure his wife obeys. I understand that. I'm not like these modern women who whine at every little thing, and I never saw him lay a hand on my daughter or their kids."

"But you found something that led you to think he might do something violent?"

"It made me suspicious. He was weird."

"Weird, how?" Turner asked.

"He always watched violent movies. We had to tell him over and over not to let the kids watch."

"May we see what you found?" Fenwick asked.

"I'm not sure." She lit another cigarette, pulled in a lungful of smoke, slowly let it out. "I guess so." She stabbed the unfinished cigarette into the ashtray.

She took them to a clean bedroom with a double bed with a black and blue quilt as a cover. She said, "This is the guest bedroom. No one is supposed to ever go in here. At least, I'm not. I'm not a snoop."

Not a snoop, Turner thought. Only if pigs flew. But at the moment you're our snoop, so I don't care.

Mrs. Smith glanced out the window at the driveway, then led them to the closet. She had to remove several boxes from the interior until she got to one on the floor in the back.

They examined the collection. Several whips, leather vests, dildos in assorted sizes and colors, a box of condoms.

Turner asked, "May we take these?"

"It's not up to me," Mrs. Smith said.

Turner said, "We'll ask your daughter."

A car pulled into the driveway.

Mrs. Smith rushed to return all of the items to the box and the box to the closet. She hustled the detectives back to the kitchen. She lit another cigarette. Headlights shut off. A car door slammed. The back door opened and shut.

Jasmine Belger hurried into the room. Belger's wife looked like a loser in a Dolly Parton look-alike contest. Her blond wig towered above her tiny head. Her skimpy halter top could barely contain her outsized breasts. If her dress clung any more tightly, she might have erupted from it at any point like toothpaste from a tube. In a brassy and unpleasant voice, she said,"Mother, you shouldn't be smoking. Who are you guys? I got a call at work. I came right home. Has something happened to the children?"

Mrs. Smith said, "The kids are fine."

"Something's happened to Trent. The friend who called, she's the wife of a cop. She said something happened."

Turner said, "I'm sorry, Mrs. Belger, your husband is dead."

"Some criminal killed him. I warned him. I knew this would happen. I knew it." She reached for a paper napkin and dried her eyes as she slumped into a chair. "What happened?"

Mrs. Smith held her daughter's hand.

Turner said, "He wasn't on duty tonight."

"He said he was," Mrs. Belger said.

Mrs. Smith nodded confirmation.

"He wasn't," Turner said. "He was found at the Black and Blue party, a leather event for the gay community." He gave her the same explanation as he had her mother.

Mrs. Belger said, "A gay event? He wasn't gay. Maybe he was working undercover."

Turner said, "He wasn't working undercover. He was in leather pants and a chain harness. He'd been whipped. He had slash marks on his back."

"I never saw any scars."

"The whipping he took tonight might have left some, but there weren't any from before."

Fenwick asked, "You ever play with leather, whips, dress up for each other?"

"Never."

Turner said, "Mrs. Smith let us look through some of his things. We found a box of leather items including dildos."

"Mother, where did you find this? How did you know it was there? You let them look?"

"I wasn't snooping in your stuff. It was his."

"I told you not to snoop."

Fenwick interrupted. "She did, and we've seen it. We think there may be a connection to the murder."

As they trooped to the bedroom, Mrs. Belger asked, "What leather items? I've never seen a dildo in this house."

Fenwick retrieved the box from the closet and opened it.

Mrs. Belger glanced inside and gasped. "What are these doing here?"

Fenwick said, "We were hoping you could tell us."

"I have no idea. I've never seen those things before."

They returned to the kitchen. Fenwick carried the box tucked under his arm and then placed it under his chair.

Mrs. Belger said, "He was a good man. A good provider. I loved him. He loved me. I don't understand any of this. He wasn't gay. Those must be..." She stopped. Turner imagined she was trying to find a plausible explanation for them being in her house. Couldn't.

"That was his closet," she said. "Other than to hang up his clothes, I never went in there."

Turner said, "Mrs. Smith said you've had some trouble with vandalism."

"Ever since that stupid, stupid incident in the bar. He should never have gotten involved. I told him to apologize. I told him to make it right. He said it would blow over. He said that bartender was a conniving bitch. And that partner of his! I didn't like his partner. I told him I didn't like his partner. He said he was a good guy. That he could depend on him. Ha!"

"How was she a conniving bitch?"

"She'd fling herself at any man. There were always guys fighting over her."

"Was that what happened that night?" Turner asked. "Were they fighting over her?"

"All he told me was that Callaghan was an asshole, and this would all get taken care of. I saw the tape. Callaghan was a brute."

"Have you met him?"

"I met Callaghan at Ninth District social events like the Christmas party. That's all. I didn't get near him. He came on to me once."

"Were there bad feelings about that?" Fenwick asked.

"I never told my husband. I'd had a lot to drink that night, too."

"Did your husband have enemies on the force?"

"No. It was always just him and Callaghan. He never mentioned much of anybody else."

Fenwick asked, "Was your husband having an affair with that bartender?"

"No, that's impossible." She placed her hands on the side of her head and began balling her hair in her fists and pulling her hair. Gently, Mrs. Smith took her daughter's hands in hers. Mrs. Belger said, "What am I going to tell the kids? What am I going to do?" She glanced at the box. "I don't believe any of this."

She was too distraught to answer any more questions. So far she'd denied all knowledge of her husband's whereabouts or any particularly odd sexual wants or desires.

Mrs. Smith said, "Maybe you should leave."

Fenwick simply picked up the box and took it with them. He didn't ask permission, didn't hide what he was doing. They'd send the box to the lab.

After the rituals in the car to induce a breeze, Fenwick said, "How can she not know that her husband was into getting whipped?"

"There weren't any scars."

"How can a wife not know? Madge has radar for noticing the slightest thing. And she's got me trained to notice things about her."

Turner knew for certain that Fenwick never missed a birthday or anniversary. He suspected it wasn't because Madge nagged, but that Fenwick deeply loved her and would go to great extremes to keep her happy. And Fenwick would rather have his tongue ripped out than admit that to another man.

Turner said, "If Ben didn't notice, then I'd be worried. How can you live with someone and miss such a thing?"

Fenwick asked, "In our years doing this how many odd and inexplicable things have we seen?"

"More than I ever imagined."

Fenwick said, "The longer I'm a cop the only thing I learn is people are more weird than anyone would care to imagine."

"You noticed her looks?" Turner asked.

"You noticed and you're gay. What's not to notice? Although I try not to use noticing and Madge in the same sentence."

Turner said, "What about that crap about the pass made at the Christmas party?"

Fenwick said, "We're never getting the truth about that. Who was drunker? Who was coming on to whom? Bullshit."

"But Madge would know if you did such a thing."

"Madge would know if a gnat landed on my ass in the middle of the night. For these guys I think maybe an elephant stampede could crash by at high noon, and they might or might not notice. We'll have to talk to his first wife. See if she's got a little better insight. I'm sure she's got a unique perspective on all this."

Turner said, "There is something odd about that incident in the bar. I think it's the heart of what's going on, but I don't feel like I've got a handle on it."

Fenwick said, "Think the bartender's awake?"

It was a little after two. "Awake or not, we need to see her this morning. It's a murder investigation and we need to be ahead of what's going on. I think we're behind. Way behind. Violence and cops? It's the way we live. We're up to our armpits in it every day."

"Without it we'd be out of a job."

Turner said, "Depressingly true. You think a cop did it?"

"Don't you?"

"Yes."

Turner said, "As a wise old friend of mine put it, fuck-a-doodle-do."

Fenwick said, "We should try the first wife as well."

Turner glanced at the still-dark eastern horizon. The dawn was hours away. "She's the next logical person." He glanced at the materials Barb Dams had sent. It listed the first wife's current address. He mentioned it to his partner.

"Barb is brilliant," Fenwick said. "She'd know the logical progression as well as we would. I'd be surprised if it wasn't in there."

They drove over the Chicago city limits to Cicero.

THIRTEEN

Belger's first wife lived on a street filled with a row of Chicago bungalows, narrow houses with gables parallel to the street, constructed of dark maroon brick with only a few feet between them. She lived just south of Pershing Road. They only had to knock once before she answered. They introduced themselves.

She said, "Wife number two called to tell me the news. I hope he suffered." She wore gray sweatpants and a blue T-shirt. She led them to her kitchen. Clean, neat with a New York Firemen calendar on the wall. She caught Turner glancing at it. She said, "My current husband is a fireman. He's on duty."

Turner and Fenwick sat opposite her.

Fenwick said, "You're glad he's dead."

"I'd love to be dancing in the street. If it wasn't so hot out, I probably would."

"The two of you had problems?" Turner asked.

"That's putting it too mildly. I was naïve when I married him. I thought the little sexual peccadilloes were something I could handle. After he hauled out the whips and leather, I said adios."

"Not your scene?" Fenwick asked.

"No."

Turner said, "I'm trying to ask this delicately…"

She interrupted, "Was our sex life normal?"

Turner nodded.

"I was seldom satisfied. I don't think he was either. Once, at his urging, I tied his wrists together. I thought it was just silly. I laughed at him."

Fenwick said, "We found him with a dildo up his butt and what looked like a cue ball stuck in his mouth."

"I can tell you he loved to have his butt played with. That was disgusting. Another time he wanted me to strap on a dildo and do him. That was even more disgusting."

Fenwick said, "Wife number two claimed she never saw the dildos or leather items."

"Maybe he learned his lesson. Maybe he went outside the marriage. As far as I know, he never cheated on me."

Turner said, "You'd think he'd have mentioned those oddities before the marriage."

"The idiot didn't. He thought I'd just go along. He thought I'd cheerfully give in to his whims. He was gross and pathetic. Total yecch. When I wouldn't give in, he got nasty."

"Did he hit you?" Turner asked.

"He tried to. He came after me one night. I beat the shit out of him." She shook her head. "He liked it! He wanted me to do more. I moved out the next day. That wasn't my idea of a life together."

"He was found at a gay leather party."

"You know," she said, "after the dildo incident I was suspicious. I mean things never worked out sexually between us, but he never mentioned guys. It's the kind of thing where you say, could he be, but by that time I didn't care enough about him. I just didn't want to think about him. Ever."

"Did you meet Callaghan?"

"I'll say. That man was a menace. That man and my husband were a lethal combination, and I'm not talking about that problem in the bar. That was a joke."

"How so?" Turner asked.

"You think that was the first time Callaghan roughed up a woman? I know he went after his wife before she divorced him. I know because she'd be over here crying both before and after I got divorced from my idiot."

"You knew the Callaghans?" Fenwick asked.

"Sure. We'd socialize once in a while as a foursome. Callaghan's wife and I were on a couple of social committees. Our kids went to the same school for a while."

"How did your husband and Callaghan get along?"

"I must have been really naïve when I was younger. I thought all partners did what they did."

"What was that?" Turner asked.

"Well, they palled around together, and sure they joked, but they ribbed each other unmercifully. The arguments would start about small stuff, sports usually. They'd egg each other on, and it would escalate. By the end of the arguments, if it had been two women, both of them would have been in tears. But they just kept being buddies."

"Why didn't either of them put in for transfers?" Turner asked.

"Because even after the most violent arguments, they'd be all buddies again the next day. The fights got fueled by late nights, shots of booze, and gallons of beer. They'd sober up, and the whole cycle would start again."

"Any actual physical fights?" Turner asked.

"Not that I know of, but no, there was one totally odd incident. This must have happened about a year before our divorce. Trent came in one night, and he was sobbing. He was sure they were going to fire him."

"What happened?" Turner asked.

"Him and his buddy had beaten up some suspect. You remember Commander Burge and how people are trying to sue him?"

Turner nodded. It was a notorious case and no cops had been arrested, yet. Suspects in Burge's old Area claimed to have had confessions beaten out of them. Turner knew cops rarely actually beat confessions out of suspects in this day and age, but some cops still walked a thin line.

She said, "This went beyond the usual. They tasered the guy. Took turns zapping him. Turned out they nearly killed him."

"Obviously, he didn't get fired," Turner said.

"Not even suspended. I'm not sure why. I don't know if he knew why. I think Callaghan might have had some powerful friends in the department. It also might have had something to do with the fact that the guy they were questioning was suspected of molesting five- and six-year old girls. Nobody's got sympathy for that. Guy deserved whatever he got."

Fenwick said, "But that kind of treatment could have gotten the case thrown out. Did they get a confession?"

She rearranged the salt and pepper shakers which had been perfectly aligned. She shrugged, "I'm not sure. The case never went to trial. The guy they were trying to arrest just sort of disappeared. At least, that's what he told me."

Turner figured either Callaghan or Belger or both must know someone very powerful. Complete cover-ups weren't that easy. You needed cooperation from high in the department.

"But you never found out the details?" Turner asked.

"Nope. He just went to work, and 'poof' everything was just great. He and that idiot partner of his kept on being buddies, but I'm not sure they were as close as before. At least, we didn't go out much socially as a foursome any more, but the two of them seemed welded together. And by that point, I didn't care much. I got rid of him, got a good divorce settlement, and moved out of the city."

Turner and Fenwick left.

In the muggy, middle-of-the-night air, Fenwick said, "Tasering somebody and the suspect goes missing? That takes balls."

"Or stupidity."

"That kind of cover-up means powerful friends. Something is very not right."

In the car Fenwick said, "He wanted her to strap on a dildo and fuck him. We found him with a dildo up his butt. Does that mean he's gay?"

"It means he wanted his wife to use a dildo on him and that

either he or the killer was getting what he wanted in the end. So to speak."

Fenwick said, "That was one of your weaker attempts at a pun."

Turner said, "More of a play on words although I have been practicing. I guess I'll never be able to catch up to you."

"For which the world is probably thankful," Fenwick admitted.

Turner said, "As long as we're talking to the women in their lives, let's check on the bartender, and we might as well add Callaghan's wife." He checked the data sheets. "Wives."

FOURTEEN

The bartender, Stephanie Preston, sipped from her mug of coffee and sat down at a table in a breakfast nook of a bungalow kitchen in Marquette Park. She made no offer to share the coffee or for them to sit down. She still had bruises around her right eye. She was a hefty woman and Turner didn't think it would take much of a stretch to call her ugly. No reporters had turned up to pester her. Yet. Turner hoped they left her alone.

She said, "This is awfully early for you to be here. Usually I don't get visits, I just get threats."

Turner said, "We know Barb Dams called you."

She took another sip, looked from one to the other of them. "The cops did it. His partner did it. That pig did it. They will do anything to get that shit-for-brains Callaghan off for hurting me."

Turner said, "We don't know who killed him. Barry Callaghan is certainly a suspect. We're trying to figure out what was going on between the two of them. We were hoping maybe you could tell us a little about both men."

She said, "I was having a relationship with him."

"With Belger?" Turner asked.

"With Callaghan."

That hadn't been in any press accounts.

"Why did he attack you?" Fenwick asked.

"Callaghan snuck up on me. Belger distracted me. I got sucker punched. Callaghan caught me looking the other way, or I'd have decked him. The cops would never have let that get on the air. Woman beats the shit out of asshole cop."

"What started it?" Fenwick asked.

"I don't know. Him and Belger were in a mood that night when they came in. Arguing about some silly shit. They were always arguing. Then they started razzing the other guys in the bar, and they kept pestering me. I got work to do. It was 'bring me this', 'bring me that', 'gimme a kiss'. I've got time for that crap? Or they'd pinch my ass." She clutched her coffee cup in both hands. Turner saw her knuckles turn white with gripping it. She took several deep breaths. Carefully placed the cup on the table and resumed.

"I hate when Callaghan does that. I had to slap his hand a couple times. After the third time, I told him if he did it again, I'd throw his ass out. He laughed. He pinched. I punched. No, I didn't throw him out. I hit him hard enough. He got the message. After that, I stayed out of his way. It wasn't the first time Callaghan hit me. Not in the bar. He shoved me around once or twice at my place. That night was the first time any kind of fight got caught on camera. I was surprised when Belger stopped him."

"Why were you surprised?" Turner asked.

"He usually laughed about it, even cheered his partner on."

"But this time Belger intervened. What was different?"

"Like I said, they were in a mood. Pissy with each other all night."

"What happened after the fight?"

"I don't know. I was knocked unconscious. By the time I came to, the paramedics were working on me in the ambulance."

"Who called the cops?"

"I don't know. I was surprised when the video showed up on the news. I figured this would be covered up by the cops."

"Had there been cover-ups before?"

"I've lived in this city long enough. I've worked in a cop bar a long time. I know what goes on."

"You ever hear about them abusing suspects, or witnesses, anybody?"

"They all told stories about how tough they were. Cops brag, male cops especially. I guess they're making sure everybody knows how tough and macho they are. I listen with half an ear and keep smiling. I get bigger tips that way."

"Did Belger and Callaghan get along?"

"They were kind of rough about teasing each other, but nobody got violent. Like a couple weeks ago, they'd been playing pool, and one of them got pissed off. They started swinging the pool cues at each other. Nobody got hit, not really."

Fenwick asked, "What does 'not really' hit mean?"

Preston said, "Well, I think maybe one might have whacked the other guy in the arm." She poked at her bicep. "Not much harder than that, and there was no blood."

Turner said, "So they'd been at each other before this."

"Even though I think him and his buddy had some kind of fight earlier that night, they didn't go after each other until about half an hour after they got there. Callaghan took his being pissed off out on me. Belger got drunker than usual. Then the incident happened. It's as much Belger's fault as Callaghan's. He shouldn't have intervened. The customer shouldn't have reported it."

Fenwick said, "The tape I saw didn't show them fighting."

"The guy with the cell phone didn't catch what went on between the two of them. He came in a few minutes after they came out of a booth swinging at each other. I tried to stop them. Callaghan decked his buddy. Then he went after me. He'd hit Belger pretty hard in their fight."

"Did you know the patron?"

"No. I'm not even sure who did the taping. That reporter, the one who does all those investigative things, the famous guy, you know the one. He put it on the air. I know he wasn't there. I'd have recognized him. There were a couple guys I didn't know in the bar that night. Doesn't matter. The guy who took the video is probably dead by now, too."

"Why do you think that?" Turner asked.

"Reporting cops in this city? You kidding? You're taking your life in your own hands."

"Were they fighting over you?" Fenwick asked.

"I doubt it. Maybe. Not over the pinching. Belger didn't care. I never actually dated Belger."

"You had a relationship with both guys?" Fenwick asked.

"With Belger, it was more of a few sort of one-night-only, one-time-only fun times together. Nothing serious."

"Maybe he thought they were serious," Fenwick said.

"Serious? With these guys? Ha!"

"How long had they been coming into the bar?"

"Since before I started working there. Callaghan was fun enough to date. He'd take me places on the back of his motorcycle."

"Why'd you break up?"

"We weren't totally broken up."

"But you didn't date Belger?" Turner asked.

"I know I'm not pretty, but neither one of them was a prize either. I went out with each of them a few times. It wasn't a big deal. At least it wasn't to me. They were both married. It was more just fun."

"Was it a big deal to them?" Turner asked.

"They never said. Neither one of them was that great in bed. It was the kind of relationship where they'd stay for an hour or two, drink a beer, watch a game on TV, sit in their boxers. It was more casual. More like 'you're not doing anything tonight, stop over.'"

"Belger was found at a gay leather party."

"Belger was gay?"

"We don't know."

"Nah," she said, "He wasn't gay. He wasn't great, you understand. Neither was Callaghan for that matter. But gay? Nah. Neither one of them was a prize. I think they'd have done it with anything that didn't move. Animal, vegetable, mineral. Or even if it objected much and moved a little, that wouldn't stop them."

Fenwick said, "Belger was in a leather outfit when we found him. He ever talk to you about using a dildo?"

Her eyes got wide. "No. That I'd remember."

"Ever hear about him being into S+M?"

She whooped with laughter. "Him? Tough? That might have been hot. If I'd known."

"Did either of them know about the other going out with you?"

"Nah. Nothing was real formal. I just wish this shit was over. Neither guy was that big a deal. This time some idiot patron called the police. Some moron do-gooder. And my boss showed up and some guy from the press. The recording got made. It got on the Internet. It got on the news. My life has been hell since then. I'm probably going to move from Chicago soon. I can't take this. I don't care if Callaghan goes to jail."

"Maybe he killed his partner," Fenwick suggested.

She shrugged. "That's not my problem."

"How did they fight?" Turner asked.

"I always thought it was more play-like, friendly, male roughness. You know how they say rude things to each other, you know your mama wears combat boots, that kind of shit. But then they started swinging the pool cues. They smashed a couple lamps so I went over to try and get between them."

"Kind of brave," Turner said.

"Or dumb. I'd gotten between them before. Usually I could kid them out of it. My boss likes when I do that with the more aggressive guys. So, I got over there and right away I could see they were really pissed. All I did was tap Callaghan on the arm. He called me a 'cheap whore' and shoved me out of the way. I shoved the mother fucker back, as hard as I could. He banged into Belger and Belger went flying. That's when the fight moved into the center part of the bar. That's when Callaghan went after me. That's when it got caught on that fucking cell phone."

Turner said, "Let me make sure I've got the sequence of events clear. They were verbally going at it, then physically fighting in and around the booth. You intervened. They stopped. Then they played pool. And fought again. And you intervened again, but the last time was the only one caught on tape."

"Yeah."

Fenwick said, "I'm confused. What the hell are you trying to say to us? What my partner just described isn't what you said at first. Are you lying to us?"

"No, absolutely not," Preston said. "I'm trying to remember everything. I've been asked a million times. I've gone over it a million times. And some of those cops have been mean. They want me to forget. They want me to doubt myself. Sometimes I'm not ever sure what happened anymore."

Hell of a witness on a stand, Turner thought.

"Did you lose your job?" Fenwick asked.

"I'm on medical leave."

"Bars have benefits?" Fenwick asked.

"This one didn't, but the owner wants this to go away. He's a good guy. He's got a conscience. He knows I got a raw deal. He probably also knows I can sue his ass."

"For what?" Fenwick asked.

"My lawyer said he'd think of something if I wanted to sue."

Fenwick asked, "Did you ever hear of them beating confessions out of suspects?"

"They never mentioned it in front of me."

"Where were you tonight?" Turner asked.

"I've got a job at a nice diner at Navy Pier. I work the six to midnight shift."

She knew no more.

When they got up to leave, she said, "I like you guys. You probably already know this, but you know you should be careful.

Cops are gonna be really pissed at you."

They thanked her for her help and left.

In the car Fenwick said, "She was banging them both?"

"According to her."

"And they're both married to other women."

"I hope they weren't married to the same woman. That would make things very complicated."

"I'm the one who tries to be funny in this relationship."

Turner said, "I can't tell you how trying you are."

Fenwick said, "Doesn't anybody keep their prick in their pants anymore?"

"I'm not sure the problem is when they take it out, as much as where they put it when it gets out."

"Oh. Right."

Turner said, "Fighting over a woman. That's motive for murder."

Fenwick said, "It doesn't sound like anybody was passionately in love."

"I'm not sure anyone has to really be passionately in love, not with this crowd. I think whatever got into Callaghan's head would be more important than reality. I'm not sure he's got a good grip on much of anything. Except a shot and a beer."

Fenwick said, "She said she thought they were omni-sexual."

"I can believe that. I could believe just about anything about these two guys."

Fenwick said, "Birds, trees, a variety of barnyard animals? How about Scanlan?"

Turner said, "A kid? I'd find that hard to believe. Whatever they were sexually, we've got no proof any of it was connected to the murder."

"If he was abused," Fenwick said.

"Earlier he certainly wasn't complaining about being abused

by them. If he complains, then we can beat the shit out of them."

"We could beat the shit out of them on general principles."

"Not today. No, I want to know what Callaghan and Belger were fighting about that night."

"Sex, drugs, rock and roll? Their favorite sheep? What do cop partners fight about? I don't know. We never fight."

"That's because I don't get between you and your food."

Fenwick said, "That's because you are a wise and sage man. Except when you disparage my humor."

Turner said, "Cops fight about petty stuff. Who's going to drive? Somebody doesn't wear enough deodorant. Somebody always wants sushi, and the other wants burnt burgers. Not enough to murder over."

Fenwick said, "We got plenty enough to murder over in this case."

Turner said, "I get no clear picture of these guys. They fought. They were friends. They sort of liked the same women. They were unfaithful to their wives. And Preston? She's a piece of work."

"She's right to leave town. Lawyers from both sides might destroy her on the stand. How many different versions of what happened was she going to tell us?"

"They didn't differ completely," Turner said.

"Enough that I bet a good lawyer could crucify her."

FIFTEEN

Turner and Fenwick stopped by Cook County Morgue on the way back to Area Ten headquarters. Three A.M. No hint in the eastern sky that dawn would ever arrive. The oppressive humidity continued.

They entered the morgue through the front entrance, where the bodies came when they first arrived. It was a twelve-by-twelve room tiled halfway up then the rest of the way to the ceiling was clear glass. Down a corridor to a classroom-sized space with desks topped by computers where morgue workers ate snacks and meals while staring at screens. Then they went through a room the size of a small gymnasium, which was filled with floor to ceiling metallic bookcases, each shelf filled with dead bodies in plastic covers. Occasionally they could see a foot or hand sticking out. The back wall was filled with four-foot-by-six-foot cardboard boxes, some labeled feet, others arms, legs. The random leftovers from the criminals of Chicago.

They entered the pristinely clean autopsy room. The ME had Belger's body opened on the stainless steel slab. The ME saw them and raised an eyebrow. "You're not dead."

"Should we be?" Fenwick asked.

The ME said, "You're investigating a cop killing in Chicago in which another cop is most likely the killer. I'd consider every new breath a triumph."

"He's kind of right," Turner said. "Breathing is part of the job description."

Fenwick said, "Okay, I'm pro-breathing. What have you found so far?"

The ME said, "We've got an interesting case here. His butt tells an interesting story."

"An unfortunate picture," Fenwick said. "That I would not give up a thousand words for."

Turner said, "Gives meaning to the term blow it out your ass."

The ME harrumphed. "Something very large, presumably the dildo, went up there just before his death. I presume it was the dildo although it could have been other things not in evidence that went up there as well. Whatever it was, it tore him up. The dildo got rammed back up his butt after he was dead."

"You're sure about the sequence."

"Reasonably sure. The lack of lubrication makes it seem someone was deliberately being vicious. There was a lot of ripping and tearing up his ass and evidence of bleeding." He pointed to a stainless steel bowl on the stainless steel counter. Turner noted the pale pink dildo with bits of blood and brown spots.

Fenwick said, "So you could say the thing fucked-up his life."

"Is that a pun?" the ME asked.

Turner said, "An attempted Fenwick pun. A class A Felony. The puns are bad, but attempted puns worse. In this state, the death penalty is considered mild punishment for that."

The ME said, "If either of you do another one of those stupid puns, I may shove something unpleasant up your asses."

Turner said, "Punless in Chicago. A dream come true."

Fenwick said, "You'd enjoy it too much."

"Getting butt fucked or never having to listen to your puns again?" Turner asked. "Hard to choose."

"Is that an attempted pun?" Fenwick asked.

The ME harrumphed again. He said, "I saw no evidence of unusual sexual activity in the distant past. There's no scarring up his butt which could simply mean all the other times weren't violent. Nor does it mean he didn't take it up the ass, but my guess is, he wasn't used to being fucked."

Fenwick said, "That dildo doesn't look that large."

"Compared to whom?" Turner asked.

Fenwick and the ME gave him a look.

The ME said, "I don't think it was that dildo that went up his ass the first time. Whatever went up there was bigger."

Turner said, "Could it simply have been a very well-endowed guy?"

"I doubt it. Too much tearing. Whatever was used would have to have a rougher surface than a human penis."

Fenwick said, "Using a dildo to stimulate his ass doesn't prove he was gay or straight."

The ME said, "I have no idea what it proves. I leave that to you guys. I just give you data. If there was that much tearing of the lining of his rectum while he was alive, he would have bled a great deal. He must have, but my guess is it happened away from where they found him. We've got bleeding at the site, but this much damage would have caused more. Also, I think he was dead when the dildo went up there for the last time."

Turner said, "Then why shove the dildo up his ass? He's not going to feel any pain after he's dead. Gotta be somebody trying to divert the investigation. Cops would have to assume we'd connect his being killed with cops who didn't like him. They might think dildos, leather, and whips would lead us to conclude the killer was gay, or he was killed because he was gay. Or it could be a smart gay guy. The smart gay guy would know we'd think it was cops. But the smart gay guy thinks, cops would be bright enough to try and switch suspicion away from themselves. Where better to place suspicion than on the gay community connected with a peccadillo of the dead gay guy. So, it goes round again and comes back to cops."

Fenwick said, "Anybody with that convoluted sense of planning, I want on my team."

"What did kill him?" Turner asked.

The ME pointed to another stainless steel bowl. "There you have the graduated series of orgasm balls that I pulled out of his throat."

Turner saw five balls, the largest slightly smaller than a pool ball, the four others diminishing in size. They were a translucent, slightly bluish color, held together with a dark blue nylon cord.

The ME said, "You saw the large one at the scene. All the others were down his throat. That's what killed him. He choked to death."

"Was he conscious when they went in?" Turner asked.

"Yes," the ME said. "Look at the fingernails. Definitely traces of someone else. We'll get DNA from them. You get a suspect, we'll match them. And he's got blood on him that isn't his."

Fenwick said, "Then his killer must have been incredibly strong to hold him down and be shoving those things in. Belger wasn't a small guy."

"Or it was several guys," Turner said. "So then we wouldn't necessarily find a site at the station with tons of blood. He didn't die from the whipping."

"Nope," the ME said.

Turner said, "So they could have killed him anywhere, at the party, in his own basement. And just maybe left a few flecks of blood as they dragged him in. The residue of the blood would be tough to find. In a place that huge. In a place that filthy. Nuts."

"Has to have been more than one person," Fenwick said. "Somebody had to be holding him down when they did this."

"You'd think," Turner said. He gazed at Belger's body. He wasn't a small man, but he wasn't in the kind of shape going to a gym five days a week would make you. Nobody said he was an athlete.

The ME said, "People didn't like him. Cop people."

Turner asked, "What's the story on all the bruising?"

"Somebody beat the crap out of him just before and after he died. He got the hell kicked out of him."

"Kicked?"

"By someone with tough leather boots. We got residue of black polish where he's bruised."

That was the limit of what forensics could tell them at the

moment. Just before they turned to go, Fenwick asked, "You sort of knew these guys. You ever hear of them tasering a suspect?"

The ME said, "Nobody can cover up that kind of thing. Not in this day and age. Can they?"

Fenwick shrugged. "We don't know."

SIXTEEN

At their desks, the first thing Turner noted was a report from the tech team at the scene. The ultraviolet light had not turned up any blood residue in the corridors closest to where the body had lain. Turner knew it would take them quite a while to go over the entire area. He tossed the report over to Fenwick. His buddy said, "Must have had him wrapped in something."

"Gotta be," Turner said. "Or your buddy the goddess is now in the body-transportation business."

Fenwick said, "You're picking on my goddess."

Turner said, "A man's gotta do what a man's gotta do." Turner flicked on his computer monitor and typed and clicked and waited for the Internet to come up. He wanted to type in the URL for the website Belger had been on. They did not have high-speed Internet access. He waited and waited. Turner swore. Fenwick looked at Turner. "I don't know why you bother to try. Just send for Steve Fong." Fong was the Area Ten computer guy. Turner called. Fong arrived from downstairs long before the computer finished booting up and connecting to the Internet.

Fenwick asked, "What are you doing here on a Saturday morning?"

"Helping you." Fong was six-foot-three and rail thin. He had a wicked sense of humor.

"Don't you get time off?"

"They got me an assistant. He's around when I'm not."

Turner explained what they needed. Fong said, "I'll set up my laptop. It's high speed wireless." It took him less than a minute to get the Internet access screen up. "You're set to go."

Turner said, "I won't accidentally erase everything on here if I press the wrong key?"

Fong said, "Just don't press this key." He pointed to the F14 key.

"What does that do?" Fenwick asked.

"It makes me the all-powerful ruler of the universe, or automatically zaps you every time you try to make a pun."

"Can you put one of those on his computer?" Turner asked.

"You can't afford it." Fong left.

Turner typed in the URL. When the site came up, he examined all the data. He said, "I've got to join this thing to get into the pictures."

"Can you use a credit card?" Fenwick asked.

"I'm not sure I want to give my credit card to some Internet porn site."

"Half the people on the planet go to Internet porn sites."

"Do half the people on the planet have Internet access?" Turner asked.

"All the people who have Internet access have gone to porn sites."

"Madge lets you look at porn sites?"

"She doesn't ask, and I don't tell."

"You don't?"

"I'm setting an example for my kids."

"Bullfooey."

"That's my story and I'm sticking to it."

Turner keyed in the information. Within moments he was on the site. Fenwick rolled his chair over next to Turner. He looked over his friend's shoulder as he navigated the site.

Turner typed in Belger's porn name into the site search box. In seconds a row of sharp, glossy pictures came up.

Turner said, "There's a little bruising, and I think maybe some slight discoloration on his back. No scarring I can see. Of course, someone could have put makeup over them. Or, well, I don't know. I'll download these and send them to the ME. He might uncover something."

As he performed the function, Fenwick said, "It turns me on when you do high tech."

Turner said, "It turns you on when the sun rises or sets, or the grass is green, or the wind blows."

"What can I say?" Fenwick said. "I'm easy."

Turner said, "I'm sending pictures. Not a big deal."

"I can't."

Turner typed in a note so the ME knew what he was looking at.

"I wonder who knew about Belger doing porn," Turner said.

"I've never heard of any cops doing porn. I thought cops who did that got fired."

"Isn't that some kind of First Amendment right?" Turner asked.

"I dunno. Or maybe it was some teacher down South who got the ax. Or was it California?"

Turner said, "There are sites dedicated to cops and guys in uniforms, military, fireman. Are you sure you surf the net for porn?"

Fenwick said, "Mostly I'm looking for women, and I prefer them not to be in uniform or anything else. And how do you know so much?"

"Practice."

Fenwick said, "How do the guys on the porn sites prove they're cops?"

"They can't really, but I doubt if your average porn-site guy is capable of Oscar level acting. I guess it's what you can convince the viewer to believe or what the viewer wants to believe."

"Kind of a definition of life," Fenwick said.

"I'm not up for philosophy today," Turner said. He pointed at the screen, "Okay, he's here, but he's not having sex with any of these guys. His prick isn't hard. Although some of these other guys are." Mostly the pictures of Belger were of him in submissive poses: on his knees head bowed in front of a leather-clad man, in a collar at the end of a leash, tied to a cross with a man with a raised whip looking as if he was ready to use it.

Molton's voice interrupted them. "This is scientific research?" the Commander asked. Barb Dams was with Molton. She steered an AV cart with two piles of file folders on it.

Turner swiveled the screen so his boss could see.

Molton pulled up a chair. "That's unbelievable."

Dams took a look at the screen, smiled discreetly, and said, "I'm not needed for this." She left.

Turner said, "We're just getting started on unbelievable." He and Fenwick filled Molton in on what they'd found out so far. When he finished, Turner asked, "Could they really taser somebody and get away with it?"

"A few years ago, maybe. Now, it would be tough. It hasn't been that long since Burge and his ilk were around. I'm sure there are more than a few who would like to do a lot of things."

"Stephanie Preston, the bartender, said the victim just disappeared."

"Even a Chicago cop would have a hard time making a victim just disappear. I'll look into that."

Turner tapped Fong's computer screen. "Would Belger have gotten fired for being on a porn site?"

Fenwick quoted, "The City of Chicago expects Department members to maintain the high level of integrity established by the Chicago Police Department Code of Ethics and the City of Chicago Ethical Standards."

Molton gaped. Turner raised an eyebrow.

"What?" Fenwick asked. "Besides being a poet, I can memorize things."

"Why memorize that?" Molton asked.

"I had a teacher at the academy who was nuts about it. Had it on a big poster above the door. Said it was a 'mission statement.' He made us recite it every morning."

"Every morning?" Turner asked.

"Every single one. So, it's not really my fault that I memorized it. His class was so boring. I didn't have anything else to do."

Molton said, "If I was Belger's boss, I wouldn't have cared except if it was taking time away from his job. If it was done at home, or hell, at lunch or before work or on break, who cares? If it was done on the job, I'd probably have given him a warning, not because I'm a prude, but because I expect people to be working. On the other hand, if people knew about it, he'd have been razzed, for sure. And it's," Molton looked closely, "a gay site so the ignorant would have let loose their homophobia."

"Which no one has mentioned," Fenwick said.

Molton said, "Then a fair conclusion is cops didn't know about it. If they did, he would have been razzed."

Turner said, "This might be salacious, but I don't think it gives a clue to the murder."

"Not an obvious one, anyway," Fenwick said. "Maybe we can find out tonight who the other guys are who he worked with in these. Maybe one or some of them were pissed at him."

Turner said, "I've sent the pictures to the ME. I'm going to try the web site for the convention registration." He typed in the information that Ian had given him. The site came up easily enough. The registration looked fairly normal, except for the disclaimers about age and consent. Turner pointed to the cost. "Ian was right. Two thousand dollars just to get in."

Fenwick said, "And the place was jammed. It wasn't for the poverty-stricken. We'll need to pay them another visit."

Molton said, "If you can drag yourself away from this enlightening visualization, I've got a present for you." He hefted two stacks of file folders onto their desks. "You need to look at these."

SEVENTEEN

Each stack was four inches high. Fenwick pushed at the one on top of his desk with the tip of a finger. "Is it safe to read this crap when it's this humid?"

Molton said, "These are copies of Belger's and Callaghan's files."

"Are we supposed to have these?" Fenwick asked.

Molton said, "I wouldn't broadcast that you have them. This is a murder investigation. I downloaded them myself. Everything is supposed to be correct. I can't prove someone didn't get there ahead of me and delete items, or doctor them last week, last month, last year, whatever. As far as I can tell, everything is there. Performance reports. Conviction records. Everything. Go through it. Be ruthlessly thorough. Plan on lots of overtime on this one. Pressure."

They knew what the one word meant. Molton wasn't the kind of boss who railed against his superiors in front of his detectives, but Fenwick and Turner were more than familiar enough with the police department bureaucracy to know the morass of hassles Molton was facing and fending off for them.

Fenwick said, "People have got to be really pissed about the mess this case will make."

Molton said, "Everybody hates me. Good. Word has already spread in the department that you're being hardasses because I ordered you to be. That will give you some cover for a short while, but not for long, I'm afraid. Another rumor is that I'm best friends with the mayor and want to suck up to increase my chances of being the next superintendent."

Fenwick said, "I didn't know you wanted to be superintendent."

"I don't. If they believe I ordered you to be tough, it might take some of the heat off of you."

"And puts it on you," Fenwick said.

"That's why I get paid the big bucks, to handle pressure."

Fenwick flipped through several pages. "Lots to read."

Molton said, "Yes, I know." He turned, walked a few steps, then came back. He placed one fist on Turner's desk and one on Fenwick's. He leaned forward and said, "I heard that a City of Chicago detective beat the hell out of a City of Chicago cop in a restroom."

Fenwick said, "Hey, don't leave me out. I crushed some asshole's nuts."

Molton said, "I'm opposed to violence, and nobody has video." He smiled. "Good for you guys." He left.

Anchoring the pages against the gale from the fans, they began plowing through the files.

Turner had Belger. After twenty minutes he said, "Why wasn't this guy fired?"

"Lazy ass commander?"

"He's had fourteen citizen complaints against him. He's got them for mistreating suspects and witnesses and, for all I know, random passersby. He got bawled out by a judge for fucking up a case with contradictory testimony. Ruined the case against a murderer."

"The guy went free?"

Turner checked. "No, the prosecutor got him on a weapons charge."

"Good for him."

Turner held up a page. "This one is unique," Turner said. "This guy fought back. Hired a lawyer. Wrote letters. Young fella." He handed a sheaf of papers across to Fenwick.

Fenwick perused it. "We gotta talk to this guy."

"Yeah." Turner noted down his name and address on the list he was keeping of people they needed to talk to. "What have you got on Callaghan so far?"

"Not as much. No complaints. No good stuff either. No

commendations for bravery."

"No complaints?"

Fenwick shuffled quickly through the stack he'd read so far. "Nothing yet."

"Funny. They were partners. If one was in it, the other should have seen it."

"Not here," Fenwick said.

"Cover-up," Turner said. He glanced through the rest of his stack. "Belger doesn't have much good stuff. He got high marks at the academy. Went to community college for a few years."

"Who has the power to pull stuff from your file?"

"Commanders, people from headquarters. Somebody with power that we don't have."

Fenwick shook his head. "I'm not real familiar with personnel files, but this doesn't seem to be complete."

"What's missing?"

Fenwick went back to hunting. Ten minutes later, he said, "I know what it is. There isn't a thing in here about the incident in the bar. Not a word."

Turner hunted through Belger's. "There's nothing here about that either."

"Somebody is being very thorough. And going very far to screen one or both of these guys."

"You can't just get rid of things from a personnel file," Turner said.

"Sure you can," Fenwick said. "You call up the file and delete or erase, or you walk to a file cabinet and pull a piece of paper. All you need is access."

"It's not supposed to be done," Turner said.

"If the world ran the way it was supposed to, we wouldn't have jobs."

Eighteen

A little before four, a uniformed cop led a woman with dyed blond hair and a man with streaked gold hair up to Turner and Fenwick's desks. The cop said, "These are Mr. and Mrs. Scanlan, Peter Scanlan's parents."

Mrs. Scanlan said, "We demand to see our son. Those people at the desk downstairs wouldn't answer any of our questions."

Fenwick turned pulling extra chairs over into an elaborate ritual. He made sure he placed the new seats so they got the least benefit from the continuously blasting fans. He finished carefully then settled himself back behind his desk. Turner knew what Fenwick was doing: taking command of time. The pace would be set by them, a subtle but often powerful way of controlling irrationally out-of-control people.

"Where is our son?" Mrs. Scanlan demanded.

Fenwick said, "He's being processed. He'll be available in a short while. We need to check some things with you."

"When do we see him?" she demanded.

"Soon," Fenwick said.

Mr. Scanlan pulled out his hanky and dabbed at the sweat on his upper lip. He asked, "Don't you people have air-conditioning?"

Mrs. Scanlan poked her husband then said, "Who cares about that?" She turned to the detectives and said, "While we're waiting, you can help us shut down that horrible event that is going on. That horrible event that is corrupting our son."

Mr. Scanlan said, "That thing is vile."

"What exactly do you know?" Fenwick asked.

"They called us to come get our son. We demanded to talk to him. We demanded answers. Our son tried to hide what he'd been up to. We looked on the Internet. We couldn't find much, but what we did find was shocking. There was a poster with all these disgusting men as if it was the Last Supper."

Turner said, "That was the photo for another leather event in San Francisco."

Mrs. Scanlan looked at him suspiciously. She said, "It was still vile."

Fenwick asked, "Did you know he was going beforehand?"

Mrs. Scanlan said, "Of course not. We would never have permitted it. Never. And we'd have had the man who took him to that so-called event arrested. And we want his name. And we want him sent to jail."

Fenwick asked, "How old is your son?"

"Sixteen," Mrs. Scanlan said. "You need to tell us that man's name."

"Your son told us he's been there every year since he was thirteen. How could you not know where he was?"

"Well," Mrs. Scanlan said, "I'm sure he was saying whatever you wanted to hear. My boy doesn't lie. You must have frightened him."

If she wasn't facing the fact that her kid lied, and Turner knew many a parent with their head in the sand about the truthfulness of their children, then the woman was not connecting well with reality.

Fenwick said, "Why didn't you know where he was going?"

"He's a teenager. You can't control teenagers."

Fenwick said, "You mean you can't control your son."

"Don't you talk about our child," Mrs. Scanlan said. "We want answers. Who was the adult who corrupted our son?"

Turner spoke before Fenwick could answer. He knew what Fenwick's answer would have been: the two of you. Not helpful.

Turner said, "Right now, the only person who could identify the man would be your son. He claims he doesn't know his name. He won't tell us. Maybe he'll tell you."

"Fat chance," Mr. Scanlan said.

"We tried to go there just now," Mrs. Scanlan said. "I wanted some answers. Those guards wouldn't let me in the door. I called the police. They came. They wouldn't do anything. They told us to come here."

Turner said, "I'm sorry, we're in the middle of an investigation. We can't give out any information."

Certainly, none that they would give these people.

Turner finished, "As soon as we find something out, we'll let you know."

"Our son is innocent," Mrs. Scanlan said. "He didn't commit a crime. I don't know why you brought him here."

Fenwick said, "He was underage at a party where he didn't belong."

"Whose fault is that?" Mr. Scanlan demanded.

Fenwick said, "Since technically you're the adults in the house, it would be yours."

Mrs. Scanlan stood up. "We don't have to listen to this crap. We're taking our son home, and we're going to straighten this out."

Good luck with that, Turner thought.

Turner said, "We'll have him brought up." Turner called down to the holding area. Mrs. Scanlan reseated herself. Five minutes later Peter Scanlan arrived. He still wore his skimpy leather shorts and work boots.

Turner watched the parents' faces. Both of them gaped. Their son flung himself into a chair. As he faced the four adults, he kept his legs spread far apart, exaggerating what the shorts did little to conceal.

Mrs. Scanlan recovered first. "What did you do with his clothes?"

"That's what he was found in."

"Impossible. I've never seen those clothes. Never."

Fenwick said, "When you say impossible, do you mean, he's not wearing them right now? Or that because you haven't seen them, he couldn't have them? Or..."

Mrs. Scanlan let out a shriek, flung herself on the floor in front of her son, and began to weep and beg. "What have they done to you?" She repeated this nearly beyond endurance. The look on Peter Scanlan's face almost made Turner sorry for the mother. The teenager's sneer of scorn would have broken the heart of many a parent.

Mr. Scanlan didn't go to his wife. Turner almost raised an eyebrow at that. Mr. Scanlan asked. "What the hell is going on?"

His son didn't answer. Turner filled the silence. "He tripped over a dead body. He was found attempting to sneak out of the party."

"Is this true?" Mr. Scanlan asked.

His son said, "No."

Scanlan looked from the cops to his son. "Peter, what did happen?" the parent asked.

"They're lying."

Mr. Scanlan said, "What are you doing in that outfit?"

The kid folded his arms on his chest and turned his back on his parents.

Nothing Fenwick or Turner could think to ask or say got any more information out of any of the three of them.

Moments later, the three Scanlans left.

Fenwick let out a long breath, then said, "You look up dysfunctional family in the dictionary, and you're going to see a poster of those three. How could they not know where their thirteen-year-old was?"

Turner shook his head, "That's not the most dysfunctional family we've seen in all these years. They're in the top ten worst of all time, but barely."

Fenwick said, "The kid knows more than he told us."

"Yes," Turner said. "We'll have to talk to him again. Unless we get some kind of forensic evidence against him, we're not going to be able to get through to him, and even then, I have my doubts. The kid is a mess."

Fenwick asked, "How did you know about that poster the Scanlans found on the Internet?"

"I made it into a gift for a friend. Downloaded it from the Internet. Took it to a photo shop. Enlarged it and made it into a poster. He loved it."

"Isn't that copyright infringement?" Fenwick asked.

"I'll call the police. Oh, wait, I am the police."

"You are perhaps kinkier than I thought."

"We've known each other a lot of years. You long ago won the kinky prize."

Fenwick said, "Maybe you're trying to catch up."

"Even if I had several lifetimes and worked at it twenty-four hours a day, I wouldn't come close to you."

"Shucks, you say the nicest things."

Five minutes later, they'd returned to the files, when Randy Caruthers burst up the stairs and hustled over to their desks. Turner sighed. Fenwick snarled.

NINETEEN

Randy Caruthers retained his relentless cheerfulness even after being on the squad for ten years. His clothes had gotten baggier, and he'd given up on going to law school. Turner had heard a rumor of divorce but didn't care enough to find out if it was true. Caruthers was the organizer of the group. If someone was retiring or having a birthday, Caruthers took it upon himself to be the one to put together a celebration. The gifts he purchased were seldom appropriate, the cakes rarely above edible, and the parties usually ill attended. Turner thought an appropriate wedding present for Caruthers's parents would have been a lifetime supply of condoms.

Caruthers said, "I just saw those poor people, Mr. and Mrs. Scanlan. You have to do something."

Fenwick said, "Maybe you could get a job babysitting. You'd be out of our hair forever. Or you could just die. Dying would be good."

Caruthers rarely ingested the comments Fenwick made about him. The bouncy detective said, "You should close down that leather sex pleasure dome."

"What do you know about leather, sex, or pleasure?" Fenwick asked.

Caruthers blushed. "I've heard."

"Exactly what have you heard?" Fenwick asked, determined to get Caruthers to do more than make vague bluster about that which he knew little.

Caruthers said, "You both know what I'm talking about."

Fenwick said, "I've never known you to know what you're talking about, fuck-wad."

"Why should we close it down?" Turner asked.

Caruthers was generally oblivious, but he'd caught on long

ago that Turner was gay and that no one else on the squad cared. Caruthers switched topics. "You got the Belger case. He was a traitor to us."

Fenwick said, "And he's dead. Why aren't you rallying around behind his tragic loss and determined to help find his killer?"

"Well, he betrayed us. None of us would do that."

Fenwick said, "Nice to know if a cop raped a nun at high noon in Daley Center Plaza, you'd be supporting him."

Caruthers said, "Everybody always criticizes Chicago cops. We've got to stick together. The press treats us like dirt. The public doesn't appreciate what we do. Nobody understands us."

"If it's so awful," Fenwick asked, "why don't you quit?"

"I like helping people."

"Caruthers, we have work to do," Fenwick said. "Go away."

Caruthers planted his butt on Fenwick's desk. Fenwick swatted at him as a tiger with an unruly cub. Caruthers stayed put, an action more daring than usual. Turner knew that this meant Caruthers' obliviousness was now intermeshed with his stubborn streak, a possibly lethal combination. Undeterred, Fenwick rose, placed a hand on Caruthers's love handles from behind, and lifted the man off his desk.

"Hey!" Caruthers said. He steadied himself.

Fenwick growled.

Caruthers kept his butt from Fenwick's space, but he continued declaiming. "We gotta be the ones who draw a line in the sand. We gotta to be the ones who stand up for what's right. We can't let them try and railroad Chicago cops for this murder."

"We who?" Fenwick asked.

"Us. Cops. Chicago cops. Belger wasn't really one of us. He got killed at some kinky gay club."

"So what?" Fenwick asked. "We've seen people get killed on church altars. We don't close the churches."

Turner said, "Now we investigate based on the venue where

the body was found or based on the sexual orientation of the victim? How does that work?"

"Well, it's important."

"To whom?" Fenwick asked.

Turner saw Harold Rodriquez, Caruthers' long-suffering partner walking up behind Caruthers. Rodriguez wore a grim smile. As the other three listened, Caruthers blathered an inane answer to Fenwick's question.

Rodriguez was a generally silent man who worked methodically and with precision. If he arrested you, you were likely to spend time in jail. He seldom made a mistake. Turner liked thorough and competent. Caruthers made no sign that he was aware of his partner's approach. Obliviousness was one of Caruthers' cardinal virtues.

Caruthers finished with, "So, are you guys going to do right by us?"

Rodriguez said, "Shut the fuck up, asshole."

Caruthers jumped. "I told you not to sneak up on me like that."

Rodriquez grimaced. "When was the last time I listened to something you had to say? Or when has anyone else for that matter? Let's go. We've got work to do."

As they walked away, Rodriquez turned back and said, "Good luck."

Turner and Fenwick continued reading more of the files but found little new of significance. Fifteen minutes later Joe Roosevelt and Judy Wilson, two other detectives on the squad, strode up to their desks. Roosevelt and Wilson did their part to insure the squad's stunningly high conviction rate. These two detectives quarreled about anything. They had been on the job since about the founding of the city. Roosevelt was red-nosed, with short, brush-cut gray hair, and bad teeth. Wilson was an African-American woman with a pleasant smile. They settled into the chairs the Scanlans had abandoned.

Roosevelt said, "You beat the crap out of Sergeant Bert Lensky?"

"Who?" Turner asked.

Wilson said, "I can believe Fenwick beating the shit out of somebody, but not you."

Fenwick said, "I crushed somebody's nuts. That's got to count for something. I must get points for that. I'm sure it's in our contract."

"You crushed somebody's nuts?" Wilson asked. "I'd pay for video of that."

Fenwick said, "I most certainly did."

"Got video to prove it?" Wilson asked.

"No," Fenwick said.

"Worse luck," Roosevelt said. "Today everybody's got video. You gotta have proof. Now, your buddy here," he hooked his thumb at Turner, "his name is now legend, and it's only been a few hours."

Fenwick objected, "But he doesn't have video either."

"Such is fame," Wilson said.

Fenwick said, "Well, I get some credit. Paul's my star pupil. He's been taking lessons for years. About time something rubbed off."

Wilson said, "There's just so much of you that could be rubbed off."

Turner said, "What I did wasn't a big deal."

The other three detectives gazed at him in silence.

Turner said, "Okay, it was kind of a big deal. I kind of enjoyed it, but it wasn't helpful to the case. It was unavoidable."

Wilson said, "Bert's not going to cause you trouble."

"How'd you find out what happened?" Fenwick asked.

Roosevelt laughed. "We heard you got the case. The logical thing would be for you to find out where Callaghan was."

Wilson said, "We didn't even know where the body was, but we know it wouldn't make any difference. Callaghan was the obvious suspect, and you'd see him as soon as you could."

Roosevelt said, "Then the news about your little tiff went around like lightning. We figured we'd better find out who attacked you and pay him a visit. The owner there is an acquaintance of mine. You should talk to him."

Wilson said, "Two older, wiser detectives paid our new best friend Sergeant Lensky a little visit. We figured he might be tempted to fuck you over."

Roosevelt said, "He was thinking of causing you trouble. We explained why that was a bad idea. How many aldermen we knew. That it would be bad for him to pursue this."

"Thanks," Turner said.

Roosevelt said, "Somebody has to show these other assholes what real loyalty means."

Wilson said, "You guys always get the fun murders."

"We must have a different definition of fun," Turner said.

"You want to trade?" Fenwick asked.

"Not particularly," Roosevelt said.

Wilson leaned close. "We were out on a case. Drug dealers. Pretty routine, but we had beat cops hurrying up to us all night."

Roosevelt said, "Yeah, asking about the case. Asking about you guys. Trashing Belger and praising Callaghan."

"You guys know Belger and Callaghan?" Fenwick asked.

Roosevelt said, "I know Callaghan a little. His cousin is married to one of my cousins. I was at the wedding. He got drunk, made a fool of himself, but then my cousin who married the asshole made a bigger fool out of herself so it kind of evened out and got forgotten in family lore."

Wilson said, "Somebody's going to leak the gay angle to the press."

"Hard to keep it out," Turner said. "That is where it

happened."

"No," Wilson predicted, "they'll give it to the Fox network news, not the local guys who are all right. Mostly fair. Those who wish you ill will try to get the national network to play up the angle of evil gay perverts snuffing a good and saintly cop."

Fenwick asked, "Who is it who wishes us ill?"

Wilson said, "The killer, and those who think or know Callaghan is the killer, and those who think the slightest besmirchment of the department is cause to man the barricades."

"Besmirchment?" Fenwick said.

"You aren't the only poet around here," Wilson said. She was referring to the used-to-be well-hidden fact that Fenwick wrote poetry and appeared at poetry recitals.

Turner said, "We can't pay attention to the media."

Fenwick said, "Don't the media have the video of Callaghan in the bar? I thought all the networks showed it endlessly."

"But you know Fox. They twist to suit their right-wing agenda."

Turner said, "We better let Molton know."

"We already did," Wilson said. "He'll handle it."

Roosevelt said, "A few beat cops made some pretty blatant threats against you."

Wilson smiled her broadest. "Joe actually knocked some guy up against a car, grabbed him by his shirt front, and said if anybody bothered you guys in the slightest, he'd come after him personally, to his house, you know the usual from our Joe."

"Shucks," Roosevelt said, "I like beating the shit out of somebody once a shift. At least as much as Fenwick does."

Turner knew for a fact he was an exceptionally gentle soul. He appreciated the support and told them so.

"It's bullshit," Wilson said. "Guy dies. Somebody killed him. We find out who. Politics can go fuck itself."

Turner wished it were that easy.

Roosevelt said, "This job is tough enough without our own turning on us."

There wasn't time for the conversational masturbation they often indulged in about the hopelessness of stemming crime and the mind-numbing weariness of dealing with the dregs of society.

Roosevelt said, "Watch out for the Commander of the Ninth, Boyle. He's an asshole."

Fenwick said, "So you could say that he was a Boyle on the ass of life."

Wilson gaped. Roosevelt fixed Fenwick with a gaze that would have shriveled the most hardened gang banger. Turner rubbed both hands against tired eyes. When he looked at Fenwick, his partner was grinning.

Fenwick said, "And we could name him Lance."

Wilson looked at Turner. "No one would testify against you. At the trial all they'd have to do is list all his puns. They'd never convict you of murdering him. They'd probably give you a medal."

Turner said, "Reading them all his puns would be cruel and unusual punishment."

Wilson said, "He's infected you. I knew it would happen." She patted his arm. "You poor thing. There's no cure, but I hear they're working on a vaccine."

They all looked at the still smiling Fenwick. Roosevelt said, "Against all odds, I shall resume. He was a lieutenant when I was just starting out. Couldn't harass the new guys enough. Made it even tougher on the women."

Wilson said, "The person to talk to is Evon Teasdale. She's been a secretary in the Ninth since dirt. She'll know everything. I can set you up an appointment with her, but outside of work, of course."

Turner asked, "You hear anything about Belger and Callaghan tasering a suspect?"

Both Wilson and Roosevelt shook their heads.

"It's not in their files?" Wilson asked.

"No," Turner said.

The four detectives mulled for a minute. They all realized the significance of files being cleared. Someone had power and was using it.

They exchanged a few more bits of conversation and moments later, Roosevelt and Wilson hustled off to finish their cases before the end of their shift. Turner doubted if he'd be ending his shift soon. He called home to let Ben know he wouldn't be there for breakfast. The kids were still asleep when he called. Paul was determined to be home at least to see them off to camp.

Fifteen minutes later Molton appeared again. He said, "We've got a meeting with Commander Boyle of the Ninth. He was Callaghan and Belger's commander. I'll help you guys with him."

Fenwick asked, "Is he gonna be a problem?"

Molton said, "I get along with all the commanders in the city."

Fenwick said, "So, he's an asshole."

"Yep. I've also got feelers out among friends around the department, hunting for information. I've even been trying to go back to Belger's and Callaghan's days at the police academy. Somebody must have known these guys. What did you find in the files?"

Turner said, "It's more what we didn't find."

"Explain," Molton said.

Turner said, "Belger has reams of complaints against him. Callaghan is pure as the driven snow."

"Possible," Molton said.

"But not probable," Fenwick said.

Molton nodded agreement.

Turner added, "And there is no mention of the incident with

the bartender in either of their files."

Molton said, "I know a clue when I hear it." Molton rested a bit of his butt on Fenwick's desk. Turner knew how much Fenwick hated any butt but his own on his desk. This was the boss. Fenwick's paw did not swipe.

"What does it mean?" Fenwick said.

"Just what you already know it means. Somebody's got power behind them. One assumes it's Callaghan because he has the cleanest record. Probably the most to lose. Of course, Belger, being dead, doesn't have much to lose at this point."

"Who's behind it?" Turner asked.

"Ah," Molton said. "That's the thing. Perhaps Commander Boyle will fill us in."

Fenwick said, "And pigs fly."

Molton said, "In Boyle's office, I wouldn't be surprised."

Before they left they paused briefly at Barb's desk. Molton approved the note they were leaving which asked her to add information on the Scanlans and others they'd talked with to the packet she'd already sent. Molton said, "Keep her up to date as you go. You'll want pictures of everybody to show back at that party."

TWENTY

They sat in district commander Dan Boyle's office. Molton said, "Dan, I'm not interested in cover-ups, emotion, and crap. I want my guys here to find out the facts, the truth, whatever it is and wherever it leads and to whomever it leads."

"I just hope it doesn't hurt us." Boyle had a whiny voice maybe half an octave above tenor. His hefty frame rivaled Fenwick's although he was at least three inches shorter than the detective.

"Cover-ups usually only make things worse," Molton said.

Turner wondered how many clichés they would be forced to listen to. Commanders were an odd breed, and usually liked to avoid stepping on each other's toes. Molton, however, was not like most Commanders. His bullshit quotient was low.

Boyle said, "Sure, sure, but these were good guys." Boyle glanced meaningfully at Turner. "We can't have cops attacking other cops."

Molton asked, "Has someone filed a complaint about someone else?"

"No," Boyle said.

Molton said, "Then I can't imagine what you're talking about."

Boyle pointed at Turner, "Your detective attacked a Chicago cop."

"Produce a victim, witnesses, a report, and paperwork."

"He attacked one of ours."

Molton said, "Until you produce what you need to, you're out of luck. Perhaps your guy attacked my guy. We'd need witnesses."

"Maybe I can find some."

Molton was up to the challenge. He said, "We could compare notes on our ability to find credible witnesses."

The commanders exchanged glares. As the silence moved

from uncomfortable to unbearable Boyle blurted out, "This is bullshit."

Molton said, "I agree. We need you to tell us what you can about Callaghan and Belger."

"The two of them just liked to let off steam. They were partners. I know they depended on each other. That's what makes a good partner; someone who can be depended on. I don't know what all that fuss over the bartender was about. Sometimes guys get out of control. So what? Nobody should have to go to jail or lose their job or anything."

"Why wasn't there a video recorder in the bar in the first place?" Molton asked.

"Lots of bars don't have them. Certainly not a bar we go to."

Turner knew lots of establishments in the city had added security cameras in the last few years.

"Did they know they were being recorded?" Molton asked.

"I have no idea."

Turner said, "Wouldn't it be logical to assume they would be recorded, especially in this day and age?"

Boyle said, "The Raving Dragon doesn't have a camera. Most cop bars don't. Maybe they didn't remember where they were, or they didn't figure it out. Or maybe they were stupid. Maybe they weren't paying attention. Who thinks about a fucking cell phone taking pictures?"

Turner thought, in this day and age, anyone with any sense.

Molton asked, "How did the video get out?"

"The guy used his cell phone. He knew a reporter. He was probably planted by one of the media outlets. You know how crazy they get whenever a cop does the slightest thing wrong."

Turner said, "Callaghan put the bartender in the hospital."

Boyle said, "And I hear she's thinking of dropping the charges. But the real problem is the guy who made the video. We think he's got even more pictures or video on his cell phone."

Turner knew they'd need to interview the guy, and they'd have to find the reporter.

Turner said, "We've talked to Belger's ex-wife. She wasn't fond of him."

"Women these days," Boyle said. "She's an ex. What can you expect?"

Fenwick said, "Something these guys weren't ready to give."

"What's that?" Boyle asked.

"Respect," Fenwick said.

Boyle said, "People make all kinds of accusations that aren't true. As cops, you know that better than most people."

Turner said, "Nobody knew anything about his marital difficulties?"

Boyle said, "Cops have one of the highest divorce rates of any profession. You know that. If I listened to every marriage squabble among the guys, I'd never get anything done. I'm sure what Callaghan did in the bar or what Belger did to his wife wasn't a big deal."

"Have you seen the video?" Fenwick asked.

Boyle looked peeved.

Molton asked, "Did you ever hear about Belger and Callaghan tasering a suspect?"

"Never. I would never permit that in my district."

His eyes shifted and Turner thought, he's lying.

Boyle said, "Maybe the person who got tasered was a suspect accused of molesting little girls? Do you think I'd much care what happened to that kind of guy?"

Molton said, "Painful as it is, we treat all suspects alike. You know that. Our job is to make sure we've got a strong case against every kind of criminal."

Boyle said, "I'll keep my Boy Scout manual on my desk from now on."

The Commanders exchanged another round of glares.

Molton broke the impasse. "Neither of their files mentions the incident with the bartender. Both of them should."

"No one has access to the files."

"Which is my point," Molton said.

"I don't know anything about the current state of their files."

"Belger had a lot of complaints. Callaghan none."

"So what?"

"Seemed odd," Molton said.

Boyle shrugged.

Turner asked, "Did you know Belger appeared on a gay porn web site?"

"If I'd've known that, I'd have fired his ass," Boyle said.

Turner said, "It was dedicated to people who liked to whip and get whipped."

"Well, he was at that place last night. It wouldn't have been hard to figure out."

"You didn't know about the web site?"

"No."

"Nobody noticed or talked about it, came to you with gossip?"

By now Boyle's face was bright red. This time his, "No," came out as nearly a squeak.

Molton spoke up, "Either of these guys ever put in for a transfer?"

"No, and it wouldn't have done any good. I don't transfer people because they don't get along. People learn to work together or they get fired."

"Either of these guys in danger of getting fired?" Molton asked.

"Nope. Everybody in my command was a top-notch cop."

Molton said, "We need to talk to the other guys on Belger's

and Callaghan's shift."

Boyle said, "I already did. None of the guys knows anything."

Molton said, "My guys will need to interview them one at a time. You know how pissed the mayor gets when there's police misconduct."

This was true. The mayor went ballistic whenever charges against cops surfaced. Molton said, "I've got approval from high up."

Boyle gave them a Karl Rove smirk. "Sure, talk to them. My men won't be able to tell you much."

Molton said, "We'll let my guys try. And their cars won't get keyed, or their tires slashed. Nobody's going to be touched or bothered, or I'll take it out of your ass, Danny boy."

Boyle's smirk changed to a slash of anger, but he held it in. Turner knew exactly what was going through Boyle's mind. This was a politically volatile situation for cops at the command level. Make a mistake and demotions could happen fast. You didn't get to the command level in the CPD without being able to play politics.

Molton said, "They'll talk to the guys on the current shift, and they'll probably have to come back again later. We want to catch everybody."

Boyle objected, "Everybody didn't know them."

Molton said, "But we don't know which everybody might have a clue."

Boyle dropped his contrariness about the personnel interviews in his district and switched topics. "Are you going to shut down that stupid party?"

Molton said, "I have no plans to make that request."

"You should. The place is dangerous."

"How would you know?" Molton asked.

"There was a murder there. What else do I need to know?"

Molton said, "It's more likely, if someone at the party had

something to do with the killing, that if we leave it open, they'll come back. You know, the killer always returns to the scene of the crime."

Turner couldn't remember which of the Commanders was ahead on clichés.

Before Molton left, the three of them stopped in the hallway for a moment. Molton said, "He was lying about the tasering." The two detectives nodded. "You'd think I'd have at least heard something about that through the grapevine, but I haven't. I'll keep hunting for info. On the interviews be smart, be careful."

"As always," Fenwick said.

Molton glanced at his watch. It wasn't six yet. "How many more interviews do you have after these cops?"

"Five or six at least," Turner said.

"If you can, do them this morning. This one is hot and it's not going away until you solve it. Sooner would be better."

Turner recognized the urgency in the request. Except for people at Caruthers' level of ability, Molton seldom gave direct orders. Turner understood Molton's suggestion. It was going to be a long morning.

TWENTY-ONE

They conducted the interviews in a generic Chicago cop station interrogation room: painted more than twenty years ago what might have been a shade of green but now looked like pasted on dinginess, no table, three chairs bolted to the floor, no outside windows, an interior mirrored-window that only the most stupid suspect didn't know was two way. All in all as sterile as a bureaucrat could make it.

Before the first cop entered, Fenwick said, "We need to find the guys from the bar last night. We need to get them alone and at rest."

Turner said, "If they don't show up in the people we interview now, we can try to get pictures from Molton."

The attitudes of the beat cops ranged from silently sullen to overtly hostile. Turner hoped one of them would be the guy who gave him information in the washroom earlier this morning. None was.

After their fifth guy, Fenwick said, "Add these guys to the list of people I don't like."

The first five, three men and two women, took less than fifteen minutes. Turner said, "Everything was sweetness and light between these guys. I might puke. Let's try a little something different with number six who is Milton Cheswick."

"What different?"

"Watch."

Milton Cheswick shuffled in. He draped his lanky frame in the metal chair and matched Turner's yawn. Without preliminary, Cheswick said, "Aren't you guys worried about being involved in this investigation?"

"How's that?" Fenwick asked.

Cheswick said, "Digging into stuff about one of our own.

Doesn't that bother you?"

Every single one of the first five had asked some similar form of that question or made the same kind of oblique mention of danger.

Fenwick said, "Thanks for being concerned about us. You have any details on that? Names? Specific threats?"

Cheswick said, "Did you really beat the hell out of a couple of cops?"

Turner ignored the question. "The guys we interviewed have been telling us that Belger was gay. That he offered them blow jobs. That him and Callaghan were lovers. Either of them ever come on to you?"

Cheswick sat up. "Nobody ever came on to me."

"We've got it from three sources," Turner said. "You were one of their targets."

Cheswick said, "What do you mean 'targets'?"

"They wanted to seduce you."

"I'm no fag," Cheswick said, "You're making that up."

Turner said, "Belger's body was found in the middle of one of the biggest gay celebrations in town. We got rumors that Callaghan was at the same party."

"They weren't gay. I can tell when a guy's gay."

"How's that?" Turner asked.

Cheswick licked his lips. "You're trying to trick me into saying something politically incorrect."

"Just trying to find out what happened," Turner said.

"They've both been married," Cheswick said.

Turner asked, "Did you know Belger appeared on a gay S+M web site?"

Cheswick said, "I don't believe that."

"Want us to wait while you check the Internet?" Turner asked.

Cheswick looked from one to the other. Turner said, "We

downloaded one picture." For once the color copier had been working. He pulled it from his folder and showed it to Cheswick who peered at it closely then looked up at the two detectives and said, "Did the killer whip him to death?"

Turner said, "He had fresh wounds. Belger was seen participating in S+M training sessions at this party."

Cheswick again looked from the detectives to the picture and back again.

Turner said, "Either of those guys ever strike you as being into rough sex?"

"No. They were both regular guys."

"Who fought a lot. Like lovers do."

Cheswick said, "Come on, that's not right. Sure I guess they could be rough around the edges. Who isn't?"

"They ever hit each other?" Fenwick asked.

Cheswick said, "This is so fucked up."

"How's that?" Turner asked.

"Shit. Okay. Look. I saw them once. It was after our shift was over. I saw them outside the Raving Dragon. They got into a kind of shoving match. I'm sure it didn't mean anything."

"What was it about?" Turner asked.

"Damned if I know. Guys are rough with each other. They weren't gay. Are you saying Callaghan is gay?"

Fenwick said, "We're just trying to understand the two of them."

But Cheswick didn't really know anything helpful. He left. As the door slammed, Turner said, "So much for my brilliant interrogative trickery."

"Or he really didn't know anything," Fenwick said.

"All too possible," Turner said.

They finished two more interviews. That was all the personnel on duty inside the station at the moment. They'd have to come back to catch the ones on Belger and Callaghan's shift. Turner sighed. More call-backs. More time. He yawned again. He was already tired. He wished he was home having breakfast with Ben and the kids. He'd be lucky to catch them at lunch.

Outside, even at this relatively early hour, sunlight had baked the car interior to nearly unbearable.

"I'm tired," Turner said.

Fenwick added, "I've got to get some sleep."

"Sleep would be good," Turner said. "But for now it's not that kind of tired. I'm sick of these people. We work with a few good people. We work with a lot more assholes. And for us it's the same thing. Day after day, we basically lie, or put on a mini-play, which is the same as lying. We do just about anything to get to the truth."

"We don't hurt or torture people."

"Except in cop bars."

Fenwick said, "I'll give you that, but we did what we had to do. Neither you nor I nor anybody on our squad hurts suspects or witnesses. Even Caruthers doesn't have that kind of nerve."

"That's because his partner would beat the crap out of him, and Molton wouldn't put up with it. Caruthers is easy compared to the assholes we just questioned. You listened to them. You heard Boyle earlier. Vague threats and bullshit. Except for a little cooperation from that Cheswick guy, and he was no saint. It's just shit. I don't know if rogue cops killed Belger. Or maybe everybody he worked with hated him. Nobody was raving about what a good guy he was. Nobody shed a tear. Nobody looked sad."

Fenwick said, "He was the embodiment of an asshole, and he's dead. What would you expect from them?"

Turner didn't respond to the comment. He said, "And Callaghan is a double shit, to use your old classification system. Fighting the criminals of society is sort of a game. So many of them are so stupid, but even then we still have to get clear evidence. But fighting our own?" He shook his head. "And I believe in the system, the ultimate fairness of the law, but times like today are too much. The bullshit level is above flood stage."

Fenwick pulled to the side of the road under the El tracks on Wells Street. The grid above provided a modicum of shade. He said, "I've never heard you be this down."

"I'm not sure I've ever been this down. Not since my first week on the job when I was at my first homicide. A guy killed his wife and three kids. All the little ones were under the age of five. I know a cop isn't supposed to cry. I went home and sobbed. Ian and I were lovers at the time. He helped. He was great."

Fenwick said, "We all get down. It's part of the job."

"I need sleep. And this side of death, I'm not sure there is enough sleep to cure what ails society. And I'm not sure I care that much about the dead guy, but it's the seedy shit that's depressing me."

"You mean like the party?"

"No, that's kind of amusing and a little fun. I might even get a few tips for late night with Ben. And don't ask." He was silent several moments then he rapped his knuckles on the torn door vinyl as he stared out the window. As he spoke, each distinct syllable got its own thump. "This is sordid. Squalid. Sleazy. Ugly in ways that make no sense." He looked over at Fenwick. "That asshole Callaghan beat the hell out of the bartender, and now it's so important for him to get away with it that people are willing to kill?"

"If the bar incident is connected with the killing."

"Neither of us believes in coincidences. Certainly people are willing to lie. Why? What the hell makes Callaghan's life that important?"

"You saying you think Callaghan did it?"

"A cop or cops."

"It could have something to do with the people at the party."

An El rumbled by on the tracks overhead. Turner felt a slight breeze. When the noise abated and the wind died, he resumed, "I know there's no solution to any of it. Crooked cops. The depression of violent death. I guess I'm just tired and hot and miserable."

Fenwick said, "You're right. There are no easy solutions. I don't have any. I could make a joke about chocolate always making things better. I don't know what does. I'm not sure what to say."

Turner said, "Maybe there isn't anything to say. Maybe it's like everything else in this world. You learn to endure. And mostly I do. I've been at this for years. This time it's getting to me. Either I endure it or I don't."

Fenwick said, "I suspect you will."

Turner said, "I suspect you're right. You heard Molton. We've got to get this finished. We've got to try and get more of these interviews done."

Fenwick said, "People will tend to be home, this hour on a Saturday morning. Let's find the complainer that was listed in the files. The one who hired a lawyer and followed up."

Turner said, "We get enough overtime on this, I can buy you donuts for a week."

"Not enough money to do that on our salaries for a month."

TWENTY-TWO

The complainant, Delmar Cotton, lived on LaSalle Street just south of North Avenue. Saturday morning just before 7:30 A.M., he answered the door in black silk boxers and a gray T-shirt.

Cotton said, "I was expecting a delivery from the bakery down the street."

Turner and Fenwick showed ID and introduced themselves.

Cotton didn't rush to change. He had extremely wide shoulders, very narrow hips, and muscular legs. "What's this about?"

"Trent Belger and Barry Callaghan."

Any nervousness Cotton might have felt with having two cops at his front door disappeared. He said, "Bullshit. It was bullshit. Those two are assholes." He led them into the apartment. His Bowflex machine sat in front of a flat screen television. Cotton's body looked like he and the Bowflex machine had a seven-day-a-week relationship. Besides the TV and exercise machine, two black easy chairs decorated the living room. They could see a large kitchen and a door which must lead deeper into the apartment.

They sat at a glass topped table in a breakfast nook. Cotton spread his legs wide and didn't seemed concerned if anyone was trying to look up the gaps in his shorts. Turner resisted the urge. He asked, "What was bullshit?"

"Are you guys finally going to do something about those two? Each one was worse than the other."

"Did you file a complaint about both of them?" Turner asked. They'd only found complaints about Belger. This would be proof that someone had doctored the files.

"I sure did. Both. I got a lawyer and everything. I didn't care how much it cost. But nothing ever happened to those two. Nothing." He shook his head. "Everybody knows the statistics now about the internal workings of the Chicago police complaint department. Everybody! Two complaints out of a thousand were upheld. Two! What bullshit. And Belger and Callaghan were the biggest assholes."

Turner said, "Trent Belger is dead."

The door to the rest of the condo opened. A well-muscled man bare-chested and wearing navy blue pajama bottoms walked into the room. He yawned and said, "I thought I heard somebody. What's going on?"

Cotton said, "This is my partner, Bill Grant." The detectives introduced themselves. Grant was taller and leaner than his partner.

Cotton said, "These detectives are here about Belger and Callaghan. Belger is dead."

"Good," Grant said. He pulled some juice from the refrigerator, offered some to the others, poured himself a glass, and joined them. "I hope he suffered."

Turner asked, "What did those two do to you?"

"We were attacked right on Belmont Avenue. This gang of homophobic teenagers got out of their cars with baseball bats. But we're in good shape and people nearby rushed to help us. It was wonderful. We got the baseball bats away from those kids. We got the keys to their car. We held them on the ground until the cops showed up. Belger and Callaghan."

The doorbell rang. Grant returned with a box of pastry. He offered them some. Turner glanced inside. Grant said, "These are whole grain, no-fat muffins." Turner declined. He watched Fenwick manage to mask his sneer. As far as Fenwick was concerned if chocolate wasn't involved in the pastry, it wasn't worth eating. And if the pastry was trying to disguise itself as something healthful, it should be sent immediately to the great garbage disposal in the sky.

Cotton offered coffee and produced four heavy beige mugs which he filled.

Fenwick asked, "Did the kids get hurt?"

Grant said, "From the way they screamed, you'd have thought we were torturing them. We got the bats away from them. That was all. They had no bruises. There was no blood. But those fuckers Belger and Callaghan." He banged his fist on the table. The box of pastries jumped. "They let the kids go." He wiped at his face.

Cotton picked up the story. "They let those snotty little, homophobic creeps go. We said we'd testify. We had witnesses. We had everything. They listened to us. Then they took the kids about twenty feet away. A few minutes later, I saw a couple of the kids giggle. I knew something was wrong."

"You were right," Grant said.

"The kids got in their car and took off. The cops came back to us. I was so furious. If Grant hadn't been there, I think I would have been arrested. Those two were as bad as the kids."

Turner said, "That was wrong."

Cotton said, "It was criminal. But there was nothing we could do. Not right then. But the next day we called an attorney. He told us how much it would cost, and what we would need to do, and how useless it probably would be. He was right about all of it, but I didn't care."

Grant said, "Nothing happened."

Turner said, "It should have." He didn't add that only one of the cops involved had gotten a mention in his file.

Cotton said, "There's worse."

"What?" Turner asked.

Grant said, "We heard rumors about them tasering gay people."

There had been absolutely nothing about this in either cops' file. Turner knew that if anything had been made of such a complaint, they would have heard about it through the department grapevine.

Cotton said, "Yep. It was after a Pride Parade a few years back. They went after a couple guys who were holding hands."

"Nobody complained?" Turner asked.

"The guys were closeted, but thought they'd be safe at the Pride Parade. They were afraid because Belger and Callaghan were cops."

"When was this?"

"Two, maybe three years ago."

"Do you have any names of the people involved?"

"No," Grant said. The answer came very quickly. Turner wasn't sure if he was lying or not. "Some friends told us about it."

An urban legend or strict fact?

"They were in uniform when they did this?" Turner asked.

"Yep," Grant said.

"It wasn't the first time," Cotton said.

Again, they didn't have names, dates or facts.

Turner said, "With officer Belger dead, any investigation into that kind of incident would stop."

"What about Callaghan?" Cotton asked.

Turner said, "We're trying to find out anything we can about both of them."

Cotton said, "I know what happened to us. I believe they did that other stuff."

"Did you call the gay papers?" Turner asked.

"We did about the tasering," Grant said. "The reporter we talked to said we'd have to have the victims come forward. We knew that wouldn't happen."

"What happened to Belger?" Cotton asked.

"Where were you last night?" Fenwick asked.

Cotton said, "A private party."

"You have witnesses?" Fenwick asked.

Grant said, "Several thousand. We were at the Black and Blue party. I'm sure you don't know what that is."

Turner said, "That's where they found the body."

Silence reigned for several moments as Cotton and Grant looked at each other.

"I didn't see him last night," Grant said.

Cotton nodded. "Same here."

"Did you know Belger appeared on a porn web site dedicated to S+M?" Turner asked.

Grant said, "We don't need to look at porn to be turned on." More nods from Cotton.

Turner asked, "What did you do at the party?"

"We looked at the display rooms and looked in on the seminars. We were signed up for some of the bondage seminars. They were pretty interesting. Do you know what a bondage seminar is?"

Turner said, "About what time did you leave?"

"We got home about two. We were going to go back tonight for more extensive stuff. Are they going to close down the party?"

"Not that I know of," Turner said. They left the two lovers to their pastry.

In the car Fenwick said, "They never look at porn on the Internet?"

"You don't. Now there are three of you."

"You don't?"

"I don't ask. I don't tell."

Fenwick said, "Those two would be plenty strong enough to drag a body around."

"And they were pissed off enough to be willing to give revenge a try."

Fenwick said, "If an angry gay person killed Belger, wouldn't that same person be out to get Callaghan? Wouldn't he be in danger?"

"Only if we're lucky," Turner said.

Turner's cell phone rang. He looked at the caller ID. It was Ian. Turner pressed the answer key. The reporter said, "I know you're going to interview the guy who had the cell phone that night and the reporter."

"Yeah."

"I have paved the way. All will be well. I have the proverbial gold mine."

"What?" Turner asked.

"The fella who did the recording is gay, and he's angry, and he's scared, and he's ready to talk. He doesn't know what the hell is going on. I think he's been threatened. I've convinced him that you and your portly buddy are the answer to his dreams."

Turner glanced at Fenwick's bulk and tried to imagine him as the answer to anyone's dreams. He knew for sure that Fenwick's wife Madge loved the man, bulk and all. After that he wasn't too sure.

Turner asked, "You got a lead on the reporter who broke the story."

"I, your sainted friend, have more than a lead."

"Saint Ian?"

"I may get my own goddess to match Fenwick's for this. I have the reporter set to come to lunch after we're done with the guy with the video."

"How do you manage all these things?" Turner asked.

"I'm a saint."

"Depends on your point of view," Turner said. "We've got a couple interviews yet this morning." They agreed to meet for lunch when Ian could fill them in on the details he found out.

"Any progress?" Ian asked.

"Yes, Belger and Callaghan were assholes."

Ian said, "I'll alert the media."

TWENTY-THREE

Turner organized their next interviews so that they'd be least geographically challenged. He also called Judy Wilson, who had said she knew the bar owner. She had set up a meeting for later that morning at the bar. She said she would call when she had the exact time.

They walked up to Callaghan's ex-wife Stacey's porch. As Turner raised his hand to knock, a teenager wearing all black rushed out the door. He ignored the cops but took the time to slam the screen door. He hopped on a bike that had lain on the front lawn and pedaled off down the street.

"Everett, come back here," came the shout through the door.

"Domestic bliss," Fenwick said. "My favorite."

Turner knocked.

A harried woman in her mid-thirties hurried around a corner and rushed down a short hallway. "You need to close this door to keep the heat out." She pushed open the screen door and tried to see around the detectives.

"Where did he go?"

"Took off on his bike," Turner said.

"Who are you guys?" She peered at each of them. "Cops? I know cops. What? Barry get killed, too? I can't be that lucky."

Turner made introductions.

She opened the door, closed it carefully behind them. It was cooler inside. As she led them into the living room she said, "You got teenagers?"

They nodded.

"You can't control 'em. Now or ever. Course, I was no saint when I was his age." Mrs. Callaghan indicated two chairs reupholstered in pink chenille. She sat on a green horsehair couch. "What's he done this time? I heard about the other one.

Course, wouldn't bother me if he was dead, except I'd miss the alimony and child support payments. I wonder if ex-wives are entitled to any widow's support from the police. Probably not. Although with divorce, I don't know. You guys know how that works?"

"Sorry, no," Turner said. He rushed ahead attempting to interrupt her flow. "We're trying to find out as much as we can about your ex-husband and his relationship with Officer Belger."

"Relationship? You mean they were gay? Nah. My very, very ex-husband was a lot of things; mean, vicious, stupid, but gay. Nah. He wasn't great in bed, but he was interested, always interested. If interest was a virtue, he'd've been a saint. Now, that Belger guy. I heard they found him at that gay thing. What is all that about? Makes no sense to me, but Belger, he was an oddball all the time."

"Did they get along?"

"I guess they did. I divorced my son-of-a-bitch years ago. I don't know how they've gotten along since then. Might be better. Might be worse. Back then, it was more like they were used to each other. Friends in a kind of forced way. A bickering kind of way. But men do that, don't they?"

Turner said, "Officer Belger attempted to hit his first wife."

"She told me that. That's when she left him. Mine came after me. I learned, oh how I learned to stick up for myself. By the end the asshole would cringe from me. Oh, he'd yell and holler and carry on, but he'd cringe. And the carrying on was about stupid stuff. He thought I'd be his mother. Bullshit. I don't think that woman ever said no to him about anything."

"His mother ever call the police on him?"

She laughed. "She's no fool. Call the cops on a cop? Ha!"

"Do you ever remember your ex getting in trouble at work? Being worried about losing his job?"

"He was always complaining about his bosses. Always. Never did much good. Never got specific."

"Why didn't he ask for a transfer?"

"I brought that up a few times. He told me to forget it. He claimed that Boyle wouldn't give transfers, but I don't think he wanted one. I think he wanted to work with Belger."

"Did he ever talk about someone protecting him, a friend who had clout?"

"Not to me. He didn't talk much to me about his job. He'd tell endless stupid stories to his cop friends. All the stories were the same; how brave they were and how stupid crooks are."

"Where were you before midnight?"

"Chasing my idiot son. He's as bad as his father. We had him when I was eighteen. My little mistake. Ha!"

They got up to leave. She said, "You seem like decent guys. Be careful. My ex-husband is a loon. He's capable of anything. He could have killed Belger easy. If he did, it wouldn't bother him to go after you guys."

In the car Fenwick said, "It's so nice everybody is so concerned for our welfare."

"Lot of good their warnings do now. Callaghan and Belger were creeps long before this."

Fenwick said, "Those two guys were up to something."

Turner nodded. "That's why there weren't any transfers. Why do you stick with someone you can't stand? It's got to benefit you in some way. They must have been in on something."

"Money," Fenwick said.

"Gotta be," Turner said.

Both detectives knew of the numerous scandals through the years about police theft rings, extortion rings, and on and on.

Fenwick said, "Was it more than them?"

Turner said, "Whose record is clean? Callaghan's. He's the one who must have the most pull, and pull means power."

Turner's cell phone rang. He listened for a moment then said to Fenwick, "It's for you. Says it's the goddess."

"Tell her I'm busy."

Turner spoke into the receiver. "He says he's busy." He listened a moment then said, "Sure." He picked up a piece of paper and scribbled something Fenwick couldn't see. Turner hung up.

Fenwick gaped at him. He said, "That may be one of the older jokes on the planet."

Turner held out the paper. "I took a message. She wants you to call."

Fenwick snatched the paper. The scribble was only a scribble.

"Who was it? Madge?"

"Judy Wilson. She and Roosevelt have the bartender set to talk to us in another half hour. We've got time to meet with Teasdale, the Ninth District secretary. It's on our way."

TWENTY-FOUR

They drove to the address they had for Evon Teasdale, Judy Wilson's contact in the Ninth District out of which Callaghan and Belger worked.

Teasdale lived in the Wicker Park neighborhood. She was a tall, slender, African-American woman. They sat at her kitchen table. She offered them tea, which they accepted.

She said, "Judy Wilson told me you'd come by. I talked to Barb Dams, Molton's secretary as well. We secretaries, us good ones anyway, keep in touch. They both said you can be trusted. How can I help?"

Fenwick asked, "What the hell is the real story with Belger and Callaghan?"

"You've read their files?"

The detectives nodded.

"That gives you a lot of the essentials."

"Callaghan's seemed pretty clean," Fenwick said.

"Nonsense. I do the filing. He had at least twenty public complaints against him. I know. I put them in there myself. I've worked in that station for thirty years. I know everything. I don't screw that up."

"They're gone," Turner said.

Fenwick asked, "Who has access to them?"

"Each person can see their file, but under supervision, and they can't take anything out."

"Who else?"

"Just Boyle. And I guess people from downtown."

"Boyle has gotta be the guy behind all of this," Fenwick said.

Teasdale said, "I wouldn't be so sure." She took a sip of tea. "Boyle is in the grand tradition of Commander Burge."

She mentioned a CPD commander notorious for supposedly covering up for officers in his command who beat suspects. "Boyle just hasn't been caught yet. He's been investigated internally, but nothing sticks. He barely conceals his ambition to be superintendent. I always thought it was such a joke, him wanting to be the top cop in the city."

"Why's that?" Turner asked.

"I know who goes in and out of his office door, and Internal Affairs and lawyers and assistant superintendents have been in there constantly. That kind of guy doesn't get promoted."

"Why haven't they demoted his ass?" Fenwick asked, "Or fired him?"

"His clout is powerful. Whoever it is must be high up in the administration."

Turner noted that she used 'clout' in its correct Chicago incarnation, not necessarily having power, but your 'clout' in Chicago was having someone who was your godfather in the department.

"Who is it?" Fenwick asked.

"That I don't know."

"What kinds of things has Boyle done to prisoners?" Turner asked.

"He certainly condoned prisoners getting the hell beat out of them."

"Kill them?" Turner asked.

"That's tougher. Like the beatings, he wouldn't be doing them himself. Boyle does a lot of bluster. He's got a violent reputation. He lives by it, but I'm not sure there's lot of bite behind it. He tried that bullying crap with me his first day on the job. I put him in his place. He's the kind who thinks he's still back in high school where drinking beer, scratching your balls, farting, and not ratting on your friends are the cardinal virtues. He strikes me more as a guy who would cover up what someone else did rather than someone who would commit the crime himself."

"Have prisoners died under his command that he wasn't directly responsible for?" Turner asked.

"I have no direct evidence of that."

Fenwick asked, "Did he cover for Belger and Callaghan abusing suspects and prisoners?"

"They'd get written up, but nothing bad ever really happened to them."

"What kinds of things did Belger and Callaghan do?"

"Mean, when they didn't need to be. Brutal, when a gentle touch would have solved a problem. Hit people."

"Taser them?"

"Once they got the reputation, it would be hard to separate fact from fiction. I believe they would do that, but I have no proof that they did it."

"And if they did, so far they've gotten away with it," Fenwick said.

Teasdale nodded, then said, "You didn't notice the other thing in their files?"

"What?" Fenwick asked.

"Too many arrests."

"Huh?" Fenwick said.

"The two of them would have contests each shift, each week, each random set of time, to see who could arrest the most people."

"I didn't catch it," Turner said.

"Me neither," Fenwick said.

"It's subtle. At first glance, they look like good cops. Maybe there are some complaints, but some supervisor looking at their records would see all these arrests. But you look a little deeper. This is the kind of thing secretaries, good secretaries, or secretaries that don't like you, notice. They arrested more people than just about everybody else. But they had the lowest conviction rate of any two other cops in the District. It would take you a while to get the exact statistics. I've worked in that District a good long time, and I'm telling you, I know what I know."

Turner wouldn't dream of doubting her. A good secretary was worth Fenwick's weight in doughnuts. A mean, vicious one could make your life hell on Earth.

Turner said, "I don't know how to ask this politely, if you knew this abuse was going on, why didn't you turn them in?"

"Who says I didn't?"

"What happened?" Turner asked.

"Nothing. I knew what that meant. After the first time, I knew to keep my mouth shut. When nothing happens, that has significance as well."

"I understand," Turner said.

Fenwick asked, "Anything else you can tell us about Callaghan and Belger?"

"I already have the rumor from the staff that you were asking the guys about Belger being on some porn site." She tittered. "So I looked this morning. I suppose I shouldn't have laughed. He looked silly with his ass hanging out of those chaps. I kept wondering if the whipping was fake or real."

"No one knew about this until now?"

"As far as I can tell, no."

"How did Callaghan and Belger get along?"

"They were competitive about everything. I mentioned the arrests. It was like watching a couple of high school boys. They just never seemed to grow up. At times they seemed to be best friends. Other times they fought like mad." She sipped more tea then said, "Here's another example. You know they both got divorced?"

Head nods.

"They competed about who was going to get remarried first."

"Gives another meaning to trophy wife," Fenwick said.

Teasdale said, "I have no idea if Belger really loved his second wife. I doubt it."

Turner asked, "But what did they win?"

"I'm not sure. It wasn't as if they had a trophy case. It was more in their heads. Or maybe they were gambling on it. I just don't know. It just seemed so silly."

"How'd they get along with Boyle?"

"Everybody got along with Boyle the same way. We avoided him. You didn't knock on his office door unless it was a dire emergency. He'd emerge once in a while, mostly to appear at community functions with local politicians. He always smiled for those. He never smiled for us. Never said good morning. Never brought flowers or doughnuts. No presents for secretaries' day or for holidays. I know those aren't really in his job description, but he was cold beyond rudeness. If I was going to pick anybody in the district that Boyle came close to being friendly with, it would have been Callaghan."

"What kind of scheme could Belger and Callaghan have hatched? Something that, despite their differences, would have kept them together?"

Teasdale thought for a minute. "I'm not sure. It would have to be money, but I heard no rumors about that. If they were involved in a property theft ring, I sure never heard about it. Then again, I doubt if they'd have confided in me."

Turner and Fenwick thanked her for her time and tea. As they got up to go, she said, "You two should be careful, you know. You're investigating cops. That can be dangerous. And this crowd is dangerous. Boyle is dangerous."

They thanked her and left.

The mid-morning humidity slammed into them. Not a leaf in the trees moved. Turner thought he might be able to give Fenwick a run for his money in the who-could-sweat-more derby. They stopped at a nearby convenience store and stocked up on bottled water. Fenwick guzzled two waters in the time it took Turner to finish one.

They stood next to the car. Turner splashed water on his face. He said, "I need sleep."

Fenwick grunted.

"We're getting nowhere," Turner said. "And we've got to catch up on several tons of paperwork to record our lack of success."

Fenwick took another swig from a third bottle. He said, "We're learning shit."

Turner said, "Hooray for education."

Fenwick said, "I think the next person who warns me about these people is going to get punched."

"They're trying to be helpful." Again, Turner poured water over his head, let it run down his neck.

"Each time it adds to the spookiness. They all know we should be frightened."

"Are you?"

Fenwick said, "No. You?"

"No. Well, maybe a little."

"Maybe I am a little, too."

"Or a lot. This thing is dangerous."

"Let's solve it."

"And maybe that will make it less dangerous. Or not."

TWENTY-FIVE

They met the owner of the Raving Dragon at the bar. Wilson and Roosevelt were already there. A floor fan sat in the open door blasting air from inside out. Upon entering, they saw a back door wide open. Rotating at full speed was another fan two feet from this far opening. The crosswind they created seemed to annoy the air rather than dispel the humidity. All the lights inside were on, but it was the outdoor light that made the difference and allowed the greatest clarity.

Lester Ballard was the thin and gangly bartender from the night before. He wore cut-off jeans and a white muscle T-shirt. In this light Turner could make out many of Ballard's tattoos. A lot of them seemed to be complex figures of medieval European and ancient Chinese dragons.

Wilson and Roosevelt greeted them. The five of them squeezed into the same booth Turner and Fenwick had been in the night before.

Ballard said, "I didn't know you guys knew Judy. I'm sorry. I might have been more helpful last night. I didn't know you were good guys."

"When did Callaghan get here this morning?"

Ballard turned to Wilson. "You're sure it's okay to tell them all this?"

"Absolutely," Wilson said. "I'd recommend it."

"He showed up a few minutes before you did."

Fenwick said, "He lied to us."

Turner asked, "Did he tell you where he'd been?"

"No. He came in with two other guys. One was the one who came up to the table, Claude Vereski. The other was the one who caused the problem in the washroom, Bert Lensky. They were drunk when they came in, laughing and carrying on. Like they were happy and partying. Of course, they were like that half the time."

Ballard didn't know the name of the cop who'd been in the washroom when the fight started nor did he know the one who had tried to give Turner friendly information.

"What happened the night of the original fight?"

"I wasn't here so I'm not sure. I live above the bar. First I knew about it was when cop cars started showing up."

"How did that video surface?"

"When the beat-down happened, nobody said anything about any video. The few not-cop patrons cleared out when the rest of the police started showing up. The cops didn't want any witnesses. They wanted it covered up. I saw the guy who made the video on television. I don't remember seeing him in here before."

"Did Boyle show up that night?"

"Sure. Half the damn department did. It was a mess. They were desperate to find out who called the paramedics. They figured it was one of the patrons, but it was way too late by then."

"Do you know the reporter who broke the story?"

"I saw him on the news. I never saw him in here."

"Had Belger and Callaghan fought before?"

"Jesus, they were always at each other. Mostly verbally."

"About what?" Fenwick asked.

"Stupid, stupid stuff. They'd agree that bosses were assholes and then they go off on some weird tangent, and they'd argue and get into it."

"Nobody caught those on video?"

"It wasn't the first time they got into it. The night my bartender got hurt was the first time somebody got knocked unconscious. I saw that video on the news. Callaghan really went after her. It was sick. The big difference was this time some idiot called it in. That was against one of the rules. Whatever happened here, stayed here. We had our own rules."

"You ever hear about them abusing suspects, other cops, their wives?"

"Hell, they all brag about how tough they are. I'd listen to their stories sometimes. If I was picking one, I'd say of the two, Callaghan was the bigger asshole. He hated every minority. He claimed he tasered a few people. I didn't believe that. Tasering suspects? You'd think somebody would complain. Or get it on their cell phone camera. I never heard about it. I kind of dismissed it. I mean, he bragged about what a stud he was with the ladies. The man was not pretty. What woman would go with him? He never left with one from here." Ballard scratched his left arm where a tattoo of a rose crossed that of a medieval battle ax.

"Stephanie Preston said she dated each of them a few times."

"She told me they were just buddies and that these guys were good tippers, and she wanted to stay on their good side. And, face it, Stephanie is no prize. She's not real pretty, and she's got a weight problem."

"Was Stephanie Preston a good employee?"

"Sure. She didn't short the till. If she gave out free drinks, she paid for them out of her tip money. She was honest. Can't say much more than that for a bartender. The place usually ran pretty smoothly when she was in charge. And that night, hell, it was a weeknight. Who expects trouble on a weeknight?"

"Did any of the officials from the District or downtown say anything about a cover-up?"

"Not to me. They all huddled together. I think they thought it would just go away. Then that video got onto the news and all hell broke loose."

Turner asked, "Did Callaghan and Belger still come here after the incident?"

"Belger, not as much. Callaghan strutted and bragged even more. He practically moved in. He was kind of a celebrity. He'd bring buddies, and they'd tie one on almost every night. They used to come in and drink pretty regular, but after that night, it was like a ritual."

"You didn't throw him out?" Fenwick asked.

"He actually brought customers in. And this is a cop bar. We don't get many patrons from the public. I've got to keep the clientele happy. The clientele who came in thought Callaghan was an okay guy. There may be a lot of cops who think he's an asshole. Hell, I think he's an asshole. I like Stephanie. I feel bad for her. But I don't pick the clientele. This tavern's been in my family for fifty years, and it's been catering to cops all that time. Not much I can do. My livelihood is invested in this place. I don't want trouble. You sure I'm not going to get in trouble for talking to you?"

Wilson said, "No one will know what you said to us. You're safe."

They began to get up to leave. Ballard said, "I think you guys should be careful. The talk after you left here this morning was pretty ugly. The guys were pretty pissed about what you were doing."

"We're trying to find a killer," Fenwick said.

"That's not how they see it."

Fenwick said, "But the way we see it is the one that counts."

Ballard said, "For your sakes, I hope that's true."

Outside, Fenwick asked Wilson, "What kind of hold do you have over him?"

She said, "I kept his son from having three felony convictions. He got two misdemeanors and a reduced sentence."

"For what?"

"For being an asshole. That's what they all are. Assholes."

They thanked Roosevelt and Wilson for their help. Wilson said, "Everybody's doing what they can to keep you guys safe, but I'd watch my back, if I were you."

Fenwick said, "Thanks for the tip."

It was time for them to meet Ian, who, if he had come through as promised, would have the person who did the taping and the reporter who broke the story.

In the car, Turner jotted down notes, as he always did. Fenwick drove as he always did. Turner yawned. Fenwick caught it. Fenwick's yawning noises sounded like a siren for a brass fire engine rushing to an inferno.

Turner said, "I want to go home."

"Me too," Fenwick said.

TWENTY-SIX

They met Ian at Cool, the latest trendy restaurant on Michigan Avenue. The place was jammed just before noon on a Saturday. As opposed to dressing in his ever-present untrendy outfit, Ian enjoyed going to and being seen at the latest 'in' place: whether it was a restaurant, bar, lounge, or concert.

Ian had a table on the third floor with the best view up and down the street: trees lifeless in the humidity, shoppers trudging through the haze, honking cabs and trucks fighting with pedestrians at traffic signals, stores luring patrons to their mega-priced wares.

Each floor of the restaurant had a bar and a four-tiered dessert case. Fenwick lingered for a moment to visit the chocolate.

The offensively perky waitress gave them menus, returned with coffee, and took their order. Fenwick asked for his dessert to be served before his meal. Neither Turner nor Ian blinked at this. They knew Fenwick's priorities, and while neither necessarily admired them, they understood them.

After the waitress and her plastered-on smile flounced away, Ian said, "I've been busy. Boy, do some members of the Chicago police department hate you guys. I'd watch around every corner."

Fenwick said, "Bullshit."

"Have I ever lied to you?" Ian asked.

At Turner's baleful look, Ian rushed to add, "About cop stuff?" Those many years ago, Ian had cheated on Turner, and had admitted it only after he got caught in their bed with another man.

Fenwick said, "That wasn't bullshit meaning you're lying. It means this is a bullshit case, with bullshit suspects, and bullshit warnings, and capped with bullshit fears."

Ian said, "Perhaps I'm definitionally challenged, but that seems to burden the word bullshit with a lot of baggage. Why not just try a dirty look?"

"Because I'm pissed," Fenwick said.

Ian said, "I do understand that."

Turner said, "You're always pissed. Let's get on with it."

Ian said, "You do have lots of friends on the department who are behind you. Unfortunately, there's lots more against you."

"What if a cop didn't do it?" Turner asked.

"You know who everybody thinks did it; Callaghan. As you well know, they're protecting their own."

Turner asked, "Have you found out anything?"

"Yes. This was not the first fight these two guys had."

"We knew they argued."

"No, I mean, knockdown, drag out, put-each-other-into-the-emergency-room fight."

"How come nobody else has mentioned this?"

"Because nobody but me knows about it."

"It's not in the files," Fenwick said.

"And that should tell you a great deal."

"You know," Turner said, "and your source knows."

"Yes, I know," Ian said.

Turner said, "Rotten stuff was in Belger's file but not in Callaghan's, but there was nothing in Belger's file that says the two of them had a fist fight. Even the disagreement in the bar isn't in there."

Ian said, "To me that means there's a lot of powerful interventions going on behind the scenes."

"We got that part," Fenwick said. "And the part where we should be very afraid. I will care when I need to."

Ian said, "The department is going nuts. The way-high-ups want this solved. As you probably imagine, the mayor is going nuts. The rank and file are split. A lot of guys think Callaghan was justified in killing him."

"They know he did it?" Fenwick asked.

"Everybody thinks so," Ian said. "Don't you?"

Fenwick said, "Silly me. I thought I'd wait for the facts."

Ian said, "Don't get steamrolled while you're waiting."

Fenwick grunted. "Vague warnings aren't going to solve the case."

Ian said, "That's one of the things that's kind of interesting. My sources are good, but I can't pin down anything definite about the case, which means either there's nothing definite to be had about this in the police department, or that you guys are in way over your heads and need to run like hell in the other direction."

"Are your sources as good as you think they are?" Fenwick asked.

"They're good. Not infallible."

"Can we talk to them?" Fenwick asked.

"If they say anything helpful, you know I'll give it to you."

Turner said, "Might dry up your sources in the department."

"Might keep you alive," Ian said. "The threats about you two are pretty specific. The least nasty I got is that if you don't do 'what's right' you would never be able to have another kid or sex again."

Fenwick said, "Very ouch."

Turner was not about to underestimate Ian's warnings.

Turner asked, "We appreciate the warnings and anything you can do. There's a couple things you might be able to tell us. You ever heard rumors about gay guys in the city being tasered?" Usually Ian was aware of any shake on the tendrils of any web involving the gay community.

Ian shrugged. "We get complaints at the paper all the time. Usually they're third- or fourth-hand accounts. The actual victims don't want to go to court or hire a lawyer."

Fenwick asked, "Won't the gay legal organizations hire one for them?"

"Not likely. They won't give garden variety legal representation. They like to take cases that are going to lead to precedents. They can't take every case, and the bigger problem here is that victims do not want the hassle. Say some teenager does get convicted or they sue some sixteen-year-old Nazi. What does a complainer get? Kids don't have cash. It's not worth it." He quoted the statistics that Grant and Cotton had given them. Turner realized that anybody who read the *Sun-Times* editorial on that day would have the statistics from now on.

Turner said, "You get any rumors of tasering by Belger and Callaghan?"

The reporter shoved his slouch fedora back on his head and said, "I have nothing on that. Tasering? That's something that would make headlines."

Turner said, "If they could prove it. If they got it on video. Obviously they didn't. Or somebody's holding back a recording."

Fenwick said, "Does anybody hold back anymore? It's too easy to make yourself famous on the Internet."

"Or," Turner said, "It happened to a frightened gay man."

Ian said, "I'll check around some more, try to pick up any rumors. For lunch I have for your interrogation pleasure, the guy who made the video in the bar, to be followed by the reporter who broke the story. That man with the cell phone," he pointed to the bar area, "is Raoul Dinning." Turner saw a tall, thin Hispanic man in his late twenties. "He is for sure gay. And he was at the Black and Blue party last night."

Fenwick said, "Ah, I can recognize new information when it bashes me in the head."

"You're sure he was at the party?" Turner asked.

"I'm sure," Ian said. "Plus, and I deserve a drum roll here."

Fenwick said, "How about a drum stick in your ear?"

Ian said, "Aren't we testy."

Fenwick said, "I thought I'd spread the threats around."

Ian said, "Thanks for sharing. Luckily for you, there's more. The gay community, specifically the leather mavens, are in an uproar. Calls from my contacts among them have jammed my cell phone."

Fenwick said, "And I care because?"

"Because rumor has it people in the gay leather community know things that would help in your investigation."

"Names?" Fenwick asked.

"I don't have them."

Fenwick gave him a baleful look.

"Yet. I do have the definite impression that whoever it is they know, must be someone powerful, or it is someone who has friends in very high places."

Fenwick said, "I hear that's the new standard in Illinois courtrooms, your definite impressions. I'm ready to make an arrest."

Ian glared.

Turner said, "I'm tired. I need sleep. This case is fucked. What do you have for sure?"

"Zuyland, the reporter who broke the story, is not gay."

"Alert the media," Fenwick said.

Ian said, "However, this next bit might cause a bit of a flurry in the press. They know each other."

Turner asked, "Dinning and Zuyland?"

Ian said, "You betcha."

"Huh?" Fenwick said. "Why would that be news?"

Ian said, "Before the video came out."

"It was a set-up," Fenwick said.

Ian said, "You betcha."

Fenwick said, "I don't like cops being set up."

Ian said, "Yes, and your point is?"

Fenwick said, "Fuck-a-doodle-do."

"You're sure?" Turner asked.

"Ahhh," Ian said, "the magic question. I have one reliable and one unreliable source."

"Any background on Dinning?" Turner asked.

Ian said, "He sees me as a concerned representative of the gay press eager to help him tell his story and right injustices around the world."

"He trusts you?" Fenwick asked.

"He's had some hassles. I've convinced him you are the saints of the department come to liberate him from his trials and tribulations."

Fenwick said, "Stuff it up your ass."

"Not right now. Mr. Dinning seems to be a regular guy. I've got more notes on Zuyland for when we're done with Dinning."

"We got time for this guy before the reporter gets here?" Fenwick asked.

Ian said, "That's the way I set it up."

The waitress appeared with their order. Fenwick's dessert consisted of mounds of ice cream, chocolate, and fudge.

Ian pointed at the Cobb salad next to the large dessert and asked, "Why did you bother to order the salad?"

Fenwick said, "Balanced diet."

Ian left the table, approached Dinning, and returned with him. They sat down, and Ian performed introductions.

Under heavy dark eyebrows, Dinning had large, sad brown eyes that looked a moment or two away from crying. His thick black hair was cut short. His brown muscle T-shirt and tan athletic shorts revealed a wiry frame of taut muscles.

Fenwick and Turner sat on one side of the table. Dinning and Ian on the other.

Dinning asked, "Do I need a lawyer?"

Turner said, "We're just looking for information. Especially on the background between these two cops. You recorded them on your cell phone. We'd like to make sure we have all the details."

Dinning rubbed his hand on his lower jaw. He said, "I am so sorry I recorded it. I am so sorry I said anything to anybody. Recording the incident was the stupidest thing I've ever done. I've had problems at my job and in my condo ever since."

Turner said, "On your job?"

"Yep. My boss got anonymous calls about me. They said I was cheating on my accounts. I wasn't. But an investigation had to be held."

"Where do you work?"

"The Jeanne D'Amato Accounting Agency. We're one of the biggest accounting firms in town, and we never take business from the city. My bosses are tough. They don't trust those politicians. They said they preferred honesty and backing their employees than kowtowing to the city. They said they trusted me. But still, after this, there will always be a shadow or a question about what I do. I'm not sure how long I can hang on."

"What happened at your condo?" Turner asked.

"I live in a nice place on Belmont just east of Broadway. Last month the electricity was shut off for three days. No explanation. It took hours of phone calls and waiting on hold and listening to crap explanations to straighten it out. After I got that fixed, the gas was turned off. It's been one hassle after another. If I parked my car on the street, anywhere on a street around my condo, I'd get a ticket. And I've got a sticker for the neighborhood. I think I've been followed. These guys are relentless."

For overnight parking in densely populated areas of the city, you needed a sticker on your windshield or you'd be ticketed/ and or towed.

"You sure it's cops?" Fenwick asked.

"Who else could it be? Who else gives tickets? What else have

I done?"

"Maybe you're just unlucky," Fenwick said.

Dinning gave him a puzzled frown. Turner thought it increased the handsomeness and sorrow at the same time. If he wasn't happily married, he wouldn't mind comforting Dinning in any affliction.

The waitress appeared and asked how they were doing. Fenwick mumbled through a mouthful of food that they were fine. He had just finished his dessert and was starting on his salad. To his credit, from long practice, when working, Fenwick could multi-task: focus on a witness and on his food.

Turner said, "We're sorry for your hassles. We'll do what we can to help."

Dinning sat back and looked from cop to cop. "Thanks," he said. "Those are actually the only non-threatening words I've heard from cops."

Turner said. "We're not here to pester you. We just need as many details as you can remember about that night."

"You think that fight was connected to the murder?"

Turner said, "We're trying to sort things out. What happened that night?"

"Well, I walked in. The bartender was kind of surly, but she'd been that way the first time. I didn't think much of it. I got my beer and left a big tip, but she didn't seem to appreciate it. I figured out later that she must have known I wasn't a cop. I just wanted to relax for a few minutes and watch the game on the television. Callaghan and Belger were playing pool near where I was sitting. They had a lot of empty beer bottles scattered along several tables."

"They'd been drinking for a while?"

"They sounded drunk, like slurring their words, staggering around. Couple times they sounded like they were angry. Then, and I kind of couldn't believe this, once when Belger bent over to take a shot, Callaghan, the big hefty asshole, takes the wide end of his pool cue and starts rubbing it up and down the crack of Belger's ass. That's when it started. Belger swung his pool cue at Callaghan. The fight didn't last all that long, but things started getting busted up because of the pool cues. That's when the bartender got in on it."

Turner knew that the fight between Belger and Callaghan had not been on the news. Only the attack on the bartender.

"Who else was in the bar?" Turner asked.

"A couple uniformed cops. They just laughed at Callaghan and Belger and got out of the way."

"Why did you start recording?" Fenwick asked.

"I don't know. I guess I just did."

Fenwick said, "You were upset enough to start recording, but you weren't upset enough to call the police? You weren't upset enough to leave the bar, but happy to make a movie? Bullshit."

"Hey," Dinning said. "I'm trying to help."

Dinning's failure to take alternate actions disturbed Turner as well.

"What the hell else was I supposed to do? There's a huge fight, and I don't know they're cops. They weren't in uniform. I didn't even know it was a so-called cop bar. The cops in uniform who were there weren't trying to get them apart."

Fenwick said, "You mentioned being in the bar for a 'first time'. And our understanding is that you knew the reporter Zuyland before that evening."

"What? Who told you that?"

"He did," Fenwick lied. He caught the man's eyes and held them. "He told us on deep background. We're not supposed to tell, but he trusted us." He'd finished his salad.

Turner presumed Fenwick was extrapolating from what Ian had mentioned earlier. Or this was one of the bigger whoppers Fenwick had let out in the past few months. It was a risk. If Fenwick's intuition was wrong, they could lose this guy.

Dinning hesitated. The three of them waited. Finally, Dinning muttered, "Some of us stopped in one time after a Cubs game. One of the guys was a rookie cop, and he took us there. I guess he knew about it. I didn't know I wasn't supposed to go in there without a cop escort. I didn't know it was an exclusive cop bar. I felt safe with the cops in uniforms. The city can be dangerous. It was nice to have them around." By the end of this statement, Dinning's head was down, and he was mumbling into the table top.

Turner said, "Mr. Dinning, we're not out to hurt you. We understand being harassed. But you've got to be honest with us."

"How far has honesty gotten me so far?"

Turner said, "We will do what we can." He caught Dinning's eye and patted his arm.

Dinning looked near tears. He said, "You can't trust anybody. Zuyland told me he wouldn't tell."

"We know," Fenwick said.

Despite the coolness in the restaurant, Dinning broke out in a sweat. He did the hand across his jaw several times.

Turner asked, "How come none of the fight earlier was given to the media?"

"I gave it all to the reporter. I guess he used what he wanted to." He shook his head. "I should never have agreed to do it."

"It was a set up? You planned to be there?"

"Yes."

"And you didn't just happen to start recording?"

"No."

"No earlier visit with a cop escort?"

"No."

"Why did you call the cops that night?" Turner asked.

"Huh?" Dinning said.

"If you were there to trap Belger and Callaghan—and that's

what you were doing. That's the proof you were getting—why'd you call the cops?"

"I didn't," Dinning said. "All of a sudden a bunch of them showed up."

Fenwick and Turner glanced at each other. "Did the bartender call the cops?"

"I don't think so. She was in a bad way. Someone else must have."

Turner knew they'd have to find out who that person was.

Fenwick asked, "So how the hell did you just happen to be there?"

"Zuyland, the reporter, talked to me."

"How did he know you?" Fenwick asked.

"He was doing a bit on the news about gay people being mugged."

"You've been mugged?" Turner asked.

"I was walking down Clark Street one night with my boyfriend. These kids walked up behind us and began screaming faggot. We started to run, but they were too quick. Zuyland was real nice."

"Is he gay?" Ian asked.

"I don't know. I never tried to find out. You've seen him on the news. He's not very attractive, but he's kind of a bulldog reporter. He's won all those awards, hasn't he?"

The detectives shrugged. Ian said, "I know he's gotten several."

Turner rarely watched the network on which Zuyland did his newscasts. He'd caught several glimpses, thought the guy was more toad-like than bulldog, especially for the pretty-boy media age, but the man had won awards.

Turner asked, "So how'd you get to know him?"

"We met a couple times for coffee. He was real helpful. The cops who responded to the call when I got mugged were Belger and Callaghan."

Turner knew plot thickener when he heard it.

"How did they handle your complaint?"

"Well, my boyfriend and I were both bloody and pretty shook up. The cops sneered at us. It was like they were in sympathy with those kids. We were furious."

"How did Zuyland get you to go along with his scheme?"

"It wasn't hard. I was still mad. He said he was investigating homophobic cops. He said he had some evidence that these guys had been rotten to gay guys. He claimed they'd tasered some gay guy in a washroom in a phony public-sex sting."

"What did he tell you about that?"

"He wasn't real clear on the details. He'd been on these guys' tails for a while, I think. Months at least. I'm not much of an activist. He said this would be simple. He had one of these ultra-cool cell phones that record beautifully. We set it up."

"How could Zuyland be sure they were going to fight that night?"

"I don't know. The more I think about it, the whole thing was a set-up, me included. After I did it, he dropped me. Didn't answer my calls. He's as much of a shit as those cops were. Zuyland is devious. That's not the worst." He gulped. "I haven't told anyone this. I didn't know who to tell. Zuyland had abandoned me. The cops were against me." He gulped again and did the hand/chin thing again. Dinning whispered, "He came to my house after the incident in the bar. He threatened me."

"He who?" Fenwick asked.

"Callaghan."

"What exactly did he say?"

"He said he'd get even with me if it was the last thing he did."

"Was Belger with him?"

"No."

"I didn't know what to do. I know I couldn't go to the cops. Not in this town anyway. I just did nothing. I knew there was nothing I could do."

"Did you tell your boyfriend?"

"We broke up right after the attack. He couldn't handle what happened to us. I couldn't blame him. He was more hurt than I was."

"When was this?"

"About two months before the incident in the bar. I've been a wreck ever since. The police get away with stuff all the time. Look at the headlines."

Turner said, "Aren't those usually about people who are caught?"

"After people have had to stick up for themselves and go through hell and file lawsuits and maybe win. And what about all the others that don't get caught?"

Turner said, "We can't help that, but we want to help you. We know it's not easy."

Turner could understand the fear. Turner could also sympathize with a gay man having been attacked. Fear of the police still had not been completely eradicated from the gay community. In some jurisdictions sting operations still occurred for nonsensical reasons.

Dinning said, "Anything you can do, I'd appreciate. Can you make them stop?"

Turner said, "We'll do what we can. We've got a few more questions though."

Dinning leaned forward.

Turner said, "We need to know where you were last night?"

Dinning said, "I was at the Black and Blue party."

"Doing what?" Turner asked.

"Whatever I wanted. I'm into a bunch of different things."

"Did you see Belger?"

"No. I would have remembered that. Am I in trouble?"

Turner said, "You sure it was just Callaghan who came to threaten you?"

"Yeah. Belger wouldn't have a reason to. My video backed him up and made Callaghan look like the bad guy."

They gave him what assurances they could. A few minutes later Dinning and his soulful eyes left.

Turner said, "Hell of a guess on his deliberately being there."

Fenwick said, "You don't just happen to walk into a cop bar. If I was right, and I'm never wrong, about there being a connection between him and the reporter, he had to have been there before. The reporter couldn't guarantee a fight."

Ian said, "Hardly a stretch. I told Paul about it earlier."

"Yeah, he told me. Okay, it wasn't much of a stretch."

Turner said, "Unless he's awfully lucky or awfully devious or awfully bright."

"Or maybe all three," Ian said. "I want to see the rest of that video."

Turner said, "It's more than a little odd the whole thing didn't get out. A cop fight and then a bartender beaten. Something is not right."

Ian asked, "I don't get the pool cue on the ass thing."

"They were gay?" Fenwick asked.

Turner said, "It started a fight."

"Belger thought Callaghan was coming on to him?" Fenwick asked.

Turner said, "Or he thought by doing that in public he was revealing something that he wasn't supposed to reveal."

"They were both closeted?" Ian asked. "They were both gay?"

Turner said, "Nobody says so. Belger may have liked his ass being played with sexually, but not in a bar by his partner. Does that action tell us who the murderer is?"

"No," Fenwick said.

"Maybe motive?" Ian asked.

"Far as I can tell these were motiveless pigs," Turner said.

"Harsh," Ian said.

"The truth often is," Fenwick said.

They speculated for several minutes but couldn't come up with anything concrete about why the reporter would hold back the rest of the video. For a few minutes Ian and Turner concentrated on their food.

TWENTY-SEVEN

Turner asked, "What's the deal on this reporter?"

Ian said, "Ralph Zuyland is to journalistic ethics as the Bush administration was to the Constitution. Neither has a lot of connection to fundamental principles like truth, honesty, or sense."

Fenwick said, "Tell us how you really feel."

"I've met Zuyland once or twice," Ian said. "I doubt if he'd remember who I was. The main thing I've heard is that he's wanted out of the Chicago markets for years. That he's tried and tried to catch on nationally or at the least in New York or Los Angeles."

"Why hasn't he?" Fenwick asked.

"Supposedly people don't like him. And you've seen him on the news?"

"Once in a while."

"As the cliché goes," Ian said, "he has a face made for radio."

"Why did he agree to meet us?"

Ian said, "Why wouldn't a reporter in this town want to meet with the two detectives working the Belger case?"

"Wouldn't he be suspicious?" Turner asked. "You barely know him."

"I told him I was following leads. That I knew you and that you might all be of use to each other."

A short, dumpy guy, tie askew, thinning hair matted down and combed over, rushed into the restaurant. While he did look even less attractive in person, Turner recognized him from newscasts as Ralph Zuyland. He stopped at the bar, placed an order, paid, waited, was served, hefted the drink, and took a large gulp. Zuyland then squared his shoulders and marched toward them. He threw a painfully ugly gold and pink plaid satchel on the table and sat. Ian made introductions.

Zuyland said, "I've checked on you guys. You're supposed to be good cops."

Fenwick said, "I love unsolicited testimonials."

Turner said, "But he solicited these."

"You guys trying to be funny?" Zuyland asked.

Ian said, "I can't tell you how trying they are."

Zuyland sipped from his drink and asked, "Are we on the record or off the record?"

Fenwick said, "Off. This is a murder investigation, and we're asking questions."

"Am I some kind of suspect?"

More than you were half an hour ago, Turner thought. Aloud, he said, "You broke the story on the attack on the bartender. We're hoping you can give us some background, maybe give us a direction to look that we haven't so far."

"I won't reveal my sources."

Turner said, "At the moment, we haven't asked you to. Why don't you wait until after we ask our questions before you decide you've got a First Amendment problem?"

Zuyland looked from one to the other of them. "What have you got so far?" the reporter asked.

Turner said, "A lot of questions and things we don't understand. We're really looking for some help."

"I'll have questions as well," Zuyland said.

"Of course," Turner said.

A waitress came by and Zuyland ordered coffee, the lunch special, and a Cosmopolitan with pomegranate juice. Turner was a bit surprised when the waitress didn't blink about what Turner thought was an odd beverage choice.

Fenwick said, "We had an interesting talk with Raoul Dinning. He says there's more video than was shown on the air. He says he recorded them fighting with each other and swinging pool cues and breaking things up. That the bartender tried to intervene."

Turner asked, "Where is the entire video?"

Zuyland took a gulp of his drink. His eyes swiveled from one to the other of them. He put the drink down carefully. Turner would bet his paycheck that what was coming was at best a lie, certainly not the whole truth.

"I..." Zuyland began and stopped.

Zuyland did this several times until Turner said, "Why don't you skip the lies and tell us what the hell was going on?"

Zuyland said, "I was investigating Belger and Callaghan."

"Why those two?" Fenwick asked.

"The station received complaints. I handled the calls. I do the investigative reporting at the station. I have a staff."

Probably one assistant barely out of college, Turner thought.

Fenwick said, "You must get lots of complaints about cops. Why did you follow up on these two?"

Zuyland took another pull on his drink. "What did Dinning tell you?" he asked.

"Everything," Turner said.

"Everything what?" Very suspicious now.

"That they'd done something to you," Turner said.

More drink-gulping ensued. He caught the eye of a waitress and ordered a third.

"This cannot get out," Zuyland said. "It just can't. I'll get fired. I know I will. You guys have to understand."

Fenwick said, "You're gay."

Ian said, "They don't fire people for that any more. Not in metropolitan Chicago."

"I'm not gay. And they don't have to fire you. You should know that. You work for that gay paper."

Turner wasn't sure if he thought Zuyland was gay or not. He

didn't have a lot of faith in gaydar. While effeminate men might be gay, and studly guys might be gay, he was never sure what might be a dead giveaway. Sure, put a rainbow sticker on your car, but deducing from that is not gaydar. He was sure he didn't care if Zuyland was gay, unless it had something to do with solving the murder.

Ian said, "I didn't think you knew the paper, or I, existed."

"I keep tabs on every paper published from Green Bay to South Bend. I watch everything. I'm not gay."

"What happened to you?" Turner asked.

Zuyland's eyes roved around the room. He leaned forward. "I can't tell you. I just can't."

"They caught you in something illegal," Turner said, "and they were using it to blackmail you."

"Who told you that?" Zuyland asked.

Turner said, "It's logical. You're afraid to tell us. You're pissed at cops. What would piss off a reporter, yet keep him from revealing it on a newscast? They got something on you."

"It's so embarrassing."

Turner said, "We're not trying to ruin your career. We're just trying to catch a murderer."

If Zuyland had had thoughts of coming away with a scoop, they seemed to have fled. He inched his chair as close to the table as his stomach bulge would allow. He whispered. The three of them leaned in close.

"It was in a washroom."

Turner kept a neutral look on his face, and he deliberately did not look at his other two companions. He kept eye contact with Zuyland. Mentioning a washroom and cops, he was now expecting a Larry Craig explanation.

Zuyland said, "I got tasered."

A bit of a twist on public humiliation. "It didn't make the news," Fenwick said.

Zuyland's new Cosmopolitan arrived. He gulped a third of it.

Turner said, "The Chicago police haven't done washroom patrols in years."

"It was cops all right. But it wasn't connected to any sting operation. I'm not sure any more they were really on duty."

Turner asked, "What exactly happened?"

"This is confidential?"

Turner, Fenwick, and Ian nodded. Turner knew they weren't out to ruin this guy.

"This was two winters ago. I was doing some snooping around about that big scandal with the NFL quarterback and his mistress and his wife when their team was in town. It was at the Hotel Chicago. I was leaving. On that level of the parking garage there was a washroom. I stopped in. I was in the stall. One of them did this ridiculous two step on the floor."

Ian said, "I'm thinking of starting a Larry Craig School of Tap Dance and Inter Species communication. People will tap dance instead of using speech."

Zuyland said, "This is not funny."

"It isn't," Turner agreed.

More drink gulping. Zuyland's latest glass was almost empty. Zuyland looked around for the waitress, caught her eye, and pointed at his drink. She nodded.

Zuyland said, "I moved my feet away. I hurried up and left the stall. I went to wash my hands. The two of them came up, one on each side of me. I moved to go to the hand dryer and Callaghan moved at the same moment. By accident, I swear, it was by accident, my hand came in contact with the front of his pants. For about a second. What followed was a nightmare. A nightmare. I wasn't trying anything."

He began to cry. Turner didn't know if the tears came from remorse, regret, fear, too much booze. Guzzling at noon on a Saturday. Was the guy an alcoholic? Not to be trusted? Of limited use? But Zuyland wasn't on a witness stand with an attorney trying to destroy his credibility. They were cops looking for an angle.

Turner said, "We believe you." What he believed was that something happened and that Callaghan and Belger were prepared to make an incident out of it.

"I explained it was just an accidental bump. They threw the bolt in the door so no one could get in or out. I begged and pleaded. They knew who I was. They were mad because of some stories I'd run. They'd been planning to set me up. They'd been following me."

Ian said, "Mr. Zuyland, that washroom used to be known as a gay cruising place."

"It was a coincidence. I'm not gay. I'm not."

"What did they do next?" Turner asked.

"They told me they were going to reveal I was gay. That I'd come on to them in the washroom. That it was two against one. That I'd touched one of them. That boob Larry Craig at least had the sense not to touch the cop. I began screaming at them. Hoping someone would hear. They tried to shut me up. I wouldn't. That's when the taser came out. I got jolted hard."

Sweat beaded on his upper lip. He wiped his forehead. The waitress arrived with his next drink and his food. He gulped the liquid and ate a French fry.

"But you didn't report it."

"They had me scared. But they weren't going to make an arrest either. I figured that out. They wanted something. They wanted all negative news reports about cops stopped. I told them I didn't have the power to do that. People would get suspicious. They told me I had to do it. I kept my word."

"But you set them up at the bar?" Turner asked.

"Yep, they were a couple of dumb cops, no offense."

Fenwick said, "Offense taken."

Zuyland frowned. "They'd been spying on me. I can play that

game, and I'm very good at it. Better than they are. I graduated *summa cum laude* from Northwestern. I got nearly perfect scores on my college entrance exams. I knew I was smarter than them. I knew I just had to bide my time. I'd get them. I'm a good investigative reporter. A great investigative reporter."

He gripped the stem of his drink and leaned forward. "I got the bastards. I found their weaknesses. I know more about them than they know about themselves. They've both had huge amounts of complaints against them from the public."

Turner said, "We only found complaints in Belger's file."

Zuyland said, "Trust me, it was both. If you didn't find complaints about Callaghan, it means somebody cleaned out the files. Sounds like he's got powerful friends."

"Boyle," Ian said. "It's gotta be him. He's the immediate supervisor."

Turner asked, "Did you find any connection between Boyle and these guys?"

Zuyland said, "He was their first supervisor out of the academy. He was a lieutenant back then. I have nothing more than that."

"What were the complaints about?"

"Abuse. Lack of respect. But there was more. Much more. The two of them specialized in death scenes."

Turner sipped his water. He'd heard of such things. Cops who found a dead body in a home or apartment went through the dwelling before any witnesses showed up and before calling it in. Some cops became very good at being able to find people's hiding places for money and valuables.

Zuyland said, "These two were known for it. You never heard of them doing that?"

"No," Turner said. "They were never on a case that we were on."

Zuyland said, "I found out that over the years, they stole tens of thousands. It was the kind of thing that was hard to prove.

The dead person was the one who'd been hoarding the cash. No relative could prove there'd even been a stash. A few tried, but gave up. There were too many cops involved. There was that blue-stone-wall of silence."

His new drink arrived and he smiled at it. He said, "I love revenge. Love it. Love it. Love it. Turns out, I wasn't the first one they caught in that washroom. I found others who they threatened. Closeted guys. Pathetic guys who would pay anything to avoid getting arrested."

Ian said, "You'd think the day of that kind of shit would be over, especially in a big city."

Zuyland said, "You can be scared in a big city or a little town. It kind of depends on you, I think. But I found several sources on it. I talked to the guys."

Turner said, "Blackmail. And they kept it quiet? How long has this been going on?"

"I started investigating just after the incident with me over two years ago. It took quite a while. People were afraid to talk to me."

Fenwick said, "But cops get sued all the time."

"By gay guys? Successfully? Sure, since that *Sun-Times* editorial, everyone knows the percent of cop complaints that are decided in favor of the complainers."

Turner appreciated the statistic, but he wasn't sure how many more times he wanted to hear it. None, he guessed. But that wasn't his choice right now.

Ian said, "Why didn't you ask the gay press for help?"

"Had you heard of this going on?"

"No."

"Then try not to take this the wrong way, but I'm big time, and the gay press is not."

Ian said, "I think I'll take it the wrong way."

Turner said, "Why didn't you report them?"

"I wanted it perfect," Zuyland said. "I could get the blackmail victims to talk to me, but they wouldn't help me set up Belger and Callaghan. I plotted and planned. Finally, I found someone who would help. What happened in that bar that night was my idea. I set up those fuckers. I knew their schedules. I followed them. I know where they went to try and take naps on their shift. I know where they ate doughnuts and where they stopped to take a piss. I knew everything. Those two were a menace to the city. I'm glad I caught them. I knew I would get them eventually. I just needed to be patient, and I was. My boss loves anti-cop stuff, and they were poster boys for police imperfection."

"So you got the goods on them," Fenwick said. "Why didn't you just do a huge exposé? Or if you didn't want to take the risk, give your data to another station or to a print reporter?"

"No. No. No. No. No. They were mean to me. They laughed at me. I was determined to make them pay. And I wanted them to know it was me. But I had to be wary. They had that damn taser incident. They've paid a little. They're going to pay more. All the rest of this will come out."

Fenwick pointed out, "Belger isn't going to pay any more. He's dead."

"Dead or alive, I'll stomp on both of them."

Turner said, "You wanted them to know it was you. Do they?"

"Not as much as they will."

Fenwick reiterated his earlier point, "Belger, not so much, him being dead and all."

Zuyland sipped from his drink.

"The tasering incident was bullshit," Ian said. "Why didn't you report them? Do something about it?"

"You know what it's like working at a local network television station? You know what it takes to hang on? To be judged every second with vultures panting for your job? In this business, you've got to be young and pretty, neither of which I am. And Ralph Zuyland as a name to sell as a young, hip, newscaster? I actually have to work hard and prove myself every goddamn minute. Those people will cut your throat out if you make the slightest slip. You know all that happy talk on camera? It's bullshit. All bullshit."

Fenwick asked, "In your investigating did you know Belger was into getting whipped?"

Zuyland gave the detectives a suspicious look. "He was found at that gay party. He was into it?"

"We're not sure exactly what he was into," Fenwick said. "I thought we'd ask you since you'd been investigating them."

"Far as I know they were straight. I got nothing on whipping or going to gay events. Why was he there?"

Turner said, "We'll give you both some information, as long as it's off the record."

"You trust me?" Zuyland asked.

"I trust you want the biggest exclusive when we find out who did it," Turner said.

Zuyland nodded. "Which is true."

He didn't tell Zuyland that Ian already knew most of this. Let the television reporter assume he was in the same boat as the print reporter.

Fenwick said, "Belger was into getting whipped. It wasn't what killed him, but was a scene he must have liked."

"He was gay? He's been married twice."

"Not an impossible thing," Ian said.

Zuyland said, "I've seen stranger."

Fenwick asked, "You didn't know Belger appeared on a gay website?"

"No, I never found that. He did?"

"Yep," Fenwick said.

Zuyland said, "If I knew, I would have used that against him."

Turner appreciated the honesty. Turner asked, "How'd you

get Belger and Callaghan to fight that evening? What did you do to set them off? And how did you know it would be in that bar? Or did you have spies at several spots?"

"I told you. I knew everything. I knew they went to that bar every Thursday. I'd left messages for Belger that Callaghan was turning on him. Then just before the end of their shift, I made a call. I disguised my voice with one of those computer deals. I told Callaghan that Belger would be wearing a wire at the bar. I thought what I'd be getting was those two fighting. I didn't think that stupid cow bartender would intervene, but from the way it turned out, that was even better."

Fenwick said, "So you conspired and lied to two guys, and your lies led to the death of one of them. That's a felony in this jurisdiction."

"Maybe I'd be guilty in some way if they'd killed each other that night. But they didn't. And Belger is dead. And I'm guessing that Callaghan has a solid alibi." He smirked when the detectives didn't answer. "My way was best."

Fenwick said, "You are a supershit."

"Huh?" Zuyland said.

"The bartender got caught in your clever web. She was seriously hurt. Your super-smart self got her beat up. What if she got killed?"

"She didn't."

Turner said, "You put an innocent person in danger. Period. You are a shit."

Zuyland looked at Ian. Got no sympathy there.

"You want me to leave? I don't have to help you guys."

Fenwick said, "You can leave if you want. You'll get no help from us. No scoop. But we're not dealing with you, not without it being real clear that you are culpable here. The taser stuff is shit. Getting an innocent person hurt, then you are shit. Be honest enough to admit it."

Silence. Zuyland looked at all three. Hung his head. "Okay," he muttered. "You're right. I screwed up that part. I'm sorry. If I can, I'll make it up to her."

Turner said, "We'll expect it."

Zuyland said, "I keep my word."

"When is the other information coming out?" Fenwick asked. "And the other part of the video?"

"Maybe soon. Maybe never. Right now, I am part of Callaghan's downfall. He tasered me. He should suffer the most. If he was dead, he couldn't suffer. Alive, he's miserable. I'll know the right time to pile on."

Or if Callaghan figured this out, Zuyland could be in danger of getting killed.

"What did you need Dinning for?"

"If I was recognized in that bar, I might be lucky to get out with a simple tasering. God, that hurt. You ever been tasered?"

They shook their heads.

Turner said, "Dinning recorded the bartender getting beat up. You weren't in the bar. Who called the rest of the cops?"

"I don't know."

Fenwick growled. Zuyland recoiled from the menace. He said, "Are you guys going to start being vicious?"

Turner said, "You've admitted to some pretty shady activities. How do we know we should believe you about any of these things? And who actually called it in could be a key point."

Zuyland lifted his drink and took another long gulp. "I don't know," he said. "At this point I'm not sure I care."

Turner said, "Bullshit. Nobody can plan something as you claim to have and then count on the cops to show up at exactly the right moment. Even if someone in the bar signaled you, and you called them that instant, there's no guarantee they'd show up in five seconds, or five minutes. Not to a known cop bar. You had to have help. You had to have cops on your side."

"I didn't call it in."

"You didn't have to call it in," Turner said. "Stop playing finesse games."

Zuyland gulped. Looked at Ian, Fenwick, and back to Turner. If he was expecting some kind of rescue from any of them, he was out of luck.

Zuyland said, "Okay. I know a few good cops. They owed me. We're friends."

"You involved them," Turner said. "If it became known you involved them, they could have been in danger. Did you even think beyond yourself about what might happen to other people?"

Zuyland stared down into his drink.

Fenwick said, "Who are the cops?"

"No way. No. No. No. No. No. Throw me in jail. I won't tell you. I won't. Telling you might jeopardize their careers. I know I will keep my mouth shut."

Ian said, "You're not as smart as you think you are."

Zuyland stabbed a finger at Ian. "At least I did something. I tried to make things right. And now Belger is dead and Callaghan is suffering. This thing isn't in his control, and that's a start, unless the cops get to you two, and you two become part of a cover-up."

Turner ignored the invitation to defend themselves. He asked, "Have people been harassing you since you did the report on Belger and Callaghan?"

"I sent the video to all the media outlets I could think of here and nationally. Of course, we had it first. The cops might have a spy in the office or at least someone sympathetic to the cops who might have told them it originated with us, but so far no one from the police seems to know the connection between me and Dinning."

"Except us," Fenwick said.

"I've trusted you."

Ian said, "And they can be trusted. You'll be safe."

Turner asked, "After the video came out, why didn't they make good on their threat about you?"

"Ah, but they don't know I planned the whole thing. They may know my station had the video first, but they don't know I was the one who got it for us. My boss did the disseminating."

"They didn't at least try to talk to you?" Turner asked. "Maybe to get you to tone down coverage?"

"Events moved too quickly. The video spoke for itself. It didn't take a lot of reporting. You just had to watch it."

"You left Dinning hung out to dry," Ian said. "He's been threatened, and you're hiding behind your media badge."

"If I could, I'd help him."

Ian said, "Maybe you should start by taking his calls."

Zuyland looked abashed. He said, "I haven't had a free and clear time of it. The ratings went way up each time I did a story on the cops. Once I was free of their threats, I wasn't about to be stopped. Every report I've done on cops since that video came out has been delicious."

"What if they came up with another plan to get back at you? You may be clever, but they were cops. They'd only be limited by their imaginations and how desperate they were."

"Ah, but you see, now, I'm one among many. It's not just me. And I'm smart, like I said. I gave some of my biggest scoops about cop corruption to other reporters and other stations. And remember, all the news outlets were doing 'bad-cop' stories. We weren't even the most aggressive. I hid myself out in the open, but in the back of the crowd. You know how it's been in this city. The cops have had problems for years now. They've been out of control since before the Democratic convention in '68 and even earlier. I was in the streets in '68. I know what it's like to watch the police be out of control. I know how the establishment rallies behind their own. You guys won't get far. You'll be stopped. Or you'll just rally around them. But it's not that easy any more. We've got the media. We've got the video."

Turner said, "Belger and Callaghan weren't cops in '68."

"I don't care. Cops are out of control in this town. And those two tried to destroy me. It's got to stop. If I can be part of stopping it, I will. You can't make threats."

Turner said, "I wasn't planning to. I'm just trying to solve a murder."

Fenwick asked, "Where were you Friday evening?"

"I'm not gay. I wasn't at the Black and Blue party."

Turner said, "You don't have to be gay to be a murderer or to have been at the party. There were ways to get into the party where you wouldn't be noticed."

"You can see me on videos of the news that night."

"Which can be prerecorded," Turner said. "Who can vouch for you?"

"I did the ten o'clock news, then I grabbed a burger and went home. My cameraman, anyone at the station can vouch for me."

Ian said, "I've got a source that says he saw you at the party."

"Who says that? They're lying. Did Dinning say that? Was he at the party?"

Ian said, "It's a confidential source."

"Bullshit. If you don't produce the person, then you're making it up."

Ian said, "Is that what you tell people when they ask about your sources?"

"I know of you, but I don't know you well. I asked around before I came. I was told you can be trusted, but you aren't a friend." He turned to the detectives. He rapped his knuckles on the table with each word that followed. "I was not there."

Fenwick said, "Aren't you still afraid someone's going to go after you? Try and hurt you? If someone finds out you were behind the bar incident, you could be in danger."

"I know. I never leave a building alone late at night. I've got a state-of-the-art security system in my condo. The doormen in my building are well compensated by me on a frequent basis. I always watch what I'm doing, but isn't it the same for you? Shouldn't you guys be afraid?"

"Of what?" Fenwick asked. "Not of the press."

"I didn't mean that. Of your own. Belger is dead. If it's a cop conspiracy, then things could get very bad for you, couldn't they? Are the cops going to turn on you? You know they are quite capable of going after their own. If they killed Belger, they'd kill you. If you need a media outlet to go with your story, I can arrange it."

Turner said, "Thanks for your concern. We'll be fine."

Zuyland stood, threw money on the table, and picked up his satchel.

Fenwick said, "Uh-uh. Where's the rest of the recording?"

"It's protected."

Ian said, "Not if you released part of it."

"You're sure?"

Turner said, "Why didn't you release it?"

"I kept the rest in case it came in handy." He paused for a moment then said, "I'll get you a copy by the end of the day."

Zuyland got a to-go bag for his nearly untouched food and left.

Ian said, "Dinning didn't tell me he saw Zuyland at the party. I made that up."

"We got that part," Turner said.

"Didn't help," Ian said.

"We got that part, too," Turner said.

"More video?" Fenwick asked.

"This is gonna get worse," Turner said.

"Will he really get it to us?" Fenwick asked.

Turner said, "We're solving a murder, not a First Amendment

rights to a reporter's recording issue."

"He isn't gay?" Fenwick asked.

Turner shrugged. "Do we believe another denial about being innocently in a washroom?"

Ian said, "I get a gold star for not busting out laughing."

"So, he isn't gay?" Fenwick asked.

"The washroom thing is a mess," Turner said. "Nobody in this city cares, do they? Has there been an arrest recently?"

Ian said, "If there was, it hasn't made it to the gay press. You'd think it would."

Fenwick said, "Belger and Callaghan were bluffing. Extortion and blackmail?"

Ian said, "Zuyland knows more than he's telling."

"Don't they all?" Turner asked.

"Who were our good cops who did Zuyland's bidding?" Fenwick asked.

Turner said, "If it becomes a problem, we'll have to pressure him."

After a few more minutes of speculation, Ian left.

In the car Turner said, "Zuyland drank a lot in the middle of the afternoon on a Saturday."

"Does that mean we trust him less?"

"It means he drinks a lot in the middle of the afternoon on a Saturday. He doesn't strike me as a happy man."

Fenwick said, "A vicious one who gets revenge. Not always a bad thing, but in this case..." He shrugged. "Do we believe him?"

"He's got a lot of crap on Belger and Callaghan. Easy enough to have gotten them fired, at the least investigated, but this is Chicago..." He matched his friend's shrug. "Belger and Callaghan were up to their armpits in people who didn't like them."

Fenwick pointed out, "We don't have a lot of cops who disliked them."

"They didn't seem to like each other, but, you're right, they had a lot of civilian enemies, but not a lot of cop enemies. Then again, it only takes one."

"Got that right."

While Fenwick drove back to Area Ten, Turner took out his cell phone, called Molton, and filled him in on their progress so far.

When he was finished, Molton said, "I've tried to find out about suspects being tasered or suspects going missing. I've got nothing. Either it didn't happen, or it's a very thorough cover-up."

"Could be either one, but that doesn't help us," Turner said.

Molton said, "I'll try checking on the theft of money."

Turner said, "There's gotta be a connection between Boyle and Callaghan for sure. Probably between Boyle and Belger as well. He was their supervisor when they came out of the academy when he was a lieutenant. Why would Boyle clean out the file?"

"I'll check. It would have to be big," Molton said.

"Bigger than theft?" Turner asked.

"Murder is bigger than theft," Molton said.

Turner said, "Can cops really cover up murder?"

Molton said, "You read the *Sun-Times*?"

Turner knew immediately what Molton was referring to. The *Sun-Times* had run a huge series of articles on a relative of the mayor who was involved in an incident. A man died outside a bar. Whether or not the mayor's relative was involved, guilty or innocent, as if by magic a whole investigation went away.

"I'll try to find out the connection between these guys. Meanwhile, go home. Get some sleep. You and Fenwick both."

After he hung up, Turner filled Fenwick in, then said, "We've got a ton of paperwork and more interviews. We've got to go back to the party tonight, but I've got to get a few hours sleep."

Fenwick said, "We've done enough for now."

"All we could."

Still, at the station they stopped to jot down notes from the last two interviews. Always after each interview they took a few moments to put down what the witness or suspect had said. It was too easy to forget. Tired as they were, they knew this was essential. After half an hour of transcribing notes, they left.

TWENTY-EIGHT

It was after two on a blazing hot afternoon. Paul Turner had several thoughts as he drove home. One, he was exhausted and just wanted to get some sleep. Two, with the boys leaving in a short while, he knew he'd have some last minute summer camp issues to deal with. At the least, Jeff in his wheel chair because of spina bifida would require extra looking into. Although Jeff had gone to the same camp for the past two years, Paul still got concerned. He himself had gone all the way to the camp the first year to make sure all was well. Jeff had even gotten a little annoyed with his hovering. Third, he thought about the boys being gone, and he and Ben having the house to themselves. His crotch stirred at the thought.

He pulled up to their house and parked. The street was alive with summer. Kids running through sprinklers. A few elderly adults on front porches. They wore summer sweaters despite the simmering heat. Watched kids and great grand kids with pride and amusement. Somewhere he heard a lawn mower cutting through the afternoon haze.

Mrs. Talucci, their ninety-three-year-old neighbor, was out by her SUV. One of her nieces was helping her stash suitcases in the back. Mrs. Talucci was off on another of her senior-approved, mild-difficulty-level adventures, a boat trip up the Amazon.

She smiled at Paul and strode over. She wore safari pants, a matching khaki shirt, and a bright red and gold scarf around her neck.

Paul said, "The only thing you're missing is a pith helmet."

She smiled. "In the car already."

Jeff trundled his wheel chair down the front ramp. Breathlessly he rushed up to them, "Dad, I need your help."

"Be in in a minute."

Jeff twirled his chair on its back wheels, eased himself by the handrails up the ramp, and rushed back into the house.

Mrs. Talucci said, "I hope you and Ben have been planning to party with the boys gone."

"For weeks."

She said, "You look exhausted."

"Cop killer case."

She patted his arm. "You always get assigned the crap cases."

"Molton has faith in us. You're leaving soon?"

"Few minutes."

"You ready for the Amazon?"

She said, "The better question to ask is, is the Amazon ready for me?"

Paul smiled.

They hugged and said their goodbyes.

Paul proceeded into the house. Their seventeen-year-old, Brian, sat in front of the television playing an action game.

The house was air-conditioned. Just that was almost as much a relief as getting some sleep.

Ben met him in the doorway to the kitchen. He'd taken the afternoon off from his mechanic shop. They embraced. Paul loved feeling his partner's arms around him. He took a whiff of Ben's smell. He loved the combination of summer sweat, engine oil from his car shop, his deodorant, and essence of Ben. His partner hadn't shaved that morning. Masculine, studly, a little rough. He couldn't wait to enjoy it without the encumbrance of clothes.

Brian said, "Get a room, you two."

They unclinched. Paul heard Jeff's wheelchair, so he strode down the hall and entered the boy's room. He repositioned the wheelchair, and then helped Jeff tie up two last boxes. He knew Ben would have helped the boy. Paul knew Jeff wouldn't have minded having Ben or Brian help. But sometimes, Jeff wanted his biological dad to pay a little extra attention. Paul was happy to give it to him. The boy was done with whining and manipulating for the moment.

Jeff clutched his favorite traveling chess set in his arms. Brian carried both boys minimal luggage, a large gym bag for each.

Paul, Ben, Brian, and Jeff assembled in the living room, surrounded by the boys' gear. "You guys ready?"

He got, "Yeah, Dad," from both of them.

"I've gotta get some sleep and then I've got to go back to work in a few hours. Ben will drive you to the drop off points."

All was settled. In the moments before the boys had to leave, Paul and Ben talked at the kitchen table. He gave Ben a brief summary of the case and the reason for his lateness. Ben felt the lump on the back of Paul's head from where he'd bashed it in the bathroom brawl. As he got out some ice, Ben said, "It's pretty swollen. You sure you don't need to stop in a hospital and get it x-rayed?"

Paul said, "It doesn't hurt. Much. I'm fine." He placed the ice on the lump. Before meeting Ben, he'd had to be strong for his kids on his own for a long time. It was great to have someone to fuss over him.

Ben said, "Being violent is so not your thing."

"I know. When this is over, I'm going to have to think about it. If nothing else, the rarity, and to be honest, how much I enjoyed doing it."

Ben said, "It means you're human."

Paul said, "I like human."

"Do you really think a cop could have done it?" Ben asked.

"All I know is, it's a mess. We've got rotten cops and dizzy leather queens and an angry ex-wife or two." He shook his head. "We'll do what we always do. Follow the facts."

Ben said, "The gay angle in your case could be tricky. You and I went to a couple of those leather events. This one sounds pretty different. If it wasn't so outrageously expensive, we might give it a try."

"Fenwick and I will be going tonight in plain clothes."

"I wouldn't call what they wear at those things 'plain clothes.'"

Turner smiled. "I'm sure I can find something. I'll borrow a few things from your stash."

"And we could wear some of them this weekend." Ben's eyes glinted.

Paul said, "Let's get the boys on their way. I hope they keep them very, very busy." He shook his head. "I need to become unbusy. I need sleep." But they sat for a few more minutes at the table. They updated schedules for kids, grocery shopping, fixing the garage door, repairing a screen on the back porch.

Finished, Paul contented himself with an enormous hug in the kitchen out of sight and sound of the boys. He loved these moments of warmth and closeness. Ben caressed the thick layer of dark stubble of Paul's unshaven face. He knew Ben liked the rugged veneer it added to Paul's look. He used both hands to squeeze the taut mounds of Ben's ass and pull him close. He got to enjoy the closeness for three seconds when Jeff's voice rent the air. "It's time to go."

They held the embrace for a few more moments. Ben nuzzled his lips close to Paul's ear. He said, "I love you."

Paul said, "I love you, too."

Ben said, "Be careful. You're more important to me than every criminal in Chicago, and all the stupid cops and good cops put together and that includes Fenwick."

Paul said, "I know. I'll take every precaution like I always do."

Paul pushed Jeff's wheelchair out to the car. He gave both boys a hug and told them he loved them. They both said love you back. Brian jumped into the passenger seat. Jeff's wheelchair was maneuvered into the back. A kiss for Ben, a wave to the boys, and they were off.

As soon as they were gone, Paul felt the exhaustion of the day. He eased himself upstairs and collapsed into bed.

TWENTY-NINE

The ringing phone dragged Turner out of an all-too-short sleep. He heard Fenwick's voice. "Fuck-a-doodle with a twist."

Turner said, "You woke me up for that?"

Fenwick said, "We need to get down to headquarters."

Turner said, "If this is the goddess, leave a message."

Fenwick's deep voice rumbled, "Does this sound like a goddess to you?"

"My goddess quotient is pretty low. Do goddesses have sex change operations?"

Fenwick said, "I got a call, now you got a call."

Turner said, "I was asleep."

"Yeah, well, weren't we all. They've arrested Peter Scanlan."

"The kid from the party?"

"Two patrolmen from Boyle's district took him in. Boyle's planning to hold a press conference. Taking credit and causing trouble."

"What's Molton doing?"

"Idiot prevention and damage control. He called me, told me to call you. We're to go in. He told me that for the past couple hours he's been on the phone with half the people at headquarters and with Boyle."

Turner said, "Boyle can't have any evidence."

"None that Molton knew about when I talked to him."

Turner said, "The kid's being set up. Boyle is covering for the killer."

Fenwick said, "That assumes Boyle knows who did it. Maybe he thinks Chicago cops are guilty, although he's not sure which one, and he's being proactive and trying to protect one of our own."

Turner said, "Or he wants to get his ass on national broadcasts. The bash in the bar made news, and now he'll capitalize on that and the murder. He wants his fifteen minutes."

Fenwick said, "Or he's the killer. A very smart killer who is using every trick to save his own ass."

Turner showered, shaved, dressed, and dashed down to Area Ten headquarters. He'd slept for little more than an hour. He was exhausted. On rare occasions he'd been bored interviewing witnesses before, but he'd never fallen asleep on one. Couldn't afford to let the first one happen on this case.

Before he left, he grabbed a few things from Ben's side of their closet that he thought would fit in at the leather fair. In his car, he turned the air-conditioning to medium. The dew point level was in the mid-seventy degree range. The weather report on WBBM-AM was for continued miserable and little chance of the heat breaking for another week.

At the station Caruthers rushed up to Turner before he could get to his desk. Caruthers said, "I knew it was some gay guy who killed Belger. Were you covering up for him because you're gay?"

Turner eyed the annoying menace. He said, "Has the doctor upped your stupid pill prescription again?"

He saw Caruthers trying to figure out what he'd just said. Light dawned and Caruthers said, "You can't insult me."

Fenwick strode in, saw them, marched over, arrived and said to Caruthers, "Go away, you numb nuts, triple fuck."

"I was just saying..."

Fenwick loomed over the shorter man. "They will have the air-conditioning working in this building before I'm willing to listen to you. That's 'never' in a simple word you might understand. Get the fuck away."

Caruthers retired muttering, "I was just trying to say."

Fenwick said, "Molton's in his office with folks from downtown and Boyle. We're invited." Fenwick did his own mutter symphony as they walked downstairs. "Doodle fuck administrators. Doodle dumb and desperate."

They knocked and entered. Molton was behind his desk. He said hello and introduced them around. Arrayed in a semi-circle in front of Molton's desk were Boyle, deputy superintendent Franklin Armour, CPD press spokesperson Phillip Nance, and attorney for the department Mandy O'Bannion. Turner and Fenwick took two chairs in the back. Molton's office had one rotating fan. Turner got a faint breeze about every twelve seconds. All the visitors showed signs of perspiration pooling on their clothes and any exposed bits of flesh.

Mandy O'Bannion asked, "You don't have air-conditioning?"

Molton said, "You get it to work, I'll put you in for a citation."

Boyle pointed at Turner and Fenwick and said, "They shouldn't be here. This should be a disciplinary meeting about them. They have no standing here."

Molton said, "Blow it out your ass, Boyle. This is still my Command. You haven't taken over."

Armour said, "We'll want to do what the superintendent wants."

Nance said, "We want to avoid embarrassing the department."

The door opened and Molton's secretary, Barb Dams, hurried to his side and whispered in his ear. Molton thanked her. She left. Without a word, he reached for a remote control and flipped on a television to his left.

"What's going on?" Armour demanded.

Molton said, "Boyle knows."

Turner thought Boyle looked smugger than a Republican at a Family Values rally.

The screen opened to CLTV news. They were showing a 'perp walk' of Peter Scanlan outside Ninth District headquarters. The reporter breathlessly announced that this was a possible suspect in the murder of Trent Belger, the partner of the notorious Chicago cop.

Nance turned on Boyle, "You dumb shit. That's going to be shown on television around the world in about ten seconds. You fool. What did you think you were doing?"

Boyle looked not a bit abashed. "He's guilty."

Molton asked, "Who interviewed him?"

Boyle said, "I did."

"With or without his parents?" Molton asked.

Boyle said, "I followed procedure."

"Charming kid," Fenwick commented.

Boyle said, "I know how to talk to witnesses. I gave him my 'Come to Jesus' lecture."

Molton said, "Paul, Buck, is he the killer?"

Fenwick said, "No. He's being set up. And anyone who is acting as part of the set-up probably had something to do with the murder."

Boyle bellowed, "That's insubordination."

Molton said, "It's also possibly true, and I happen to agree with it. How did those cameras know to be there?"

Boyle said, "I have no idea how the press learns these things."

Nance said, "If that arrest is a mistake, we're going to look awful. The superintendent wants this to go away. The mayor is furious over this whole thing. He doesn't want the gay community implicated, but he doesn't want a killer to go uncaught. If the killer happens to be gay, fine. He wants an honest arrest."

Turner didn't quite get the fine distinction. If the person was a killer, gay or straight, how did that reflect on the gay community either way? To mark a whole group with the actions of one was a classic sign of prejudice, but he didn't see that kind of problem here. Politicians and press spokespeople. They were all nuts.

"We've got to be careful," Armour said.

Molton said, "My guys are being careful and thorough. They are the most careful and thorough detectives I know. If they haven't made an arrest, then there is not enough evidence right now to make an arrest. Boyle, what do your guys have as evidence? It better be specific and clear."

Boyle said, "We have a whip with Belger's blood on it and Scanlan's fingerprints on the handle. DNA confirms it is Belger's."

Turner said, "Where did you get that? We found no such device at the train station."

"My guys searched more thoroughly than your guys."

"When?" Fenwick demanded.

"This morning."

"Who sent them?" Molton asked.

"I did. A cop is dead. We've got to find out who killed him. We can't lose respect in the community. The thing's got the blood. It's got the fingerprints. We've got a case."

Turner doubted this. He looked at Molton. Molton said, "One, that's not in your District. Two, and more interesting, how did you get DNA, blood test, and fingerprint results so quickly? It's only been a couple hours. It takes us up to two weeks."

"I'm not accountable for your inefficiency."

Mandy O'Bannion said, "I find this whole thing extraordinary. I don't like extraordinary. I, too, was at the meeting with the mayor and the superintendent. We can't have mistakes on this case. We can't do anything premature. Boyle, we need you to back off."

"A little late now," Boyle said. His smirk was back.

Armour said, "That's an order. If we see any more perp walks, you can look forward to a demotion. These detectives need to be allowed to work. You send any more cops to interfere, you're going to have problems."

Nance jerked a finger at Turner and Fenwick and said, "But they better come up with some answers soon. This is a powder keg. The people in the department are up in arms. The gay community will be furious."

O'Bannion said, "This is a direct order, Boyle, from the very top. Cease and desist. You two detectives, come up with the real murderer, or we're going with Scanlan."

"How long do they have?" Molton asked.

"Not as long as they'd like," O'Bannion said.

Fenwick asked, "Who is Matthew Bryner's contact in the city?"

"Who?" O'Bannion asked.

Armour and Nance said nothing.

Turner thought, Armour or Nance or both of them knows who it is.

Fenwick said, "We've got the guy who runs the Black and Blue event flaunting himself in our faces. He'd only do that if he thought he had powerful people behind him. We'd like to know who, and we'd like to interview that person."

Nance finally spoke up, "I have no idea what you're talking about."

Liar, Turner thought.

Molton spoke to his detectives, "Can any of our assembled guests help you in any way?"

Turner said, "We have lots of citizen complaints against both cops."

"Overblown horseshit," Boyle said.

Molton said, "Not when one of them is dead, and the other is the prime suspect in the case."

Fenwick said, "We got rumors of tasering."

"We'd have heard that," O'Bannion said.

Fenwick listed the complaints. All the others claimed to know nothing. Boyle sat with his arms crossed over his gut and said not a word. The smirk did not go away.

Fenwick said, "We've got rumors of theft." He explained.

O'Bannion said, "Bring the people connected to all those rumors to us, and we'll do something. I'll have them checked."

Boyle said, "I've gone over both of their files. Belger had complaints. He's dead. We don't want to go into those, do we?"

"If it leads to a killer we might," Molton said.

Boyle said, "Callaghan didn't have any complaints."

"Odd," Turner said. "We've got people who said they did file complaints about Callaghan."

"Send me their names," O'Bannion said.

With a few more warnings to Boyle to back off and to Turner and Fenwick to get results, the others left. When they were alone, Molton said, "Sometimes I don't like people."

Fenwick said, "Assholes..."

Molton cut him off. "It's not going to do any good to rage about them. Not to me. I've got to work with them. I'll assign Roosevelt and Wilson to help you. You want Caruthers and Rodriguez?"

Fenwick said, "Only if Caruthers is a corpse."

Molton said, "Maybe I can get your buddy Boyle to arrange it."

Turner said, "Boyle is guilty or he knows who did it, and he's covering for him."

Molton said, "Don't underestimate his desire for publicity, and his mania for wanting to be superintendent. Or to embarrass you or me or to impress the people at headquarters."

Fenwick said, "O'Bannion et al didn't sound impressed. They sounded pissed."

"Not if he's right," Molton said.

Turner added, "Or the evidence he's manufactured holds up."

Fenwick said, "If all the cops are conspiring and all these cops are doing illegal things to suspects and civilians, why aren't they being investigated?"

"I know Internal Affairs is not investigating them," Molton said. "I know people there. They wouldn't lie to me. The Feds are another question. They may be investigating. Maybe they aren't ready to go to a grand jury yet. I will try to find out. I can't guarantee I'll find anything. The Feds are not our friends." Federal investigations of Chicago cops were nearly to the point of being routine in the past few years.

Fenwick said, "We'll need to talk to Scanlan again as well."

"I'll arrange it," Molton said, "And go back to the fucking party. Find out what was really going on. Yeah, I think cops did it, but that whole party thing just seems wrong to me. And go undercover. Find something. This is getting nuts. What did these idiots really want? I'll handle Boyle and all this crap. You guys can go." He was already reaching for the phone as they walked out the door.

THIRTY

It was nearly five. Fenwick and Turner were at their desks, but Fenwick couldn't sit still. He swore. He thumped his fists on the desk top. He twisted in his chair, even forced the ancient, creaky thing to swirl for several inches on its protesting ball bearings.

Caruthers began to approach them, but Fenwick's venomous glare backed him off.

Turner slammed his desk drawer shut after grabbing a stack of forms they needed to fill out on their interviews. He broke the tips of three pencils as he began to write. He tossed the fourth one into the center of his desk. He said, "We're screwed, but Molton must be in one hell of a mess."

Fenwick said, "He backed us up. He did right."

Boyle rushed into the room. He stopped next to their desks and leaned over. "Watch your backs, mother-fuckers. Watch your backs. Molton's not going to be able to protect you for long. And there are ways. I'll be watching you." He did the stupid two-fingered point at his eyes, then swiveled his hand, fingers pointing toward them.

Fenwick laughed. Turner picked up his phone and dialed the in-house number for Molton. When the Commander picked up, Turner said, "We've got Boyle up here making threats. You want Fenwick and me to handle it, or do you want to?"

"Stop Fenwick," Molton ordered. "I'll be right up."

But it was far too late. Fenwick was beyond command from friend, foe, or boss. Seldom sanguine with suspects and criminals, he was volatile about administrative/command assholes. And being threatened by one was more than he would take.

Fenwick's laugh died. He stood up. He took a step toward Boyle who took two steps back.

Boyle said, "Start something, mother-fucker. I want you to start something."

Fenwick took another step forward. Boyle retreated farther.

Turner stood up.

Boyle looked from one to the other.

Fenwick took another step closer to Boyle. The much shorter but even stouter man summoned his courage and his bluster to stand fast. "Don't touch me!" Boyle's warning was a decibel short of a screech. "You touch me and your job is gone!"

Fenwick leaned close until his nose was an inch from Boyle's. He paused for several beats and then delivered his next line in a soft rumble, "Boo." Then Fenwick took a step back.

Boyle began shouting rapidly and inarticulately and waving his fists in the air.

Hearing the noise, a crowd had begun to gather. They stood at a distance. Screaming commanders was new to Area Ten. In moments Molton arrived.

Boyle screamed, "He threatened me."

Molton said, "I see you waving your arms around. Neither one of them is near you." He turned to Fenwick and Turner. "Did either of you threaten Commander Boyle?"

Both detectives said, "No."

Molton said to Boyle, "You got a witness?"

He turned to the rapidly-scuttling-away crowd. Seconds later only the four of them remained in the squad room. Boyle said, "They're going to be sorry."

Turner asked in a very soft voice, "Commander Boyle, what is your connection to Officer Callaghan, and why have you gone so far to cover up for him? For years."

Boyle's face turned so red, Turner thought he might be about to have a stroke. When he got his voice back, Boyle jabbed a finger in Turner's direction and said, "I will destroy you."

Molton, calm in the face of bullets or brinksmanship, raised his voice and pointed his finger. His shouts reached every corner of the old station. "Get the fuck out of my squad room. Stay the fuck away from my detectives. You dumb fuck, son of a bitch. Get out and stay out."

Turner and Fenwick stared at their always calm Commander. This was a side of their boss they'd never seen.

Boyle's defiance deflated only somewhat. He backed away, tripped over his own feet, grabbed at a desk with his left hand, missed, plopped to the floor, but jumped right back up. He said, "You'll be sorry. You'll all be sorry." He turned and almost fell.

Stumbling and tripping in a pratfall is not the way a victor leaves the field. For several moments Boyle managed to look like Charlie Chaplin on fast forward.

Nobody laughed, although Fenwick did sneer.

Boyle disappeared down the stairs.

Molton breathed hard for several minutes. Turner and Fenwick eyed him carefully. Finally, Molton said, "I gotta stop doing that."

Turner said, "I've never seen you do that."

Molton said, "The amount of fun I had doing that should be declared illegal." He shook his head. "There's nothing you can do about this. There's nothing I want you to do about this. What are you doing next?"

Turner outlined their next set of work and interviews. "I've got to check the email to see if the reporter sent us the entire video. Then we want to try and find some of the cops who were in that bar the night we went there."

Molton said, "Solve the damn case." He left.

THIRTY-ONE

At the computer Turner called up his email. He had one with an attachment from Zuyland, the reporter. He didn't even try to open it. Neither of their computers would be able to download such a huge file. He and Fenwick trooped down to Steve Fong's office. Fong had his feet up on his desk where his laptop computer hummed away. He was halfway through devouring a slice from a wheel of pizza.

Fong swallowed and said, "You need high-speed access." He tapped a couple keys on his computer and the Internet opened up.

Fenwick said, "As long as you've got high speed access, you'll always have friends."

"A dream come true," Fong said.

Turner called up the email and downloaded the video. He, Fenwick, and Fong watched it unfurl.

The first thing they noted was that the recording began before any fight. It showed the two cops playing pool. The sound quality was not the best. Fong did several magical things with the computer, but they still couldn't make out the dialogue.

They recognized only one other cop. The one whose balls Fenwick had attempted to crush earlier this morning.

They watched it to the end.

Fenwick said, "The only thing this confirms is that it was a set-up. He was recording from the beginning."

Turner said, "There's something wrong with it."

Fong said, "I checked the video. That's all that's in the file that was sent."

Turner said, "I'm not sure what it is." They ran it again. Toward the end, he said, "Stop."

"What?" Fenwick asked.

Turner tapped the computer screen. "This is the point where the other cops come in. What hasn't Belger done all this time? He hasn't tried to stop Callaghan from attacking the bartender. Now he does, when other people show up. Belger wasn't a hero."

Fenwick said, "He enjoyed the encounter until he could put it to some use to screw his partner."

Turner said, "Nothing anyone has told us so far leads me to believe that Belger was capable of that much thought or planning. Certainly in that short of time. Something is odd there, though. I'm just not sure what it means yet."

They saved a copy of the file to a jump drive, thanked Fong, and went back to their desks. Barb Dams strolled over with several thick folders. She said, "Pictures of Chicago police officers from all the districts near the bar. Molton said you'd need them to find out the identity of the other cop in the bar."

Fenwick said, "He's good."

Dams said, "It's obvious. I threw in a few others I thought might be helpful." She left.

Fenwick said, "We've already got Lensky and Vereski's name from the owner. The only one we don't have is the guy who was trying to be friendly."

Turner and Fenwick divided up the pictures. On the top Dams had included photos of Boyle, Armour, O'Bannion, and Nance. After a few minutes of leafing through pictures from the Districts, Turner found a picture of Karl Wendover, who'd been the one who gave him a friendly bit of information in the bar. They also found Bert Lensky, the sergeant who had assaulted Turner. They found Vereski, the bulky cop whose scrotum Fenwick had mushed. He walked a beat in the next district over from Belger's.

"We better get to these guys," Fenwick said.

"Karl Wendover must have figured we'd find out who he was."

"Maybe he wanted us to know," Fenwick said.

Lensky was off duty. They got his home address. They got Molton to find out Wendover's work schedule. He was about done with a shift. Molton had central Dispatch get a message to Wendover to be at the Melrose restaurant at 5:30. Vereski was supposed to be at work, but no one could find his current location.

Walking up Broadway, as they passed Unabridged Bookstore, Turner asked, "Is Boyle's 'Come to Jesus' lecture to Scanlan the same thing as having a goddess?"

"Not hardly. But I liked your last question to Boyle. There is some connection between these guys. We gotta figure out what it was."

They saw Wendover pacing in front of the Melrose. He saw them as they began to cross Melrose Street. For a moment, he looked like he might bolt. The detectives hurried up to him.

"What is this?" Wendover demanded.

Turner said, "Let's get off the street."

Wendover thrust his lanky frame into the darkest corner of the booth farthest from the restaurant entrance. He peered at the nearest patrons then hunched over the table toward the detectives. They all ordered coffee.

Wendover asked, "What the hell is this?"

Turner said, "You tried to help earlier this morning."

"How'd you find me?"

Fenwick said, "We Googled scared young Chicago cops who want to be helpful. Your picture came up."

"Fuck," Wendover said.

"That sums it up nicely," Fenwick said.

Turner said, "Thanks for trying to help."

Fenwick said, "You didn't stay when the violence started."

"That was a sergeant. I'm a beat cop. You were both superiors. I'm not a fool. I'm not getting into the middle of that."

"Why'd you help?" Turner asked.

Wendover said, "Used to be I wanted to be a cop who helped people. I'm a shit. Worse than a shit. It's all Belger and Callaghan's fault."

"What'd they do?"

"What didn't they do?"

Fenwick said, "We need details."

Wendover asked, "Am I going to be fired?"

Fenwick said, "What have you done wrong?"

"Are you helping the Feds?"

Fenwick said, "We know nothing about a federal investigation of these guys. Do you?"

They stopped talking while the waitress delivered their coffees. She took Fenwick's pie order and left.

Wendover said, "There were rumors. There were always rumors about those guys. I never wanted to work the same shift with them. I was the one who always had to clean up their messes. They'd get accused of something, and they'd try to pass it off on someone else. They'd do something stupid, and the rest of us paid."

"Like what?" Fenwick asked.

"I carried money from point A to point B."

"Not good," Fenwick said.

"I'm screwed."

"Get a lawyer and a union rep. Talk to them now. Today if you can. Monday at the latest."

"Is there anything I can do?"

"We need help with the murder investigation," Turner said. "That won't be likely to help you, but it may help us."

Wendover nodded. "You heard about those cops who were trying to get other cops killed? The corrupt cops going after the good cops? I tried to walk the line. To keep them satisfied and to keep myself honest."

"Was Boyle in on it?"

"I sure thought so. How could they have gotten away with anything if they didn't have bosses backing them up?"

"How come Callaghan had no complaints in his file and Belger had a slew of them?"

"Boyle liked Callaghan best."

"Why?"

"How the hell should I know? All I know is, I got screwed. All I know is, I don't want to be a cop any more. I for sure know I don't want to go to jail because of these guys. I'll do whatever I can to stay out of jail."

Turner asked, "Did they taser anybody?"

"Oh, shit man, yeah. They'd laugh about it."

"They weren't worried about getting in trouble?" Fenwick asked.

"Callaghan never seemed concerned about anything. I think Belger was kind of a worrywart, but if he did worry, it wasn't enough to stop him."

"What would he worry about?" Fenwick asked.

"Getting caught."

Fenwick's chocolate cream pie arrived. He dug in.

Turner asked, "Did he mention specific things they'd done that he was worried about?"

"No, he'd just say things, like, 'are you sure we can get away with this'. That kind of stuff."

Turner said, "So the specific crime was stealing money?"

"At least that." Wendover described one incident where they robbed a victim at a death scene. Then he talked about sloppy police work, witnesses and suspects being intimidated, excessive arrests and few convictions, all the things they'd already heard about.

"How'd they expect to get away with all that?" Fenwick asked.

"They had for years. Callaghan especially acted as if it was no problem, not in the past, not now, not ever."

"Did you hear that Belger was into gay S+M?"

"Never heard that before today."

"Did they fight?"

"Constantly. Like a married couple main-lining steroids, like the two of them were permanently on fast forward. They were nuts, but they were buddies."

"Any of the people who complained particularly vocal?" Turner asked.

"Those two gay guys. They were pretty persistent. But even that, it just went away."

Turner asked, "Do you know Bert Lensky or Claude Vereski?"

"They're in the Raving Dragon pretty often."

"Did they drink a lot last night and this morning?"

"I wasn't watching. Some beat cop came in with the news of the murder. That shook the place up. Everybody wondered where Callaghan was. They knew he'd be a suspect. The general feeling was that Belger got what was coming to him."

"Did you hear Lensky and Vereski discussing what they planned to do?"

"No. I heard you beat the crap out of Lensky. Did you?"

Turner said, "I did what I had to do to defend myself. Did the guys in the bar talk about us showing up before we got there?"

"Not to me. When Callaghan and his crowd came in, a few guys huddled together with them."

The waitress took Fenwick's empty pie plate, refilled their coffees, and left the bill.

"Do you know who sent the guy to attack me?"

"I don't know. I think it was spontaneous. They felt righteous and justified."

Fenwick said, "In this case, nobody does anything spontaneously. A lot of this seems planned although maybe not well planned."

Wendover said, "Well enough planned that you haven't caught the killer yet."

Fenwick said, "It's been less than twenty-four hours. Give us time." Turner made sure they left the waitress a large tip. They'd taken up her booth for quite a while and hadn't ordered much. Turner didn't think it was right to short her. Wendover stayed in the back booth so he wouldn't be seen leaving with them.

Outside, Fenwick said, "Let's pay Sergeant Bert Lensky a visit. After pounding the hell out of someone, it's always nice to examine one's handiwork."

"Advice from a master. All this and heaven too."

Fenwick said, "My experience also tells me it isn't the worrywarts of the world who get themselves in deep shit. It's the confident ones, the ones who think they're smarter and cleverer than the rest of us. Those are the ones who make the fatal mistakes."

"Good theory, except this time the worrywart is the one who's dead."

"I hate when my masterful theories go in the crapper."

Thirty-two

They drove through the unrelenting humidity to the southwest side of the city. It was nearly 6:30 in the evening. Lensky lived alone above a garage in a studio apartment he rented from an aunt of his who said, "Have you come to evict him?"

Fenwick said, "Aren't you related to him?"

"You ever heard of tough love?" Her red hair swirled about her head in ways that did little to hide the hideousness of the dye job. Her feet slopped over the side of her shower clogs, now trendily called flip-flops. Edith Bunker would have thrown out the house dress that the aunt wore.

Lensky had his own entrance up a short flight of stairs on the side of the garage.

Fenwick pounded on the door. When no one answered, he pounded some more. The aunt had said her nephew was home. His car was in the driveway blocking her, and she had to go to the store.

They heard mumbles behind the door then a voice growling, "Go away."

Fenwick pounded some more.

The door finally swung inward. Lensky said, "What the fuck?"

Fenwick pushed his way in. Lensky fell backwards, stumbled to the far wall, righted himself, picked up a lamp in his left hand, and came at them. His right hand fumbled behind his back.

"Gun!" Turner shouted.

Fenwick's movement's belied his bulk. Moving quickly, Fenwick punched the guy in the gut, then kneed him in the face as Lensky bent over from the first punch. Lensky bellowed and flung his hands against his nose. A gun clattered to the floor. Lensky followed it down. He held his bleeding nose and moaned. His body was in as tight a ball as his overweight bulk could manage.

Fenwick picked up the gun and said, "How's your day going?" He dragged over a plastic covered kitchen chair and sat down. Turner checked the mini-refrigerator and found, in a frost-encrusted freezer, a bag of corn two years past its expiration date. He tapped Lensky's shoulder with the cold mass.

Lensky moaned but took the vegetables and covered his nose. Then he moaned some more.

Turner stood at Fenwick's right shoulder.

Fenwick said, "We're going to wait and have a nice chat. Maybe I can be convinced not to beat you to a pulp. But I doubt it."

Minutes passed before Lensky's moaning halted. He moved the vegetable package and glared at the detectives. "You broke my nose."

"That was the point," Fenwick said.

"It hurts," Lensky said.

"Good," Fenwick said, "And don't whine at me."

Using the wall for support, Lensky tried to get up. He plopped back down, but managed to ease himself into a sitting position.

Turner asked, "You always carry a gun at home?"

"Only for you." He shook his head. "I talked to two detectives, Roosevelt and Wilson. They threatened me if I tried to report you guys. I should report all of this."

Turner said, "You attacked me in the washroom of the bar. Why? Who told you to?"

"Nobody told me. I knew what to do."

"Why?" Turner reiterated.

Lensky said, "You can come and beat me up. Fine. You have no idea what and who you're dealing with."

Fenwick said, "Meaning you have an idea of what and who we're dealing with?"

"Fuck you. Whether or not you catch the killer, your careers are over."

Fenwick said, "I love threats. They give zest to any investigation. You telling us the killer is a cop?"

"I'm telling you fuck you."

Fenwick said, "I'm going to enjoy this too much."

Turner said, "Torture doesn't work."

Fenwick said, "I don't care if it works on him. I'm doing it for me so I feel better."

Turner said, "I was the one attacked."

Fenwick said, "Feel free."

Turner said to Lensky, "If a Chicago cop didn't do it, why would anyone on the CPD care?"

"Because Belger was a shit."

"Did you know him?"

"I knew enough."

Turner said, "How did you know to attack me in the bar?"

Lensky said, "Man, I can't have this kind of pressure."

Turner said, "You don't think beating me up is pressure?"

"I was doing what I was told."

Fenwick said, "Make up your mind. You can't have it both ways. Either somebody did or didn't tell you to beat one or the other or both of us up. Come to think of it, why didn't somebody try to beat me up? I keep getting left out."

"He was the fag. He'd be easier. I had orders."

This was a poor excuse to use in front of Turner, but it was a flashpoint comment for Fenwick. The bulky detective moved across the room and towered over the still reclining Lensky. "You were following orders? You absolute numb nuts, fuck-a-doodle moron. Do you take stupid-asshole lessons? You mother fucking son-of-a-bitch. How dare you? This is one of your own. Orders! Whose orders?"

Lensky cowered.

Fenwick said, "Do not imagine that we are going to leave here without finding out who sent you."

Lensky said, "I can't."

Turner said, "Let's make it simple. Who would know about what happened and who would have the clout to make a call or pay you a visit? Had to be someone who would have access to information as it was coming out. Who has that? For sure the Commander of the Ninth District. Who else?"

Lensky remained mute.

Fenwick said, "Has to be Boyle."

Lensky turned pale. "He'd kill me."

Fenwick said, "Nobody is going to actually kill you."

"Look what happened to Belger."

Turner said, "Are you saying Boyle ordered Belger killed?"

"I don't know. I didn't do it. I'm not involved."

Turner said, "We've found out about all kinds of crimes Belger and Callaghan committed. Somebody had to be covering. Who was doing the covering up, and what crimes did they cover up? You're their immediate supervisor. You saw them every day. You had to know what was going on. The least you could have known was that there was some kind of cover-up going on."

"You guys wearing wires for the Feds?"

Fenwick said, "You want to pat us down?"

"I don't trust anybody."

Fenwick said, "We're just trying to solve a murder."

Turner said, "Do you imagine the Feds don't have tapes of you guys already?"

Lensky said, "Boyle told us..." He eyed each of them blearily. Turner wondered if he'd had a completely sober moment in the past year.

Turner said, "Boyle's covering his own ass."

"I don't know who to trust."

Turner said, "You can trust us to find Belger's killer. Did you kill him?"

"No." Petulance and begging mixed in the tone of his answer.

"Do you know who did?"

"I figure just like everybody else. Some cop did."

"What schemes were Belger and Callaghan working?"

Lensky sighed. "I need a drink." The detectives didn't stop him. Lensky stood up. "It's in the kitchen." The detectives followed him. Turner imagined that Lensky at this point could run, kill himself, or find another gun and kill them. When Lensky noted them following, he said, "I can get it."

Fenwick said, "We'll help."

Lensky gave up arguing. In the kitchen he fumbled in a cupboard. Turner and Fenwick put their hands on their guns. Lensky pulled a pint bottle of bourbon from the back of a shelf. He saw them ready to pull their guns. He leered. "You're safe for now." He slumped into a kitchen chair.

Fenwick said, "What is this bullshit 'safe for now'?"

Lensky said, "You guys don't get it. I heard you were a couple of suck-ass wimps. Don't you know how this department works?"

Fenwick said, "Why don't you tell us?"

Lensky drank deeply, wiped his lips with his left sleeve. "You two won't survive this. Hell, I could tell you stories that would make you weep, and you won't be alive long enough to tell anyone."

Fenwick said, "I haven't had a good weep in a while. Why don't you tell me?"

This time, Lensky sipped from his bottle and then gave them an impish grin. "Sure, Belger and Callaghan intimidated witnesses. Beat people up."

"Tasered them," Fenwick prompted.

"Sure. But you gotta be careful with this shit. We're lucky. Everybody these days claims they are victims of police brutality. It's great, because then the real victims look less credible." He cackled and drank and resumed. "The ones we could cover up, we covered up. It's not hard. We've all been doing it for years. If you guys claim you haven't, you're lying."

The detectives kept silent.

Lensky kept his eyes on them as he drank. He said, "I'm really drunk." He drank some more. "My nose really hurts." He did an elaborate sleeve wipe, then said, "If we couldn't cover it up, we put the complaints in their files."

Fenwick said, "Callaghan doesn't have any complaints in his file."

Lensky leered, cackled, and drank. "I didn't know that. You guys are so fucked."

"Did Boyle know about all this?" Turner asked.

"Sure. We all knew about it."

"Including stealing from the dead?" Turner asked.

Lensky said, "You'd be surprised how few corpses complain."

"Boyle knew about that?" Turner asked.

"Boyle knows everything."

Turner asked, "If the cops knew about all this, why did Belger die?"

"Beats the hell out of me. I had nothing to do with that. I don't know. Boyle is nuts. He'd do anything. Yes, he tortures prisoners. No, nobody is supposed to know about it, and not many people do. And yes, he's racist, and homophobic, and sexist. It's nuts. It's out of control. Boyle is out of control, but he's the Commander. Nobody stands up to that. Nobody wants to stand up to that."

Turner said, "Trying to beat up on me is standing up?"

"I was supposed to have help." He pointed at Fenwick. "When I saw him, I knew we'd have to get you alone, but I didn't know when that would be. When you went to take a piss, I decided I had to do something. Then you'd be on your own. I could do it and get out. I wouldn't need help because you're a fag."

Turner said, "I hope it hurt."

Lensky said, "The doctor says my jaw isn't broken, but I've got teeth loose."

Fenwick said, "Boyle called you."

Lensky nodded. "But don't think I'm going to go public with this or testify against him. He's got lots of ways of getting even. He gets revenge and it sticks. And no matter what you do, you aren't going to be able to stop him."

"What about a federal investigation?"

"Don't you learn from all those headlines about rotten cops? They're the stupid ones. The ones who got caught. You know how long this has been going on? You know how powerful the Blue Code of silence is? It's gone on for years. It will go on for years. You guys are fucked."

After getting nothing more than bluster and threats for the next few minutes, Turner and Fenwick left.

THIRTY-THREE

They drove back down the newly refurbished Dan Ryan Expressway to Area Ten. At least an hour before the heat from the pavement could ooze into the sunless air.

Fenwick said, "That's why I read murder mysteries."

"Why's that?" Turner asked.

"The bad guys get caught, which is a good thing, but the bad and slimy guys come to an even more awful end."

"Welcome to reality," Turner said.

Fenwick asked, "Does he really know who and what we're up against?"

"Don't we? Rogue cops. We just don't have proof to bring the dumb shits to justice."

"Did he kill Belger?" Fenwick asked.

"I don't think so, but I can't tell if he knows who did."

Fenwick said, "Boyle is up to his armpits in some kind of shit."

"All kinds of shit," Turner corrected. "Him and Callaghan. Probably half the damn department."

Fenwick said, "Time to find Claude Vereski. We can see if his nuts have recovered."

"I'll leave that to you," Turner said.

"I always get the tough, gritty jobs."

"I'm not sure I've ever known anyone tougher or grittier than you are."

Turner called Molton to find out if Claude Vereski had turned up. Molton said, "I talked to the Commander up there twice. He gave me nothing, but I've got connections. I made more calls. Word is, in summer he likes to patrol along the beach around Belmont Harbor. His lieutenant thinks he can do less harm there.

He figures the guy gets distracted by all the women in skimpy bathing suits. Keeps his mind off of doing something stupid."

Turner said, "Isn't that known as a pretty gay part of the lake front?"

"I guess there's enough there that he stays interested."

Or he's another closet case, Turner thought.

Molton was continuing. "Before you hang up, I've got some curious results to my questions on Boyle getting those tests run so quickly."

"He cheated," Turner said.

"Much stranger. Nobody would admit they did the tests. No one will vouch for him, which means he didn't think to cover his tracks."

"Or think he needed to," Turner added.

"Right, so he's over-confident or stupid or both."

Turner said, "Or he doesn't have as much clout as he thought, and people are abandoning him because they think he did it, or they see his power waning and don't want to be caught in the backwash as he sinks."

"Or they're getting even with him. Boyle's an asshole. He can't have made a lot of friends among the regular workers at the lab. Maybe he's even got some enemies."

Turner said, "Or Boyle was telling blatant lies."

"But why?" Molton asked. "He knows if the case got to court, even the most incompetent lawyer would have the forensic people up there. If they denied doing the test, the case would go up in smoke."

"Maybe he never expected the case to go to court."

Molton said, "I wish this made more sense. I haven't been able to find any significant connection between Boyle and Callaghan. They aren't related. They didn't know each other before Callaghan started on the department. I'll keep looking."

Turner and Fenwick headed to Belmont Harbor. Even at seven

thirty on a Saturday evening, cars filled the parking lot. Crowds of people crammed onto the few boats left in the Harbor.

A police car occupied the shade under one of the few trees that overhung the parking lot. The detectives strolled south. No lake breeze disturbed the ghastly hot air. After about a quarter of a mile, they saw a cop talking to a group of three young women. As they neared him, Turner saw it was Vereski. When Turner and Fenwick were about ten feet way, Vereski looked up. His laughter stopped abruptly. He glanced around wildly. He could have tried a dash to his car, but the detectives were between him and it.

Fenwick addressed Vereski's coterie of scantily clad admirers. "Excuse us, please. We need to speak to officer Vereski."

They left in a haze of humidity and giggles.

Vereski smiled after them, then scowled at the detectives.

Fenwick said, "Working hard?"

"You're lucky I didn't turn you in."

"Ashamed to show the evidence? Maybe you've got a pinprick dick. Didn't feel like much squishiness there."

"Fuck you!" Vereski began walking away.

Turner got in front of him. "Did you think we couldn't find you? Do you think someone's going to come along and protect you from us, or from yourself, for that matter? We found you this time and could find you again. You're going to have to talk to us."

"I don't have to talk to you. I don't have a union rep here."

"But this isn't a misconduct investigation," Turner said.

Fenwick said, "Think of it as some friends who want to get to know each other better."

Vereski scowled. "I don't know anything about the murder."

Turner asked, "Why were you so quick in the bar this morning to rush to Callaghan's defense? And why would you tell a lie that was so provably false?"

"You wouldn't have known if somebody hadn't told."

"Who told you to lie for him?"

"Everybody knew what was going on. Everybody knew Callaghan needed an alibi. I wanted to step up. I wanted to show people I'm willing to protect one of our own. Unlike you guys who are traitors."

"Just following the evidence," Fenwick said, "which for the moment runs right between your legs."

"My balls still hurt. They're blue. If I wasn't so embarrassed, I'd sue your asses. I should see a doctor."

"How well do you know Callaghan?"

"We're bar buddies. We play pool sometimes. He's okay."

"How about Belger?"

"I never guessed him for a fag."

"You know he was gay?" Turner asked.

"He was found at that party."

"Did you suspect before that?"

"Well, looking back at it, there was a lot of stuff, like he'd stare at a guy's crotch sometimes."

"That sounds like a criminal offense," Turner said.

"Yeah, well."

Fenwick asked, "Did you hear about them tasering guys?"

Vereski looked uncomfortable.

Turner said, "You know you've got a pretty cushy beat here. All the scantily clad women you could want to watch, or did you request the gay section of the beach because you're a closet case?"

"I'm no fag."

Fenwick said, "But we could fix it so that you lose this beat. No more naps in the winter or strolls among young lovelies in the summer."

"You don't have that kind of power," Vereski said.

"You want to risk it?" Fenwick asked.

Vereski stared at the jiggling flesh of a woman strolling by. He turned his attention back to them. "You hear all kinds of stupid rumors. Guys brag. Most of it's bullshit."

"Was it with these guys?"

"I never saw them do anything."

"But you heard?"

"Yeah."

"How about them stealing from crime scenes?"

"Hey, who cares if some drug-crazed gang member loses a few bucks? They're dead, and they won't care. It's not like somebody's going to say 'You stole my drug money'."

"How much did they take?"

"I have no idea."

"They share it with you?"

"Every time they lost at pool."

"Who was protecting Callaghan?"

"I have no idea. Belger was always complaining that the world was out to get him. Callaghan was much cooler. He didn't act like he ever had much to worry about. Some guys are just that easy going. I guess."

He knew no more. Turner and Fenwick left.

THIRTY-FOUR

Molton called and told them he had a contact from the police academy who knew both Belger and Callaghan.

"He'll meet with you at the third pillar on the left at Pierre's at midnight."

"Finally," Turner said, "some mystery and intrigue in this case."

Molton said, "Could be important. Could be nothing. You gotta check everything."

"How'd you know to call him?" Turner asked.

"He called me."

"That's odd."

"Yes."

Turner said, "Everybody is petrified about revealing themselves and their connections to these guys or this case. Why not this guy?"

"Connections within connections," Molton said. He gave them the real address.

They met ex-Commander Billy Dossett at a bar on lower Wacker Drive that had even fewer lights than the Raving Dragon. Except for Dossett and the bartender, the establishment was empty.

Dossett was trim and neat with a salt and pepper goatee. He wore a green knit shirt and khaki shorts. He had a shot and a beer in front of him. The bartender delivered Fenwick and Turner's coffee order then proceeded to ignore the three of them.

Turner and Fenwick introduced themselves. Fenwick said, "Can you tell us what the hell is going on? Why the hell is everyone so frightened about talking to us?"

"You already know the answer to that."

Fenwick said, "I'd rather hear it stated."

"You're breaking all the rules. You're not from our brand new Independent Police Review Authority. You're regular cops doing your jobs and that's the most frightening thing of all. People know you. They know your reputation. Some want to protect you. Others want to get you. They know you've got friends. Rumors swirl back and forth. Molton knows people. The other detectives on your squad are looking out for you. Some just want to run as far away from the situation as possible. They're petrified you'll find the killer, and it'll be a cop."

Fenwick quoted Walt Kelly, "'We have met the enemy and he is us.'"

"Yes," Dossett said.

"Did a cop kill him?"

"I have no idea."

"But you're willing to talk to us."

"I'm retired. I like Molton. I like your reputations as honest cops."

Fenwick glanced around the booth then at the bar. Turner knew what he wanted; diet sugar for his coffee. Fenwick lumbered up to the bar, gazed up and down, headed for the far end. He came back with two pink and two blue little packets. Fenwick dumped them all in at the same time. Stirred. Drank. Smiled in satisfaction. As he performed these rituals Turner examined Dossett.

No wedding ring. A widower? He was in his late sixties or early seventies. Maybe he just didn't wear a wedding ring. Or he was gay and rallying around an embattled gay police detective. Or maybe it was simpler; he was the kind of guy who did the right thing because it was the right thing to do.

Fenwick said, "If they don't know it's a cop who did it, why are they so scared?"

Dossett said, "Because they all presume Callaghan did it. Because they all presume Callaghan was justified in killing his partner. Because everybody was pissed."

Fenwick said, "But they must know there's more to the story than was on that video."

Dossett said, "They could have the entire video with commentary and transcripts in front of them. It makes no difference. In their eyes Belger committed the ultimate crime. Belger was at fault. Callaghan is the wronged innocent."

"He was a jerk," Fenwick said. "They all know he was a jerk."

"But he was our jerk. And they don't want their partners to turn on them. Who would be more likely to know all the dumb stuff you've done on the job than your partner? Who could turn you in? The message is to themselves. Never turn on your own. This could happen to you. Loyalty to the guy next to you is paramount. You've got to be able to depend on him. If somebody pulls a gun on you, you've got to know he'll back you up."

Fenwick said, "An asshole is more likely to be dependable than an honest guy?"

Dossett said, "You can debate whether it *should* be the reality, but you cannot debate what *is* the reality. You guys should be very afraid. You've got friends. Powerful friends. But somebody will turn on you. Some low life asshole will make your life miserable, or hurt you, or try to destroy you, maybe kill you."

"None of that's a surprise," Fenwick said. "We've been on the job. We know. Reality and facing it aren't our problems."

"I don't know you. So I'm making sure you know. I can only give you possibilities. I'm not going to leave something out because I think you might be the brightest cops on the planet. It's best to cover all bases."

Turner said, "We appreciate it."

Fenwick said, "We were hoping you could help us with information about the two of them. We heard they were quarrelling even before the night of the bartender incident. We've got reports they were into illegal stuff."

"Evidence or rumors?"

"Rumors."

"I can possibly confirm some of those, but I have no more evidence." He sipped some coffee. He spread his hands on the table in front of him. "Sometimes former students come back to me. They talk. In the past few years a couple guys mentioned their discomfort with Belger and Callaghan."

"Just a sec," Fenwick said. He got up, went to the end of the bar, took the drip coffee pot, grabbed more diet sugar packets and returned to the table. The bartender ignored him. Fenwick poured coffee and diet sugar. Stirred. Looked at Dossett and, as if there'd been no interruption for his foray into beverage attaining, asked, "Like what?"

"Tasering was one."

"Names?" Fenwick asked.

"Of the victims? No, these young cops didn't care about the victims. It was more how much trouble they would get in if they ever tried that. I always told them assume what you're doing is going to be on the news. These days you have to."

"Stealing from the dead?" Fenwick asked.

"Money and drugs all of a sudden disappear. Amazing how few major drug dealers who die have any drugs in their houses or apartments especially when Belger and Callaghan were involved."

"But nobody complained?"

"Nobody caught them. Or if they were caught, it was covered up. And if it was covered up, it's got to involve the command structure."

"And nobody complained?"

Dossett laughed. "How many complaints have been filed against Chicago cops in the past ten years? You know the answer: a thousand. How many were found to be valid? Two. Two out of a thousand. Even if they complain, it's useless. And a drug dealer complaining his illegal stash is gone? You know that's a non-starter."

"But you can't give us names of the victims?"

"No."

"How about your sources?"

"I'll see what I can do for you."

Turner asked, "There's gotta be some significant connection between Boyle and Callaghan. Maybe between Boyle and Belger as well. Do you know what it is?"

"No idea. You still going to investigate?" Dossett asked.

"It's our job," Turner said.

Dossett smiled. "I wish I'd had you in my District when I was a commander. Good luck."

"Any suggestions on what to try next?" Fenwick asked.

"Yeah, if you find out it was a cop, make sure your evidence is rock solid. Do you think it was a cop?"

Turner said, "We're keeping our options open. We've got a lot of questions to ask a lot of people."

In the car Turner said, "That all just seemed slightly off to me."

"How so?"

"I get the impression that the whole conversation was designed to get to his last question, do we think it was a cop."

"Molton trusts this guy."

Turner said, "This guy called Molton out of the blue. He didn't really give us information. No specific names or places or dates. Was he looking for information on our investigation?"

"Remember what we've been told, trust no one."

Turner said, "That's the easy part."

Fenwick started the car and they headed back to Area Ten.

After several moments of silence and as they sat at the light on the corner of Broadway and Hollywood, Fenwick said, "You're depressed again."

"I'm depressed again."

Fenwick let the silence go on. Turner would talk about it or he wouldn't. After they turned onto Lake Shore Drive, at Hollywood, Turner said, "We're supposed to be the finest. Helping people. It's all so fucked up."

"We knew that."

"But most of the time we can pretend we're doing something to help. Who have we helped in this case?"

Fenwick waited patiently.

Turner said, "Nobody."

After several miles of silence down to Belmont Avenue, Fenwick asked, "Are we doing our best to find the killer?"

"Yeah, I guess, sure."

"Do we always give it our best shot?"

"Is it really good enough?"

Fenwick said, "If our best isn't good enough, whose is? And no, that isn't egotistical." Turner glanced at him. "Well, maybe a little. But by any measure you can think of, do we not do an excellent job? We bust our butts. Bad guys go to jail."

"I'm depressed about us, our guys."

"Me, too. But we're not in charge of our guys. We're only in charge of what we do."

"I know. I know. It's just this is fucked up."

Fenwick let the next silence go until they were passing Oak Street beach. He said, "Do you keep a list of all my dumb stuff?"

Turner said, "If I kept a list of your oddities and peccadilloes, and the symphonic chorus of odd noises you make, I'd have no time for my job, my husband, or my kids."

Fenwick said, "I've got a list of yours."

"Congratulations. You could sell it on eBay and if you had a brass ring, you might make enough for a cup of coffee at Starbucks."

THIRTY-FIVE

Back at Area Ten they filled Molton in on what they had. Molton asked questions and sympathized, then said, "I ordered the schematics of the train station. It might help you guys. That place is confusing."

"Thanks," Fenwick said.

Molton said, "The Scanlan kid has been released."

"We wanted to talk to him again," Fenwick said.

"Somebody downtown took care of it."

"Over your objections?" Fenwick asked.

"Over a lot of people's objections," Molton said.

Fenwick said, "With luck, that family will be out of our hair."

Molton said, "You're expecting luck on this case?"

Fenwick said, "The goddess promised me."

Turner said, "The kid is as good as dead. He's involved in this some way. He's being used."

Molton and Fenwick looked at him.

"No, I don't have proof," Turner said.

Molton said, "You going back to the party?"

Turner said, "It's next on the agenda, but it's still early. The place won't really get going until after ten. We told them we'd be back between ten and eleven. Until it's time to leave, we can start catching up on the paperwork on this case."

Molton said, "Go then. Find. Fix. Solve." He left.

The forensics report was waiting on their desks. Turner yawned as he opened his. He wanted to sleep.

The last page had the information about the entrance the kid, Scanlan, had taken them to.

Some of the smudges found in the dirt there were the same

blood type as Belger. They'd sent their materials for DNA analysis. Turner knew it could take a week or two to get those results. He gave Fenwick the news.

Fenwick said, "Fuck-a-doodle-do. We need to get that kid back in here."

Turner called the parents. They didn't know where the kid was. The mother dissolved in tears after she told him that. The father came on the line. He was angry and demanding. Turner didn't think either reaction helped much at this point, but he understood parents being distraught about their children.

He hung up and told Fenwick who asked, "Already? How can they not know where their kid is?"

"He's a teenager," Turner began.

"And they are idiots," Fenwick finished for him.

Turner said, "They were quite willing to blame us."

"Idiots," Fenwick repeated. "Moronic, too stupid to live idiots."

Turner wasn't sure he would be quite so harsh in his judgment as Fenwick. The point was they needed to talk to the kid.

Turner and Fenwick began plowing through the mound of paperwork. They would take even more care than usual. Neither wanted the slightest slip-up.

An hour later the lab called. The tech said to Turner, "We've been told to rush everything that has to do with the Belger case. We got that box of sex toys you sent over. I can tell you the sex toys have Belger's fingerprints on them and no one else's."

Turner waited. The silence lengthened. Turner said, "That's it?"

"That's all I got. No blood. No dust. Oh, sorry, and the clothes from the kid."

"Yeah."

"They were the kid's clothes."

"That's it? No blood? No anything?"

"Sorry, that's it."

He hung up and reported to Fenwick who said, "Either someone cleaned the stuff we found, or he was always fastidious with his sex toys."

"Isn't everyone?" Turner asked.

"I thought you were the one opposed to delving into personal sexual habits in this investigation."

"Just making an observation."

Fenwick said, "And the kid wore his own clothes."

"Another alert the media moment."

THIRTY-SIX

It was ten. Turner and Fenwick went to change. Just before they left for the party, Molton walked up to them. He raised his eyebrow at Fenwick's outfit. "You're disguised as a what?"

Fenwick growled. He wore black jeans and hiking boots and a black muscle T-shirt that clung to every bulge in his torso. Turner wore black leather pants and a chain-mesh T-shirt he'd borrowed from Ben just before he left home.

Molton handed them the latest envelope filled with information they'd requested from Barb Dams. It was fairly heavy now with a surprising array of pictures and data sheets. It must have taken hours. She was a great cop, and they knew she was behind them. And she was a friend. And she was stunningly thorough. If data could catch a killer, it could very well be in the stuff she'd compiled.

Out in the humidity, Turner's pants were miserably uncomfortable.

As the air-conditioner in the car fought more with itself than the humidity, Turner said, "At the fair you might see odder stuff than even you're used to."

"How much odd stuff have we seen as cops?" Fenwick asked.

"You want that chronologically or alphabetically?" Turner asked echoing Robert Downey Jr. in his first Sherlock Holmes movie.

"Take too long either way," Fenwick said. "You and I have seen more corpses and crushed humanity, physical and emotional, that we can count. If any cop who's been on the job as long as we have is shook by what he or she sees, he or she should quit. I'm a tough Chicago cop. At the fair, if it's still breathing, I can handle it. If not, I'll get Madge to explain it to me when I get home."

Images of some of the horrors that were part of their job almost daily flashed through Turner's mind. He knew what

Fenwick meant. Turner said, "Just thought I'd mention it."

Fenwick said, "Ain't just gay people who are kinky."

Turner said, "Kinky is universal. I'll add that to my list of Fenwick's familiar quotations."

"A fine list I'm sure it is."

In the air-conditioned upper reaches of the former train station the humidity was bearable. Sanchez and Deveneaux, the two beat cops from the night before, were with them on the detail. Turner thought Sanchez looked exceptionally hot in low-rise leather pants and no shirt. He never knew Sanchez had a tattoo of an eagle stretching from shoulder blade to shoulder blade on his back. Normally, Turner didn't care much for tattoos, but on Sanchez, it was hot. Sanchez's gun was in his left boot. Deveneaux wore faded and torn blue jeans and a bulky black T-shirt that concealed his gun. The detectives had strapped theirs to their ankles, to be armed but discreet.

Denver Slade, who'd first met them outside the door twenty-three hours ago, began prattling as soon as they arrived in his presence. "Now, you can't be mean. You've got to be kind. These people have paid a lot of money."

Fenwick asked, "Why hasn't Bryner fired you? He said he was going to when we questioned him."

Slade said, "See, now that was mean. Why would you say such a thing? He hasn't said a word to me. He and I are friends. I'm the one who really runs this thing. Sure it's his money, him and his rich buddies, but I know how to organize."

Fenwick asked, "Where is Bryner?"

"He knows people in this town. Him and his powerful buddies have been calling each other and having meetings. I haven't seen him since around four this afternoon."

Fenwick said, "He confided in you?"

"No, not really. Rumors swept through the community, this morning, that the rest of the party was cancelled. Then that it was on again. It's been a crazy day. I've never seen Matthew

Bryner sweat, but he was sweating today. He may have wanted to fire me, but I know every single detail of this fair. He doesn't. I know how it runs, who the vendors are, how to get things done."

Turner thought it would be a good idea to keep Slade around. It would lessen the alarm from the impact of police asking questions, and with luck it might get potential witnesses to open up.

Turner eyed the mass of people. "The murder doesn't seem to have hurt attendance."

"Not yet," Slade said.

They asked Slade to find someone he trusted to go with Sanchez and Deveneaux who were, first, to show photos of all the people they'd dealt with on the case to any person at the fair who had anything to do with registration or guarding the place. Turner glanced at what Barb had assembled. She'd even included pictures of the Scanlan kid, his parents, Lensky, Vereski, Dossett, the police brass from late that afternoon, and more. She was a gem beyond worth. Second they were to question people in the more private whipping rooms below the main level. Slade found someone who left with the two police officers.

First, Turner and Fenwick stopped at the booths selling sex toys. Turner and Fenwick had no guarantee that the killer had purchased the dildo and whip used on Belger at the party, but it was a start.

The walls and partitions of one formerly-shuttered store front were now lined with sex toys. In addition they saw display carrels of dildos, orgasm balls, chains, whips, harnesses, socks, gloves, hoods, and masks. Rows and rows of pleasure instruments lined every surface. Turner found and purchased a dildo the size of the one stuck in Belger's ass.

At a book stall the tables were strewn with piles of books. Turner noted a few titles: *Ties That Bind, Carried Away, Master's Manual,* and thirty or forty others. Turner thought the covers were rather repetitious. Guys tied to various apparatuses, or blindfolded, or being led on leashes. These got repeated in lots of variations by a whole lot of admittedly not very attractive men; overweight, out of shape, scraggily bearded, wearing only black socks. One whole line from one publisher used blurry covers. Turner didn't know if this was an improvement or not. Maybe that's what turned guys on who wanted this kind of book. Turner knew they didn't turn him on.

Fenwick pointed to one with the title *Butt*. He said, "That's one thing I don't get."

"What's that?" Turner asked.

"Getting fucked. I think it would hurt."

"I like it. Being top and bottom."

Fenwick turned to his friend.

Turner said, "Nor do I intend to discuss that with you further. You're the one in this relationship whose peccadilloes get mentioned, described, and analyzed beyond all relation to their importance and regardless of their grossness. I'm not starting."

Fenwick said, "Pity."

Turner asked, "You sure this stuff doesn't make you uncomfortable?"

"Why would it?"

"It's about as gay as you can get."

"And you're not?" Fenwick asked.

"I just thought it might be a lot different than you're used to."

Fenwick said, "You're the one who just said he didn't want to talk about his intimate stuff. Yes, I blab. Because you know all the stuff I do blab, doesn't mean there isn't other stuff I don't blab."

Turner looked at his partner. "I don't know if I should take comfort in that or not."

They kept the dildo with them as they picked out a set of orgasm balls that matched the ones that had been found. They took them up to the counter and showed them to the manager and Slade.

The manager, Earnest Drinkwater, had a shaved head and a face with wrinkled skin that showed he must have spent his life outdoors in the hot sun. His leather pants drooped on his thin frame. He kept yanking at them to hold them up.

"You sell any of these in the past couple days?" Fenwick asked.

Drinkwater said, "Over fifty of the dildos. Maybe ten or fifteen of the orgasm balls. And I'm not the only one selling them."

Turner took out the photo array that he'd tucked into a slim, black-leather satchel. "Any of these people look familiar?" He showed him the pictures.

The man looked. He shook his head. He called over his two helpers who also said they didn't recognize anyone. They got the same result from the other sex-toy vendors.

Turner and Fenwick proceeded to the whipping booths. As they strolled along the path they passed several men with their penises protruding from their pants. These were all older men whose entire costume seemed to be a limp, shriveled prick sticking out of the zipper opening in their pants. Turner guessed these guys might actually have nothing to do with the leather community. They'd just found a venue where they could expose themselves in public and not be arrested. The one time he and Ben had vacationed without the boys at a gay clothing-optional resort, Turner thought that those who exercised the option, shouldn't. He thought the same rubric applied to these guys.

"This is legal?" Fenwick pointed at one such drooping dick.

Slade said, "Technically this is a private party. People can act as if they were in their own homes. It's sort of public, but actually private. That's why we have the guards at the door. That's why people need to sign up on the Internet and prove their identity and not just that they are over eighteen. They have to prove their age and identity again at the registration area. We don't let just anyone into these things. It just can't be done."

Many of the leather clad patrons they passed wore pants or

shorts, but no shirt. One oddity Turner quickly noted was that the muscled, studly men with tight abs tended to be younger and to keep their chests at least partly covered, and that the more portly men tended to let their bellies bulge out for all to see.

On their way to the whipping booths, they passed the pissing booths. In one of them two men were on their knees. Their jeans and tight T-shirts were soaked. One of the men opened his mouth as a man stepped from the crowd and began to piss on him. Instantly, over half the members of the crowd produced cell phones and began taking pictures.

Fenwick said, "Not quite your basic home entertainment."

"Depends on your home, I guess," Turner said.

Several drag queens swept by. Rainbow-hued from toe to crown, their shoes, gowns, make-up, and hair flashed far beyond the point of exaggeration. They laughed and pointed and sipped from multi-colored drinks topped with little umbrellas. Hairdos stopped three feet above their heads. Heavy makeup and bright smiles and evening gowns clung to hefty figures.

Fenwick nodded toward them. "I thought there was a dress code."

Turner said, "You ever try and stop a drag queen?"

"You mean you don't know how they got admitted."

"They're here for effect. They own the place. They're related to the mayor. How long of a list do you want?"

Fenwick asked, "What are they doing here?"

Turner said, "Having a good time?"

Swaying on his ten inch heels, one of the drag queens lurched up to Turner. With a smile that almost cracked his ten layers of makeup, he put out one excessively manicured nail and touched Turner just above his belly button. "Hi, Mr. Man."

"Hi, yourself," Turner said.

"You busy later?" the drag queen asked.

Turner said, "I'm always busy, my dear, sorry."

"Too bad," said the drag queen and looking more like a drunken stork than anything else, stumbled away.

Fenwick said, "You always have all the fun."

"The next one can be yours."

"More fun than I'm up for."

The detectives descended to the lower levels. While edging their way through the crowd, they saw in one store-front window a man draped backward over two sawhorses with someone dripping hot wax onto his nipples.

Fenwick pointed, "Isn't that uncomfortable?"

"The wax?"

"No. The way his body is bent sort of backwards."

"Maybe it only sort of hurts. He's not trying to get away."

They stopped at the porn-site booth where Belger had been involved in the whipping demonstration. At a table at the front, two men took in money and explained rules and regulations. Preening in front of a mirror behind them was a porn star that Turner figured the booth had hired as part of its advertising. He thought the guy was built as if he stopped using his gym membership about six months ago. As they moved into the store, they saw, along the two walls, various devices people could be or were tied to. A portly gentleman with a white beard explained the finer points of whipping to a group of fifteen or so. A man sprawled face first on a giant cross obviously ready for the next demonstration. The gentleman lifted the whip and struck. The crowd murmured and nodded approval.

They found Frank Jordan, the owner of the porn site, whom they'd interviewed earlier. He said, "I got all the people who worked at the booth here like you asked. Some aren't real happy about it. You're fucking up our business. They're afraid you're going to screw up their lives or try to arrest them."

"Not unless they're killers," Fenwick said.

Slade said he had chores to attend to. The detectives told him if they needed him, they'd send for him.

In the back they found a walled-off section that might have been used as an office in an earlier incarnation. It contained a door that lead to a small bathroom.

Turner said, "Why don't you send in the man who organized the whipping, took the money, and the paperwork."

Jordan returned a few minutes later with Dave Ordman, who wore a knit black cotton-mesh jockstrap and nothing else. He looked to be in his mid-thirties. He sat down casually and spread his legs. His hairy chest sloped down to narrow hips. Turner thought perhaps he could have used a size or two larger jockstrap. Or perhaps the size he had on was the point. Ordman raised two shaven eyebrows at them, and in a voice from the lowest bass register said, "What can I do for you guys?"

If Turner hadn't been totally in love with his husband, Ben, there were quite a few things he thought this man could do for him.

Turner said, "Tell us about Jack Rammer."

"Belger?"

"You knew it was him when he came in?" Fenwick asked.

"He came to us before he got famous. I recognized him from TV after it happened, but he never mentioned it, and I never brought it up. It had nothing to do with the site."

"Do you remember what he said when he first showed up?" Turner asked. "How he behaved?"

"The first-timers are an odd bunch. There's the confident ones who are there to show you how studly they are. They're all on their way to being major porn stars, and you should be grateful that they're bothering to stop by and grace you with their presence. Then there's the shy ones who want to make a little cash, think this might be a little fun. Belger was closer to one of those. He was real reluctant to give his name. I told him, like I tell all of them, they don't have a choice. We need a real name, real photo ID, the disclaimer filled out. We don't take chances. No sensible porn site does. Why bother? There's always another guy who wants to take his clothes off."

"Did you know he was a cop?" Turner asked.

"He said he was. Even showed me his badge once. But he looked the part, a little older, in decent shape, certainly not a muscle queen. A believable persona makes it hotter."

"How would a viewer know he was a real cop?"

"We specialize in cops and military guys or at least we have them tell the camera they're cops. Some really are, but don't come across as believable on screen. Others aren't but are really convincing. Others aren't and wouldn't fool much of anybody, but if you're watching the site so you can jack off, you're not looking for academy award performances. We interview them on screen. Some guys you can just tell. It seems natural. I try to get them to tell stories about their jobs. Nothing too specific so they'd give away details that would get them discovered, but enough to show they are what they say. I guess it's like anything on film. It's what you can get the audience to believe."

"Do you remember anything distinctive about him?"

"He was one of the ones who insisted that he wouldn't touch any guys. Said if somebody tried to kiss him he wouldn't be responsible for his actions. I made sure the guys in scenes with him were careful."

Turner asked, "Would he let them touch him?"

"Only to blow him, but it was the whipping that he was interested in. Kept asking about that over and over. He was really into it. That's why he stood out. He couldn't get enough. He was great at the booth here. Really in demand. He'd let guys get really into it. We keep medical supplies on hand, and we won't let anybody really hurt somebody."

Turner said, "We were told by at least one woman that he wanted her to strap on a dildo and screw him."

Ordman said, "And I heard he was found with a dildo up his butt. He never said anything to me about dildos or his butt."

"Anybody who paid a lot for a chance at whipping him? Anyone who was especially tough or cruel?"

"For Belger we had guys lining up. He was one of our main attractions. He projected a believable persona as a straight guy."

"Do you think he was straight?" Fenwick asked.

Ordman scratched his balls while he thought. "I try not to get into these guys' heads. I'm not sure why they do this. Being an exhibitionist, gay or straight, helps. Being into pain is kind of a requirement. Otherwise you wouldn't be here. Whether it's gay or straight, I can't say for sure. I think they're all gay, but I've got no proof. I came on to him once. He turned me down."

"Was there anybody angry at him?" Turner asked.

"You get guys who are doing the whipping. Sometimes I don't think it's acting. There might have been one or two with Belger. I don't remember names. We don't keep records on those doing the whipping. They pay their ten bucks a hit and have at it."

"Nobody stood out?" Turner asked.

"Nobody whose name I remember. I was at all of Belger's performances here at the party."

"Did you tape them?"

"Usually. A lot more people in the audience use their cell phone cameras to record stuff that turns them on."

Fenwick said, "I'm confused. I thought this was a private party where everybody was desperate not to let anyone know they were here."

Jordan said, "We don't want the police to know. We tape the demonstrations to put on our own web site. Those who perform sign releases. We're careful."

Fenwick said, "But if they've all got cell phone cameras."

"We aren't responsible for that. People know what's going on. If it's that vital for them not to be filmed, they don't have to be here. The police are a different matter entirely."

Fenwick said, "Seems like a double standard."

"I get it," Turner said. A firm, definitive tone Fenwick knew he seldom used.

Fenwick glanced at him. Turner saw his partner nod. He knew Fenwick was going to drop it, surrendering to Turner's knowledge of this world.

Turner said, "We'll need to see the tapes you do have."

"I don't know."

"This is a murder investigation."

"I dunno." Ordman scratched his right butt check. "I guess."

Turner said, "There was one guy on the website who gave him a blow job."

"I can get you the guy in charge of that." He left.

Fenwick said, "I feel left out."

"How's that?"

"Nobody has this kind of thing for straight people."

"They don't?" Turner asked.

"Not that I know about."

"Maybe there is and you just don't know about it," Turner said.

"I thought I was comfortable with this, but I'm just not into it."

"Nobody said you had to be."

"Maybe I'm missing out."

"You could ask Madge."

"She'd probably really beat the hell out of me."

"And you don't deserve that?" Turner asked.

"Not all that much."

"Or you'd enjoy it too much?"

"Don't push your luck."

Turner knew from his observation of the couple over the years that they were a loving pair although he suspected Fenwick revealed even more of his oddities and peccadilloes to his wife. At least Turner hoped he wasn't the recipient of the most major ones in Fenwick's life.

"You mean this is too gay for you?" Turner asked.

"No. That's not it. Maybe it was when the guy scratched his balls through his jock strap."

Turner laughed. "When we play poker with some of the guys, what do straight guys do?"

"Huh?"

"You never noticed? They do three things. They belch, fart, and scratch their nuts."

Fenwick thought a moment then asked, "And your point?"

"That's all this guy did."

"He didn't belch or fart, and we don't wear see-through jockstraps."

"You bragging or complaining?"

Fenwick grumbled.

Turner asked, "Is that an annoyed grumble, an angry grumble, a frustrated grumble, or a go to hell grumble?"

"I think it's a let's switch topics grumble."

Turner obliged. He said, "We'll have more tapes to look at."

"I'll let you handle it. You're into this stuff."

"More like I'm familiar with what it is."

A few minutes later two men crowded into the small space: one an older man, Jasper Thiel, with iron gray hair, the other much younger, Ken Zibel, with dyed blond locks.

Thiel said, "I'm in charge of putting people together on the site."

"How does that work?"

"I find out what they will or won't do, and I partner them with people who will or won't do the same things. I show guys pictures of other guys or I introduce them. We try to get a chemistry that will work. Ken here saw a picture of Belger and was really into him. I told him it was hopeless."

Fenwick said, "We should probably talk to Mr. Zibel alone." Thiel left.

Turner said, "Mr. Zibel, what can you tell us?"

Zibel spoke in a mild tenor voice. "I only knew him as Jack Rammer. He wouldn't tell me his real name. But he was so hot. Rugged. Masculine. That turns me on. I really was into him. I like sex rough. I talked to him a few times on the set. Just to be friendly. I offered to do all kinds of things for him not on the set. In private. He kept saying no, but I persisted. Finally, I met him a couple times in like regular places. He was nice to me. I'm sorry he's dead."

"Where did you meet him?" Turner asked.

"Coffee shops mostly. At first."

"When was this?" Turner asked.

"The last couple weeks before the incident in the bar. I really was into him. I got him to talk to me. He even finally talked about being a real cop. Helping people. Tackling a gang banger who just shot someone." He sighed. "I wanted to see him in his uniform."

"And did he oblige?" Turner asked.

"Finally. He came to my place. At first he wouldn't let me touch him. I could just look. It was still so hot. He let me jack off while I watched him." Zibel blushed. "Should I be telling this to real cops? Of course, he was a real cop. You don't look like real cops." He pointed at Fenwick. "You look kind of out of place, which I guess at the Black and Blue Party fits in."

"But he did let you blow him on the site?" Turner asked.

"He let me do it in private once and on the site a few times. I couldn't touch him above the waist or anything. He'd stop my hands if I tried anything."

"Why?" Fenwick said.

"I don't know. I hoped I'd get to do more. I guess I was in love with him. Or in lust with him. Then the incident with the bartender happened, and he got real cold. I figured it was that, because of the bar incident, I knew his real name."

Fenwick asked, "All the time he saw you, he didn't tell you his name?"

"No. After the bar thing, he wouldn't see me. He'd only do website stuff. He wouldn't talk to me or tell me anything."

"He ever talk about fights with anybody? His partner Callaghan."

"Oh yeah, Callaghan. Man, he hated that guy. Belger would talk to me about him."

"He told you his real name?" Turner asked.

"He never did, but after the bar incident when he was on TV, I figured out who he was and who Callaghan was."

"What would he say?"

"He'd get real mad. Said the guy couldn't be depended on. Said he was the one always getting in trouble with Callaghan doing dumb stuff, but they'd always blame him, Belger. He never said more than that. I don't know anything about what happened in that bar." Zibel got teary-eyed. "He was hot." He wiped his hand across his eyes.

"When's the last time you saw him?"

"After his performance here. He said he'd be back. I had other stuff to do."

After he left, Turner said, "That was only the second tear we've seen for Belger. The current wife and this guy."

"That's actually kind of sad or truly weird," Fenwick said. Turner said, "An asshole pig, dies and some nearly anonymous kid is practically the only one who cares."

Fenwick said, "Somebody cares, if you call wanting to kill him caring."

They talked to the rest of the men staffing the booth. Several of them said they remembered seeing Belger. No one remembered him after his performance the day before.

After they finished with the staff, they sent for Frank Jordan. Fenwick asked, "Did you notice any change in Belger after the bartender incident?"

"I didn't associate him with it. These guys come and go. Some need money and call day after day begging to be on. A few are semi-regulars. It's not odd for them to just drop out of sight and never be seen again. Or they call once in a while. Some we call because they're popular. Belger we'd call at least one or twice a month. I don't remember anything odd."

Fenwick said, "They had this many people working on the site?"

Jordan said, "During the Party we have a full staff. There's only about five of us on permanent retainer and only three get full time pay and benefits: me, Jasper, and Ordman."

As they were leaving the booth area, Ordman, still clad only in his mesh jockstrap, motioned Turner over. When the cop was close, Ordman leaned so his lips were less than an inch from his ear. Turner could feel his breath and smell his sweat. It was not unpleasant. Ordman said, "I'd be happy to have you at the booth or the site."

Turner shook his head.

"Or maybe even have a private show at my place. You don't have to be into this."

Turner blushed. "Thanks. I have a husband and I love him."

Jordan smiled. "My loss."

Turner said, "I appreciate the compliment."

"If you change your mind." He produced a card from a backpack under the table near the front of the store. Turner said thanks.

"What was that?" Fenwick asked when they were in the grand concourse.

"An invitation." He crumpled up the card and threw it into the nearest trash can.

Fenwick said, "What did that guy mean, I don't fit in?"

Turner said, "Buck, why don't you make friends with a

mirror?"

"Is that a dig?"

"Yes."

Fenwick said, "Belger had some kind of connection to Zibel."

"Yes. There's a sort of relationship there that Belger permitted. Something was going on."

They tried the other two whipping demonstration booths, but no one in either of them claimed to know anything.

As they climbed the stairs back to the main exposition booths, Deveneaux and Sanchez rushed up to them. Sanchez said, "Scanlan is here. I grabbed him, but he fought like mad for a couple seconds. He yelled for help, that he wasn't a slave, this wasn't a scene."

Deveneaux said, "I was just coming back up to the main concourse. I heard Sanchez yelling and came running."

Sanchez said, "People intervened. One huge guy grabbed me and said, 'If the kid doesn't want to play, let him go, find somebody else, like me.' By the time I'd identified myself, he was gone."

"Which way did he go?"

"Not out," Sanchez said. "At least not toward the exits up here. He was headed downstairs."

THIRTY-SEVEN

They sent for help, and told Deveneaux and Sanchez to guard the main exits above. As assistance arrived, it would be sent to all entrances and exits. They'd seal off as much of the perimeter of the massive old edifice as they could. As Turner and Fenwick prepared to descend into the bowels of the old station, Slade rushed up. He said, "I saw someone running toward the halls that lead to the entrance the Scanlan kid used. None of our party stuff is down there. I didn't recognize who it was." They left Slade behind.

It could be a random fool, or a gate crasher, or something insignificant, or Scanlan. They borrowed flashlights from arriving beat cops. As they left the better lighted areas, they switched them on. Without a guide, they quickly found the vast corridors and innumerable turnings confusing.

Fenwick said, "Molton has that schematic on order."

"Doesn't help much now," Turner said. "We'll follow each major path then double back."

Fenwick halted in the middle of a corridor. He shone his flashlight as far forward as he could then back. He said, "Are we being set up?"

Turner said, "Not by Sanchez and Deveneaux. We've known them too long."

Fenwick repeated the mantra, "Trust no one."

Turner said, "We gotta trust our judgment at some point. How many cases we worked with those guys?"

"Several zillion."

Turner said, "If those two are plotting against us, I think maybe I don't want to be a cop anymore."

Fenwick asked, "By Slade?"

Turner shrugged then reached down and unstrapped his gun.

Fenwick followed suit.

As they descended farther, the sounds of the party diminished. The coolness from the air-conditioning faded more as they turned each corner. Faint breezes stirred at random intervals. Random openings? Ancient ductwork? Puffs of air did little to disturb the dust and nothing to relieve the stuffiness. As they got farther down, an occasional cricket let out a forlorn chirp. As they had the first time down here, they heard the faint skittering of nocturnal creatures.

In another ten minutes they came upon crime scene tape strewn on the ground. Fenwick said, "It fell or somebody ripped it down, or it just got in somebody's way?"

"Yes," Turner said.

They followed the crime scene tape which now marked the route to the entrance near where Scanlan had been found.

Fenwick said, "Hell of a long way to carry a body."

Turner said, "Maybe there's a more direct way from the entrance to where the body was. Remember, the kid brought us here, but the maze that this place is, who knows? Hell, the body's resting point could be ten feet from here. We have got to get those schematics."

A piece of metal clanked.

The detectives glanced up and down the corridor. Nothing to be seen. Lots of closed doors and halls leading off left and right. Nothing visible beyond the glow of their flashlights.

Fenwick said, "I got nothing funny, poetic, or gritty."

Turner said, "For that I am grateful."

As they turned the next corridor, a low moan echoed down the dark passageway in front of them. Crouched on opposite sides of the corridor, they switched off their flashlights. They stood still for a few moments so their eyes could adjust to the darkness. A far hall light added vague shadows to their forms as they inched forward. Moments later they came to the door of the room the secret entrance was in. The dimmest light seeped from the room.

They heard someone breathing heavily.

Turner tapped Fenwick on the arm. They nodded to each other. "Police," Fenwick announced. Gripping their firearms, first Turner then Fenwick rushed through the entrance and threw themselves in opposite directions inside the room.

The light was sufficient for them to see Matthew Bryner stooping over a body on the floor.

"Drop the dildo," Fenwick commanded. "Hands where I can see them."

The offending sex toy thumped to the ground. Bryner then quickly obeyed the second command.

Turner switched his flashlight on while Fenwick kept his gun trained on Bryner. Turner approached the body. It was Peter Scanlan. Blood seeped from his ears, nose, and mouth. Turner handed Fenwick his flashlight then took out his cell phone, punched in 9-1-1. While they were quite far down, the room was a direct exit to the street only a few steps away, so he could get reception. Turner used the other hand to feel for a pulse. Nothing, but the kid was still warm. The blood was still spreading.

Bryner said, "I didn't kill him."

THIRTY-EIGHT

An hour later, just past two, Fenwick, Turner, and Molton huddled with the ME in the room where they'd found Scanlan. Molton rarely came to major crime scenes. He trusted his detectives, but they all knew that this case was big enough to warrant extra attention. Down the hall, Bryner was in handcuffs.

Fenwick asked, "Did you find out who let Scanlan go?"

"Boyle ordered it. He came to some kind of deal after he met the parents. I have the impression that he wanted to trash this party more than he wanted a suspect. And they couldn't hold the kid. I got downtown to put pressure on getting the tests done quickly. Real tests with real results. Nobody would admit rushing them for Boyle, which put Boyle out of luck. He claimed he had test results which no one conducted. So his whole case went kaflooey. My guess is he's going to be in trouble over that little fiasco."

"Not enough," Fenwick said. "Or at least not soon enough."

Turner said, "Why the hell did the kid come back here?"

Fenwick said, "You met the parents."

"But wasn't he released into their custody?" Turner asked.

Molton said, "I wasn't there."

The ME said, "Scanlan died just minutes before you arrived. He choked to death. The dildo Bryner dropped has bits of saliva and flecks of blood, presumably the corpse's since Bryner was not bleeding. Although they could come from an unknown third person. I'll have to examine and test all that, and I'll need time to take prints from the dildo. Right now, I'm calling it the murder weapon. I assume, and I'll be able to tell you for sure later, that the thing was jammed down his throat until he died. The kid fought. Thrashed, scratched, he even bit on the dildo. Assuming those are his teeth marks. I'm guessing from the wound on the back of his head, at some point, probably after the struggle had gone on for a while, he got his head banged against the floor. Real hard. After that, I think the fight would have gone out of him. Also, you might have a problem about the scratch marks."

"What's that?" Molton asked.

"Your prime suspect doesn't have a mark on him." He bent down, picked up Scanlan's right hand, and tapped one of the fingernails. "Even without a microscope I can see bits of flesh under several of these and more of those delightful bits of blood. I don't think they're going to be the victim's. Your killer's been wounded."

Fenwick said, "We already checked. Bryner didn't have any."

The ME said, "Unless your victim was scratching and fighting someone who wasn't killing him, Mr. Bryner is not your killer."

"Fuck-a-doodle-do," Fenwick said.

"Couldn't have said it better myself," the ME said.

"If the kid was fighting," Turner said, "then his attacker..."

"Could have been more than one," the ME said.

"Had to be strong or more than one," Turner finished. The ME left to take the body to Cook County Morgue.

Molton said, "I brought the schematics for the station and a map of the convention."

The three of them pulled the new materials close to the arc lights and examined them.

Turner said, "Remember when we first got to this place. We went back almost all the way we'd come and then all the way to that even older section, but look." He pointed. "If you took this opening and that corridor, you'd be there in less than fifty feet. That's how they got in."

Fenwick said, "The killer or killers didn't have that far to carry the body."

"If they knew about this entrance," Turner said.

"And the schematics of this place," Fenwick added.

They checked with beat cops who had been interviewing the security personnel, door wards, and registration clerks. None claimed to have seen Scanlan enter.

Turner and Fenwick strode down to interview Bryner.

Immediately upon seeing the detectives, Bryner let his fury fly. "I was the one who tried to save him. I didn't try to kill him. I saw the dildo stuck in his throat. I took it out so he could breathe. I was trying to help. Of course, my fingerprints will be on it. It was horrible. I took it out and there was blood, vomit. I don't know what all. He wasn't breathing. I don't know CPR. I'm not sure I could have done it on him anyway. The mess was vile."

Fenwick ignored the defense and asked, "What were you doing down here?"

"All morning and afternoon I've had people down here trying to close up any entrance or exit. I didn't want a dust mote to be able to get in here. I went out for a few hours to meet with some friends. I needed a break. It was a long scheduled break. I came back to check on the work I'd ordered. I saw the crime tape down. Then I thought I heard scuffling and muffled screams. I came very slowly."

"Why didn't you go for help?"

"I thought it might be a scene that guys were into. I didn't assume something bad was going on. I went carefully so I wouldn't disturb them. And, yeah, I guess I wanted to watch. By the time I got here, it was too late."

Fenwick asked, "Who are your powerful friends in the department?"

"Certainly I'm not going to tell you that. That would be insane. They're protecting me."

"Right now they are. Or at least they haven't turned on you. They might, in light of this latest development."

"What development? I didn't kill him."

It was easy to observe from Bryner's see-through T-shirt and short leather pants that his flesh was unmarred by recent activity with the deceased. Turner and Fenwick unhandcuffed him, but ordered him to stay, and left a beat cop on guard.

They consulted Molton. Moments later the crew from downtown who had been in Molton's office appeared: deputy superintendent Franklin Armour, CPD press spokesperson Phillip Nance, and attorney for the department Mandy O'Bannion.

All three officials raised eyebrows at the outfits the detectives were in. Neither Turner not Fenwick felt the need to explain.

The entire aggregation retired to the large room in the tower where they'd first interviewed Bryner. It was one of the few places quiet enough, with chairs enough, and large enough to fit everyone comfortably.

It was very early in the morning. Molton presided from behind the desk.

Franklin Armour was into full-force dither and blame. He wanted to know what was wrong with the police detectives, and when they would settle the case, and had they done every interview, had they talked to this person and that, and had they done their paperwork.

Philip Nance was in a full PR panic. Molton let him rant about closing the party, saving the CPD's reputation, and Bryner being innocent and abused.

Mandy O'Bannion was into full legal legerdemain. She was concerned about everybody's liability and rights, and that obscure legal niceties got taken care of.

All of them wore formal attire, ties, uniforms, long sleeves in evidence. If Scanlan had wounded one, some, or all of these three, it was going to take more than orders from a couple detectives to get shirts off.

Turner asked, "Whose decision was it to let the kid go?"

Armour, Nance, and O'Bannion turned a variety of annoyed glances on him.

Turner said, "It's a simple question. Boyle arrested him. Who made the decision?"

Molton said, "Perfect question."

Armour said, "I have no idea."

O'Bannion said, "The legal department wasn't consulted."

"Leaves you, Mr. Nance," Turner said.

"Don't be absurd."

"So we'll have to question Boyle."

"Yes," Molton said.

The others didn't contradict him.

The three from downtown began to wrangle. Molton interrupted and said, "Buck, Paul, you can go back to work. We'll settle this among ourselves."

Squawks issued from all three of the others, but Fenwick and Turner simply walked out. Even on the other side of the door, they could hear the chorus of wrangling.

Fenwick said, "Fuck-a-doodle-do up all their asses."

Turner said, "You couldn't be more right." They used the stairs to descend from the tower. "More to the point, where are Callaghan and Boyle, and do they have an alibi for the time of this murder? We found the body just after midnight. We've got a pretty narrow time frame."

"How are we going to interview Boyle?"

Turner said, "Very carefully."

Fenwick said, "My guess on Callaghan is he's back in his favorite bar."

"Good a place as any to start."

As Fenwick went through the car-starting ritual, he asked, "Why is Peter Scanlan dead?"

Turner said, "It's connected to Belger's murder."

"Unless somebody knew the kid. Any adult who knew him would be justified in mowing him down."

Turner said, "I'm not sure that's an accepted defense in the legal system."

"Look under teenagers, asshole. It's in there."

"Gotta be connected to Belger."

"Gotta be."

"How? Why?"

"Beats the hell out of me."

"Useless speculation would pass the time," Turner said.

"Feel free."

"He knew something and the murderer had to silence him. The killer thought he knew something. He was blackmailing the killer. It's a huge conspiracy and it's coming unraveled, and the co-conspirators are turning on each other. Someone knew Scanlan was the killer and stepped in to save the legal system the mess of a trial. Feel free to jump in any time here."

"You're doing a fine job."

"It's all fucking useless."

Fenwick said, "The kid's dead. There's gotta be a reason."

"No, there doesn't. Maybe he's just damn dead."

Fenwick nodded.

They plowed through the post-midnight humidity to Area Ten, where they changed, then moved back out into the night to the Raving Dragon bar.

THIRTY-NINE

As they entered, Callaghan had his back to them. He and a chorus of cops belted out a drinking song from a B movie that Turner couldn't name. The others in the circle around Callaghan noticed the detectives and fell silent one by one. Callaghan's lone voice finished the last chorus by itself. He turned and faced the intruders. The aggregation clustered together behind Callaghan. Turner and Fenwick faced the clump of inebriated cops. The owner was nowhere to be seen.

Turner noted that none of them had obvious scratch marks on their arms from someone defending themselves. Didn't mean their legs or torsos weren't messed up, but nothing Turner saw hinted they'd come across someone who could be arrested.

Callaghan swung a beer bottle against the bar and smashed the top off. He held the jagged edge toward the detectives and bellowed, "Fuck you both." The others looked ready to join in any attack.

Fenwick took out his gun, let off a round into the floor, then brought it up and pointed it at the group. He said, "Everyone who isn't Barry Callaghan, get out." He fired the next round into the bar a foot to the left of where Callaghan stood. Turner pulled his gun, sidled quickly six feet to Fenwick's right, and said, "Now would be a good time to obey a direct order."

None of the drunk assemblage reached for their weapons. The obviously irate detectives, guns ready to be used, were not going to be denied. With scowls, snarls, and drunken stumbles, the crowd fled. Fenwick barred the door behind them. Turner kept his gun on Callaghan with one hand and with the other used his cell phone to call Molton, who promised that he and other members of the Area Ten detective squad would be there in minutes.

Callaghan's eyes followed Turner's movements. Fenwick remained on the far side of him so Callaghan couldn't watch or attack them both at once. Still holding the broken bottle in one hand, Callaghan's other hand dropped a fraction of an inch toward his firearm. Was the drunk really going to try and shoot it out? Turner held his gun steadily three feet from Callaghan's face. Callaghan froze. If Callaghan touched his gun, Turner would fire. But with the idiot fixated on Turner, Fenwick simply walked up behind Callaghan and tackled him. The offending and offensive patrolman hit the ground with a satisfying amount of force. Callaghan bellowed. The beer bottle in his hand smashed. Turner took the man's gun. Fenwick sat on him.

Turner said, "I've wanted to see you do that to a suspect for years."

"Really?"

"Have I ever lied to you?"

"Recently?"

Callaghan squirmed and squawked. Fenwick entwined his fingers in his overweight opponent's hair and twisted, an old cop trick that was surprisingly effective. He had been taught it by a wise old school teacher.

Fenwick said, "You haven't bathed since the last time we saw you. I'd gain several more pounds just to punish you for that alone."

Callaghan spent several minutes trying to catch his breath. Turner leaned against the bar. Fenwick said, "You always let me do the fun things. I appreciate it."

"I live to meet your needs."

Fenwick thumped Callaghan on the side of the head. "Where were you tonight?"

Callaghan gasped. "Get off me!"

Fenwick squiggled, rolled, and adjusted his butt, and said, "I'm just getting comfortable."

"My hand is bleeding."

"Good," Fenwick said.

"You can't torture me."

Fenwick said, "You got witnesses?"

"Guys will vouch for me."

Fenwick said, "Not after all the command personnel from downtown get here. You're an embarrassment. They'll want to cover their own asses."

"My guys are loyal," Callaghan said. Someone began pounding rhythmically on the door. The detectives ignored it. They knew it wasn't Molton. He'd call first, not just knock.

Fenwick said, "And you're not. It's your partner who's dead. You're the one not rallying around trying to find out who killed him."

Turner crouched down so he could meet Callaghan's eye. He said, "We found a boatload of people who don't like you. All those people you beat up on. They're going to sue. They've been afraid to come forward. Not anymore. They are organized. They've hired lawyers. They're going to the Feds. You're going to be in jail, and you're going to be broke, and you're going to cost the department a ton of money." While not based on explicit knowledge, Turner's claim had the ring of enough truth to hold a real threat.

Callaghan managed to squeeze out a half-snort of derision.

Fenwick said, "Do you think anybody in the CPD has enough clout to save your ass now? We've got two corpses." The detective lifted his legs off the floor so now his entire weight rested on Callaghan.

Callaghan rasped, "Didn't kill."

The pounding became intermittent.

"Who did?"

"Don't know."

"Where were you tonight?"

"Here."

"When did you get here?"

"I've been here for as long as I need an alibi."

Fenwick bounced up and down on him.

Callaghan gasped. "I swear. Here. Who's dead?"

Abruptly Fenwick got up. Callaghan curled into a ball and pulled in gusts of air.

Fenwick picked him up by his uniform shirt and deposited him in the nearest booth. Callaghan's bulk seemed to have little effect on Fenwick's ability to swing him around with impunity. When the recalcitrant Callaghan was ensconced in the corner, Fenwick got in next to him, and Turner sat opposite.

Turner's cell phone rang. Reinforcements were in the alley. The back door of the bar opened and Molton, Wilson, and Roosevelt walked in. Molton noted the pounding on the front door, marched to it, unbarred it, and swung it wide. The cops outside, seeing a Commander in full regalia, scattered. Molton shut the door and barred it again. Molton, Wilson, and Roosevelt pulled up bar stools next to the booth the other three were in.

Turner said to Callaghan, "Peter Scanlan is dead."

"Who?"

Turner actually thought the bewildered look on Callaghan's face was genuine. Turner explained.

Callaghan said, "I didn't know the kid."

Fenwick said, "Who is covering for you? Who would go to that much trouble for such a royal fuck-up?"

Callaghan said, "You'll all be sorry."

Turner said, "Nobody has enough clout to get even with this many people. Do you really think you're worth the energy and expense of that kind of fight? You're one guy who has got to be a liability to someone. Who?"

"Boyle had the kid in custody. Why don't you talk to him?"

Fenwick pounced. "If Boyle was protecting you, are you now saying he had something to do with Scanlan's death?"

Ignoring the question, Callaghan said, "You fucks have been

running around telling people I was gay."

Fenwick said, "Cheswick blabbed." He was the cop in the Ninth District Turner had tried to lure into giving them some truth with the hint that maybe Callaghan and Belger were gay.

"Did you kill Belger?" Fenwick asked.

Callaghan didn't demand a lawyer. He didn't whine, complain, or bluster. He just shut up. Ultimately, it was his smartest choice.

They got nowhere.

They let Callaghan go.

They left the bar.

Outside in the humidity, Molton said, "Boyle's next. You want me with you?"

"No," Fenwick said.

Molton nodded. "I trust you. I'll find out where he is and get back to you."

Roosevelt said, "Call us immediately if you need help. You want us around, we'll be there."

Wilson nodded agreement.

FORTY

It was after three. Turner and Fenwick returned to Area Ten headquarters. Caruthers was mercifully absent. Molton reported that Boyle was not to be found.

They had the recordings from the whipping booth. Turner wheeled the ancient television cart with its usually working VCR and cableless television next to his desk. The remote was actually on the cart and working. Turner was fast-forwarding through the third video when Ian showed up. Turner hit pause. The screen showed a mass of people standing around.

Ian pointed at the screen, "Riveting?"

Turner said, "Mind numbing. And useless. So far."

Ian said, "You've got a new corpse."

Fenwick said, "We prefer new corpses. The old ones get moldy and smell awful. And really, a used corpse? Is that the kind of image we want to present to the world?"

Ian said, "Pretty close to teetering over the edge, are we?"

Fenwick said, "This 'we' is not even close to the edge. You don't want to see over the edge."

Turner said, "Ian, what have you found out?"

Ian said, "I have uncovered unpleasant things about Bryner. I know what happened in Iowa. It's very strange." Ian glanced at his notes. Turner wiped at his forehead. Perspiration flooded from their bodies, leaving damp patches on clothes and any surface they touched.

Ian said, "At a college graduation party fifteen years ago, a young freshman died. Bryner's boyfriend."

"He killed his own boyfriend?" Turner asked.

"Nothing was ever proven. Nobody was ever arrested. They were both at the same party, but no evidence existed beyond that simple, ordinary fact. Amazingly, I couldn't find evidence of any kind about the case. Either the Des Moines police are exceptionally closed mouthed..."

"Or you're losing your touch," Fenwick said.

Ian said, "Back off, Elizabeth, there's a brick in this purse."

"Or," Turner said, "there was someone very powerful who got the whole thing buried."

Ian added, "Or the Des Moines police are totally incompetent and messed things up completely."

Turner said, "Zuyland said Belger and Callaghan specialized in frightening closeted gay men. Could the two of them have found out about Bryner?"

"In Iowa? I suppose it's possible, but the problem would have been the same for them as it was for me. For whatever reason, there isn't anything there to find. Even the small bit of information I've told you, came from two people who had been at the same party, but who claimed not to know Bryner."

"Dead end there," Fenwick said.

Turner said, "Unless Belger and Callaghan got beyond the cover-up, maybe cop to cop. We could talk to Bryner again."

Ian said, "Then I checked into the possibility Fenwick mentioned at Dunkin' Donuts that maybe some other leather people might be trying to wreck this convention out of malice or a desire for vengeance or an attempt to destroy the competition. Nope. My sources say the organizers of the other leather events around the country, and even internationally, informally boycotted this one. Nobody specific was behind it, that I could find. What Bryner told you when you interviewed him the first time seems to be true. Just none of them showed up. And it drove them nuts that thousands came to this thing."

Turner said, "I got it. The killer is not among the elite leather crowd in this country."

Ian said, "Right. What happened with Scanlan?"

Turner filled him in.

Ian said, "Bryner for sure didn't kill Scanlan?"

"The evidence says not."

Ian said, "Sentence first, trial later said the red queen."

"Or not at all," Fenwick said.

Turner said, "Boyle has to be in the thick of covering up Callaghan's mistake. Has to be. What's the connection between those two?"

Ian said, "Callaghan must have pictures of Boyle naked at high noon with a prostitute in Daley Center Plaza."

Fenwick said, "Or a connection that's at least as possible or plausible."

"They aren't relatives," Ian said.

Turner cocked an eyebrow at him.

Ian said, "I figured Boyle had to be in on this. I checked. It is not familial."

"They're both gay?" Turner asked. "They share secret rendezvous? They're into illegal drugs and guns?"

Fenwick interrupted, "Or they're fucking morons."

"Or all of the above," Ian said.

"Boyle will never talk," Turner said.

Fenwick said, "Gotta be something or someone who can break through his wall."

Turner said, "I'm open to suggestions."

They had none. Ian left to try and scrounge up information on Scanlan's activities after he'd been released. Turner got back to the tapes, and Fenwick returned to doing paperwork.

A half hour later, Turner said, "What the fuck?"

Fenwick looked up. "What?"

Turner moved the cart so Fenwick could see the television. Turner ran the tape back for a few seconds then ran it forward.

Turner said, "Scanlan was at the booth with Belger."

They both examined the tape frame by frame. Scanlan had no visible interaction with Belger, but it was definitely the young man.

"What does this mean?" Fenwick said.

"That kid was knee deep in shit. He's dead because he knew something."

"Logical conclusion. Doesn't help. He's dead."

Turner tossed the remote aside and said, "Where's Fong?" Without waiting for Fenwick to answer, he picked up the phone and dialed the computer guru's extension. He got someone he didn't know. "Send him up to the detective squad room when he gets in," Turner ordered.

"Is there something I can help you with?" The voice sounded to Turner like that of a fifteen year old.

"Can you put what's on a tape onto a cell phone?" Turner demanded.

"Sure. I'll be right up."

Turner gazed at the receiver, then hung up.

"What?" Fenwick asked.

Turner said, "Something in this station works."

"You can count on Fong."

"Wasn't Fong."

A minute or two later a skinny, red-headed guy who looked like he was still in high school walked up to Turner's desk. He had a bundle of wires and small plastic gadgets in his hands.

"Who are you?" Turner asked.

"I'm the night shift guy for Mr. Fong. Wendell."

Turner asked, "You do computer stuff?"

"Yes, sir."

"As good as Fong?"

"Sure."

Turner relented. He explained to the young man what he wanted. Wendell thought for thirty seconds after Turner finished. As Turner's heart sank, Wendell said, "I can do it. No problem."

Fifteen minutes later, a spaghetti bowl of wires connected the television, a laptop, Turner's cell phone, and other electronic devices. Five minutes after that the kid said, "All done." He showed Turner how to work the cell phone to get the video of the portion of Scanlan at the party.

Turner said, "It works."

Fenwick came over. He clapped Wendell on the shoulder with a big hand. The kid almost fell over. "Nice job," the detective said.

Wendell beamed. "You let me know if you need anything else."

"I want to look at that video again of the original incident."

Fenwick said, "Better than slogging through this crap."

And so they watched. After the third time through the extended-version six-minute melodrama they had from Zuyland, the reporter, Fenwick said, "What exactly are we looking for?"

"It's wrong," Turner said.

"You think somebody edited it to make them look worse? How can they look worse? It accomplished what Zuyland wanted it to accomplish. Callaghan got in a heap of trouble."

"But the trouble made no difference to him."

"Well, yeah, not yet, it's still going through procedures."

"Look at that damn thing. Any normal guy would be worried about losing his job. Callaghan isn't."

Fenwick said, "We're going to look at it again, aren't we?"

"Yep."

Eighteen minutes and three more viewings later, Turner said, "That's what's missing." He rewound the tape. "Look, just before the fight, Belger and Preston the bartender. They're conferring. Then it looks like Belger started in again on Callaghan. The real fighting started later, but in the very beginning Belger provokes Callaghan." He hit play then thirty seconds later, he hit pause. "See, it's staged."

"I don't know," Fenwick said. "Looks pretty real to me."

"Parts of it. And Belger and Preston didn't have to do much acting. Belger and Preston were in on it with Dinning, the recorder. And if they were in it with Dinning and Dinning knew Zuyland then Belger and Preston were in it with Zuyland. The whole thing was staged to get Callaghan."

They got Dinning's address from their notes. Turner and Fenwick headed up to Belmont Avenue. "If it was a conspiracy," Fenwick said, "and Belger is dead, why aren't the others dead?"

"But maybe we're the only ones who figured out it was a conspiracy. Callaghan might not know. The idiots of the world can show a remarkable amount of cunning and a strong sense of self-preservation. And because they're idiots, doesn't mean they aren't predators, and maybe the danger is more random for the lack of finesse. They just strike out at any random thing. It might not be well planned, but it is still just as deadly."

"Belger's death wasn't random."

Turner said, "His corpse does kind of complicate things."

FORTY-ONE

They pulled off Lake Shore Drive. Moments later they were parked illegally in the bus stop on Belmont near Broadway. They walked back to Dinning's. It was four AM on Sunday. Not the slightest whiff of a breeze interrupted the misery of their damp torsos.

It took five minutes for Dinning to answer Fenwick's pounding. Anxiety and fear filled Dinning's eyes as he opened the door to them. Besides a frown that deepened the sadness of his brown eyes, he wore only a pair of tight, white athletic shorts that emphasized the slimness of his hips. Moments later they heard a voice ask, "Raoul, who is it?" Ralph Zuyland entered the room in a yellow T-shirt, maroon shorts, and flip flops.

"Getting an exclusive?" Fenwick asked.

"This isn't what you think," Zuyland said.

Dinning's hurt tones thrummed as he said, "You told me there wouldn't be any more lies."

Turner said, "I think it's exactly what I think it is. We're going to talk."

Zuyland and Dinning sat on opposite ends of a leather couch. Turner and Fenwick faced them in armless easy chairs, the kind Turner hated.

Fenwick asked Zuyland, "Are you gay?"

"What difference does it make?"

"What were you doing in that washroom when you got tasered?" Fenwick asked.

"Nothing. Using the washroom. Because I'm gay in a washroom doesn't mean I'm preying on random straight people."

Fenwick said, "They just happened to trap you."

Zuyland said, "Yes."

Turner said, "But the incident in the bar didn't just happen. It was a total set up."

Zuyland said, "I told you it was."

Turner said, "Preston and Belger were in it with you."

Zuyland said, "You can't prove that. They haven't said anything."

"You just did," Turner said. "Belger can't, but Preston will. It'll all unravel."

Dinning said, "I can't take this. Yes, yes, it was all a set up."

Zuyland gaped.

Dinning turned his sorrowful eyes on him. "You may be used to this, but this is it. I was made a fool of. I won't be used anymore."

Zuyland had the grace not to plead some flimsy excuse.

Turner asked, "Why did Belger and Preston go along with the conspiracy?"

Zuyland said, "I told you. I'm a good investigative reporter. They had grievances. They had problems. Belger hated his partner. He hated Boyle. Hell, as far as I could tell he hated everyone including himself."

"But weren't you angry at him as well?" Turner asked.

Zuyland smirked. "One at a time. One at a time."

"Did you know the bartender had sex with both of them?" Fenwick asked.

The smirk disappeared in a jaw-dropping gape. "She told me she didn't like them. She told me she needed money. I gave her a great deal. Belger helped to convince her."

"Why did Belger go along?"

"I convinced him that I could prove his partner was setting him up. Belger was paranoid anyway. I just fed his fear. And he wasn't the brightest bulb."

"And was Callaghan setting him up?" Turner asked.

Fenwick added, "With the Feds? You have an 'in' to the Feds?"

Zuyland said, "I have an 'in' everywhere. And I'm willing to use any edge I can. And if I don't have it, I'm willing to make it up. I'm used to investigating. Don't get all high and mighty with me. You cops make it up as well. Usually I'm believed. I have kept my job all these years based on my reputation for getting it right. And Belger was a worrier. He's the one who worried about them being caught." He thumped his chest. "I told him only he had complaints in his file, not Callaghan. He figured he was going to be put out as the fall guy. I helped that notion, along with stories I told him that intimated that I had an inside track on the latest Federal investigation of Chicago police. All I did was stoke his own paranoia."

"Maybe it got him killed," Turner said. "If it did, you're an accessory to murder."

Zuyland said, "I didn't kill anybody."

Fenwick said, "You were challenging cops. You may or may not have known how dangerous that was, but you involved innocent people in your anger and your conspiracy."

"We were all angry. We'd all been fucked over by the cops. We knew what we were doing."

"How'd you know about their files?" Turner asked.

"Friends and sources and people on the side of decent people who wanted these guys to go down. To bring them down in any way it could happen; through the law, through screaming headlines, through news video, whatever it took. Callaghan first. Then Belger."

Turner said, "You're also responsible for Callaghan turning on Belger. You gave Callaghan false information as well."

"Are you saying Callaghan killed Belger?" Zuyland asked.

Fenwick said, "This isn't a scoop, and if I were you, I'd worry more about being a suspect than a reporter at this moment."

"Did you kill Belger?" Turner asked.

"Don't be absurd."

Fenwick said, "But you betrayed Belger."

Zuyland said, "I'd have betrayed anybody."

Dinning gasped. "Including me?"

The ill-clad Zuyland gaped at his barely-clad overnight host.

Turner asked, "Do you guys know Delmar Cotton and Bill Grant?"

They spoke simultaneously. "Yes," Dinning said.

"No," Zuyland said.

"Well, well, well," Fenwick said. "You were all in on it. I guess we'll have to talk to Cotton and Grant again."

Zuyland said, "They were just among the guys who had grievances."

Dinning said, "Don't lie. They were part of the planning."

"Fine," Zuyland said. "They helped us plan the bar incident. That's all. We didn't, and they didn't have anything to do with the murder."

Dinning said, "I never heard anybody plan murder. Ever."

"What about the cops who helped you that night?" Fenwick asked.

Dinning said, "You told me they just showed up."

Zuyland blushed. "I didn't mean to lie. They have nothing to do with this. Nothing. And I won't give you their names. I won't. They're not gay. They weren't at the Black and Blue party. I just won't. Arrest me if you need to, but I won't."

Fenwick and Turner let a silence build. Dinning refused to look at Zuyland. Turner didn't hold out much hope for wedding cake and a commitment ceremony. He asked, "When did you guys start your relationship?"

"This afternoon after you talked to us," Dinning said.

"Newlyweds," Fenwick said.

The detectives left.

Fenwick asked, "Zuyland is gay? And all of our guys left

something out. I hate that."

"I'm going to have to have my gaydar chip examined. It was never very good in the first place. I just hope they don't take the toaster back."

"Toaster?" Fenwick asked.

"The one we get when we sign up for being gay."

"Attempts at humor at this hour of the morning are a Class A felony."

Turner yawned then said, "If you arrest me, will I be able to get some sleep?"

"Not unless I get some, too."

Turner said, "We gotta go back round and round again, but I dunno. I don't picture those guys being able to plan murder. Grant, Cotton, and Dinning are ordinary guys who would be showing some level of upset at committing murder."

"Zuyland?" Fenwick asked.

"I think he'd run over his grandmother with a bus if he needed it for a story or to get even."

In the car Fenwick said, "Dinning is hot. Zuyland is not. Explain them being together."

"I don't have a clue. Ask the goddess. Or ask Madge why she stays married to you."

"Zing."

Turner said, "Grant and Cotton lied to us."

"They all lied to us. They were all in on the conspiracy."

"Organized by Zuyland."

"They kill Belger?" Fenwick asked.

"He was part of the conspiracy."

"Maybe some of the planners weren't telling the whole truth to the rest of the planners."

Turner said, "It was a dual conspiracy."

"Huh?"

Turner said, "Boyle et al were out to get Belger. Zuyland et al were out to get Belger and Callaghan. Their paths crossed. Their conspiracies crossed."

"They were all in on it?"

"All of them were mucking around. Some in over their heads like Dinning or maybe he was just on the periphery, maybe the same for Cotton and Grant. That doesn't account for Callaghan's clean file and who is protecting him and why."

Fenwick said, "We can't prove any of that."

"We'll use your method," Turner said. "We'll shoot them all."

Fenwick said, "Finally, a convert."

Turner said, "Grant and Cotton first." It was five in the morning but the two men weren't home. Turner checked his notes and found Grant's cell phone number. The two men were still at the Black and Blue party. He ordered them to wait there for them.

This time the detectives simply bulled past the door wards. Turner's exhaustion was as palpable as the humidity. They took Sanchez and Deveneaux with them.

Cotton and Grant waited in the tower room with Slade. Cotton and Grant wore black leather chaps over tight jeans and black leather vests over taut chests. The front of Cotton's pants was soaked and smelled of urine.

Slade started to burble. Fenwick pointed at him and said, "Get out." There was no denying the fury and command in Fenwick's voice. Turner guessed his buddy was as fed up and exhausted as he was.

With barely another murmur, Slade left. As Slade passed through the doorway, Fenwick said to Sanchez, the beat cop, "Would you locate Mr. Bryner and bring him up here."

Turner asked, "Did you finish showing the pictures to all the registration people?"

Sanchez nodded, pulled out one of the pictures. "They thought this guy came in with Bryner. You know who he is? He looks familiar."

It was Franklin Armour. Turner told him who he was and his position in the department. Sanchez whistled. "He's here now. With Bryner. The guys at the door said they came in together."

Turner said, "Bring them both."

Fenwick said, "Now we know who his clout is in the city. Did they kill Belger?"

Turner said, "Awfully suspicious, but one set of suspects at a time."

Cotton and Grant sat on chairs. They held hands, their arms and legs pushed together.

Fenwick said, "You fuckers didn't tell us everything."

Cotton said, "You fuckers never did anything to stop those assholes. We did nothing wrong. We got a shit-ass cop off the streets. Something nobody else in this city seemed willing to do."

Fenwick said, "You talking about Belger or Callaghan?"

"We had nothing to do with Belger's death."

"Did you know Peter Scanlan?"

"Who?" Cotton asked.

Turner thought his mystification was genuine.

"Kid was killed here earlier."

"Why would we know him?"

Turner asked, "What was the plan with Belger and Callaghan?"

Grant and Cotton confirmed the story they'd heard from Zuyland. "We knew of the plan at the bar. If that didn't work, we were ready to try other things."

"Murder?" Fenwick asked.

"No, never," Grant said.

The detectives went over every detail of Grant and Cotton's story. The two men claimed every word they said was true. Turner and Fenwick let them go.

Sanchez ushered in Bryner and Armour.

Armour said, "What the hell is going on?"

Fenwick said, "Did you kill Belger?"

"What nonsense is this?"

Fenwick glared.

Armour said, "I'm leaving."

Turner said, "No." Fenwick could bluster with the best of them, but when Turner gave an order with that quiet command, few chose to disobey.

Everyone sat.

Bryner said, "Well, you got your wish. This whole thing has been shut down."

Fenwick asked, "Your clout in the city couldn't save you this time." He turned to Armour. "You've lost your touch."

"Fuck you," Armour said.

Turner said to Bryner, "What happened to your boyfriend in Des Moines?"

Bryner instantly flared into rage. "How dare you bring that up? That has nothing to do with this convention, with these murders."

Fenwick asked, "How'd you get the whole thing suppressed?"

Bryner could barely control his breathing as he spoke. "No one, no one, accuses me of killing my boyfriend. No one."

The detectives let the silence build. Bryner looked from one to the other.

Bryner asked, "Do we sit here in silence until we die of boredom?"

Fenwick said, "If you'd like, you could sit until you keel over."

Bryner said, "You think this is funny?"

Fenwick said, "What I think is funny is you getting away with murder in Des Moines. What I think is not funny is that there are two murders at your convention. Why do people die around things you touch?"

"I had nothing to do with them. Nothing. To. Do. With. Any. Of. Them. Nothing." He collapsed back into a chair and said, "You two can sit there like great Buddhas, but I'm done talking."

Turner said to Armour, "What's your role in all this? Why were you at the meeting with Boyle?"

"I was told to go."

"Bullshit," Fenwick said. "You manipulated yourself into it."

"Speculate all you want. Speculation doesn't get you a conviction."

"Conviction," Turner said. "Yes, you need to be convicted. You guys got the Scanlan kid killed."

Armour said, "I got him released."

Turner said, "Which got him killed. Why did you release him?"

"He didn't do anything," Armour said.

Turner said, "He was an underaged kid at this party. That's a lethal dose of publicity right there. Was protecting this party worth getting him killed? Death was better?"

"For these guys," Fenwick said.

"Fuck you," Armour said.

Fenwick said, "Did you guys kill Belger?"

Armour said, "Whatever for? He may have been an embarrassment to the department, but he certainly wasn't to me. Not while he was alive. Not while he's dead. Him I don't care about. You're going to have to look elsewhere for your killer. You've got nothing on us."

"Not yet," Turner said. "What's the connection between Boyle and Callaghan?"

Armour said, "All I know is Nance was always sticking up

for Boyle. You can look into that yourself. I know nothing about Boyle and Callaghan. I don't deal with personnel issues."

"Why would Nance stick up for him?" Fenwick asked.

"He's his clout," Turner said.

"What do you know about them?" Fenwick asked.

"Nothing," Armour said.

Fenwick growled, "There's gotta be something. Speculate."

Armour said, "Unlike you two, I'm loyal. I'm not saying anything more."

And not another word would they say even after a lawyer showed up.

In the car Fenwick asked, "They kill Belger?"

"They who?"

"Take your pick."

"I don't think so. I'm just not sure so."

Fenwick asked, "Was that piss on the front of Cotton's pants?"

"Do you really want to know?"

"Should we have questioned them separately?"

Turner sighed. "I really don't want this to be about a gay revenge squad. I really don't want a gay person accused of murder. Yes, I know gay people commit murder. Just, I don't want it to be this time. We're going to question Boyle. That asshole has a lot to answer for."

"We tell Molton first?" Fenwick asked.

"Is there a choice?" Turner asked. "I'm angry, but I'm not stupid."

Fenwick agreed. Turner put his cell phone on speaker so Fenwick could hear his conversation with Molton.

When Molton answered, the Commander said, "I've got news. I have test results."

"So soon?" Fenwick asked.

"Unlike other Commanders who shall remain nameless, I actually do have friends in the crime lab, but even then I wouldn't have asked if this wasn't a huge priority."

"What did they get?"

"The whip Boyle had with Scanlan's prints and Belger's blood?"

"Fake?" Fenwick said.

"Real. It did have Scanlan's prints and Belger's blood. Several prints were in the blood."

"Scanlan killed him?" Fenwick asked.

Turner said, "The whipping didn't kill him."

Molton said, "But Scanlan whipped him."

Turner said, "But Armour let him go, not Boyle."

Fenwick said, "Boyle had the whip."

Molton put in, "Said his people found it."

"Bullshit," Fenwick said.

Molton said, "I do believe that is the correct medical term."

Turner said, "Scanlan was on the tape for the booth Belger was at. Proximity doesn't get you a conviction, but it puts you on your way."

"He's dead," Fenwick said.

"I hate that in a witness," Turner said. He explained that their next step was to confront Boyle.

Molton said, "Get him."

"You're not going to try and stop us?" Fenwick asked.

Molton said, "You will be fine. You are among the best detectives I've ever seen. I have absolute faith in you. This hour of the morning, he'd be at Gracie Heaney's Diner."

Fenwick said, "Never heard of it."

Molton said, "It's a hangout for brass."

"They don't let us low lifes in?" Fenwick asked.

"It's very exclusive," Molton said. He gave them the address.

FORTY-TWO

Gracie Heaney's Diner had all the charm of a roach-infested garbage dump but was less well lit. They found their quarry in a tiny booth in the back of the nearly deserted diner. The humidity was as close indoors as it was outside. Exclusive maybe in terms of cop brass clientele, but not in décor.

In the booth with Boyle was Phillip Nance, the department's press spokesperson.

Turner said, "And now we have it confirmed who Callaghan and Boyle's clout is in the city."

The detectives pulled over chairs and effectively blocked egress from either side of the booth. Boyle said, "Get the hell out of here."

Fenwick said, "I love commands in the middle of the humidity."

Boyle shoved his jaw an inch from Fenwick's. The Commander said, "Let's see how brave you are now. I have squads of my men who'll take you on."

Fenwick said, "They're all waiting outside just for you to summon? Ha! You going to taser us? Ha! Threaten somebody who's going to take you seriously."

Boyle said, "Your ass is going to be fired so fast. And you will be in real pain before I'm finished with you."

Fenwick said, "Is real pain different from fake pain?"

Turner said, "You really think it makes sense to threaten us in front of witnesses?"

Fenwick said, "Nance is in it with him."

Nance gulped and gaped.

"It's not the first time he's tried this," Fenwick said. "It's going to be the last." There was no mistaking the thrum of menace in his voice.

Nance said, "Really we should stop this."

Boyle snapped at him. "Stop what? They started it."

Fenwick laughed uproariously. Their two antagonists frowned at the maniacal note mixed amid Fenwick's guffaws. Fenwick said, "I'm back in second grade."

Turner said, "Mr. Nance, what's your connection in all this?"

"You can't question me," Nance said.

"I can and will," Fenwick said.

Boyle made to shove his way past them. Fenwick blocked him with his bulk. Boyle might as well have been trying to move a mountain.

Turner said, "Mr. Nance, why have you protected Commander Boyle all these years? And if you've protected Boyle, you've protected Callaghan and probably Belger. They were rotten cops. What hold on you is so strong that keeps you silent? Were you part of their theft ring?"

"No, I had no connection to that."

"How about murder?" Fenwick asked. "You got a connection to murder? Why help cover it up?"

"I am not covering up for Belger's murder."

"Shut the fuck up," Boyle said.

"You're covering up for another murder?" Turner asked. "Or do you mean someone else is covering up for Belger's murder?"

Nance turned very pale. Something there, Turner thought.

Turner said, "Your connection to all of Boyle's and Callaghan's and Belger's criminal activity is going to come out. You are going to be hounded. When what you're covering up comes out, you're going to be vilified, arrested, tried, and convicted."

Nance said, "You don't have that kind of power."

Fenwick said, "I'd claim we have the power of truth, but that's almost as funny as what you guys said. I'd go with us blabbing to the press, but you're a master at twisting the truth. I'd go with

Molton being beyond any corruption you can attempt to enmesh him in, but I'd never underestimate your power to taint integrity. But you do not have absolute power, and you have no power over me."

"We can fire your ass," Boyle said.

"No," Fenwick said. "You can't."

Turner asked, "What is the connection with Callaghan and what about him is so worth protecting, covering up, lying, and murdering?"

"I didn't kill anybody," Nance said.

Turner said, "You didn't kill anybody, but you know who did?" Turner saw that the man had sweated through his uniform coat. He was onto something.

Boyle jabbed his finger at Nance. "Don't say anything, you idiot."

Nance ignored him. "What about those two gay guys who complained? They were at the Black and Blue Party. They were into S+M. Why haven't you gone after them?"

Turner said, "We never asked about two gay guys. How do you know about two gay guys and that they were into S+M?"

Boyle said, "Shut up, you fuck." He tried to rise.

Fenwick shoved him back down.

The press spokesman glanced around. Used a napkin to wipe at sweat on his neck. The white paper turned damp gray. Nance said, "Uh, there were lots of gay guys at that party. That's what I meant. Gay guys at the party. That's all."

Turner said, "But a limited number who complained and who were at the party and who you know about. How is that? Why is that?"

"What is your connection to Callaghan and Belger?" Turner asked.

"I don't know them."

"You dumb fuck," Boyle said.

"But you've said enough," Fenwick said. "He needs to remain silent only if he's guilty. If he's innocent, he could tell us everything. He's slipped and you're fucked. That's the way I like things."

Turner said, "Don't you guys get what was going on?"

Boyle looked pissed. Nance looked puzzled.

Turner said, "There was a double conspiracy. Zuyland, the reporter, was out to get the cops who screwed him over. You two and Callaghan were out to get Belger. Each side involved a lot of innocent people in hare-brained schemes. You can't have conspiracies that convoluted and hope to keep them quiet."

Fenwick added, "You could even make it a triple conspiracy if you want to include Armour and Bryner so busy protecting their goddamn party."

Nance said, "What?"

Boyle said, "Bullshit. Zuyland and them couldn't have planned to get cops. They'd never have the nerve. They'd never get away with it."

Fenwick asked, "Callaghan's job going to be here when all is said and done? Not likely. They've got the video. You've got power. Not enough. This time you're not going to win. Not after we get through with you."

Boyle said, "You're bluffing."

Turner took out his cell phone.

Boyle said, "You going to call your boss and tattle on us? That won't do you any good much longer. He'll be out."

Turner said, "Your mistake was involving Scanlan."

"He's dead. He can't testify against anybody."

"Ah me," Turner said. "But videos live on eternally. Once it's in cyberspace, it's out of your control. You've never been to a leather event, have you?" He didn't wait for a response. "Everybody's got a cell phone out. Everybody's got a camera. The booth Belger worked taped everything for their web site.

We've got your buddy Scanlan..."

"He did that on his own," Boyle said.

Turner knew they'd seen Scanlan at the same booth as Belger, but they'd seen no connection. He presumed there had to be. He was certain of it. He said, "He whipped Belger to the point of bleeding. He wasn't strong enough to do it on his own. Somebody was holding Belger. Somebody was planning. Scanlan was part of your conspiracy. You probably planned to kill him anyway, but Armour and Bryner screwed up, and unwittingly helped you. Unintended consequences."

Turner flipped open his phone. He pressed the buttons Fong's assistant had shown him. Scanlan at Belger's booth appeared. Boyle looked and grabbed for it. Turner was too quick. He yanked it out of reach.

Nance said, "They've got tape? They've got tape!"

Turner turned the screen so Nance could see it. "That's Scanlan at the booth." And then he bluffed and took a risk. "We've got more. Much more."

"No," Nance said.

"Shut up," Boyle said.

Fenwick added, "You idiots, Belger was in on it with Zuyland and Preston the bartender and Dinning the recorder from the Raving Dragon. They were all in on it. Zuyland has the goods on Callaghan and Belger and you two. He knows about the stealing you condoned. He's got all of it. He's getting ready to go on the air with it."

"Why didn't he come forward before this?" Boyle asked.

Turner said, "Belger's killing got in the way. He wanted to get Belger and Callaghan equally. He'd gotten Callaghan. He was waiting to turn on Belger. You got him first."

Fenwick said, "While you were conspiring to get Belger, they were conspiring to get you. They gotcha."

"No," Nance said.

"Shut the fuck up," Boyle said.

"No," Fenwick said. "No one is going to shut up. No one is going to keep quiet. It's all coming out. It's all going to be shown on the air. All of it. You've lost."

"No," Nance said.

Boyle shoved at Fenwick and tried to rise.

The door swung open and Molton, followed by detectives from Area Ten, swarmed into the diner. Wilson and Roosevelt had Callaghan in cuffs in between them.

Boyle swore. Nance wept.

FORTY-THREE

Ultimately, it was the quivering Nance who blabbed. Back at Area Ten Callaghan was in one interrogation room, Boyle in another. Nance, who had refused a lawyer, was in Molton's office with Turner and Fenwick.

Turner asked, "Why kill Belger?"

"Not because of what he did in the bar. Who cares about that?"

"The woman he beat?" Fenwick asked.

"In this department? Don't make me laugh. Belger could reveal all he knew about the theft ring. About torture and tasering prisoners. Everything. He had to die before he could ruin the rest of us."

"Who actually killed Belger?"

"Boyle, Lensky, and Vereski held him while Callaghan shoved those things down his throat. I watched. I didn't kill him."

"Why'd they kill him?" Fenwick asked.

"Are you stupid? He was a traitor. And he was going to testify against us. We had to stop him. Boyle and I were beat cops together. I started covering for him and then it escalated. Over the years we involved others. Belger was in on everything." He looked up. "If I name other names, will they go easy on me?"

"How many others?" Fenwick asked.

"A lot."

"The shit is going to hit the fan," Fenwick said.

"How'd he meet Scanlan?" Turner asked.

"The kid saw Belger on the site. He wanted to meet him. Did so. Last year. They met on occasion. One time the kid was doing Belger in the alley behind the Raving Dragon. In the back of their patrol car. Callaghan caught them. He didn't turn Belger in.

He just wanted to share. The kid loved it."

Turner said, "It was right there on the video. Callaghan rubbed the pool cue up and down Belger's ass crack. Belger was into getting his ass played with, but Callaghan was into fucking anything that moved. He and his partner had a relationship?"

Nance said, "I wouldn't call it a relationship. They used each other. I think they were straight. At least, they kept getting married to women."

"They were both doing a kid," Turner said. "They were using their power as cops to ruin him."

"Who knows? Who cares? Maybe he was in love with them. He was a teenager and an asshole. He used them. They used him. The whole fair thing was a bonus."

"That's why Scanlan was so confident and aggressive," Fenwick said.

Turner said, "He lied to us."

"Well, duh," Nance said.

Turner said, "He talked about a guy in a leather hood."

"That was probably Lensky convincing him to do the scene."

Turner said, "Scanlan didn't look real upset that Belger was dead. More surprised."

"Callaghan and Boyle got Lensky to use him to lure Belger to the lower level. You found money on Belger? Hundreds? They got Scanlan to offer Belger money to let him, Scanlan, whip him. Belger would do anything for cash. Scanlan actually thought it was a real scene."

Turner said, "He was sixteen, probably fifteen when he met Belger. Didn't that bother Boyle and his cronies?"

"Belger liked being used. He didn't care who by. And they were planning murder. Do you think they cared about the kid? They used him like they used everybody else. Like they used me."

"You're an adult," Fenwick said.

No prizes for that today, Turner thought.

"I couldn't stop them. The kid left before the killing."

"And that makes what better?" Fenwick asked.

"And the whipping?" Turner asked.

"The goal was to draw blood. The kid started it. He kind of got into it. He seemed pissed at the world. They all got into the whipping. I didn't. It was them. Then later they convinced the kid that he did kill Belger. Then it got on the news how Belger really died. Things moved fast. Boyle and the rest couldn't know what Scanlan would do. When he got arrested, I watched on the two way mirror. He wasn't sad. He kept snarling and sneering. Huge ego mixed with monumental stupidity. He had to die."

"Why'd he get released?"

"That's your whole double conspiracy thing. We thought everything was fine. Then he got released. We couldn't kill him in custody. That would be too suspicious. You guys were hot after all this. We could only get away with so much. Released, he'd be vulnerable. On the other hand, Boyle thought he was invulnerable. I told them the kid was a problem. But remember, the kid didn't actually see the killing. He whipped. He left. The others whipped him, shoved a two-by-four up his butt, killed him."

Turner said, "The ME said something large went up his butt. Where'd you get the two-by-four?"

"The room was run down, half renovated. There was dirt and shit everywhere. Rotting wood, old tools, all kinds of crap." He closed his eyes. "He really squealed when that went up there."

They were all silent a few moments. Nance reopened his eyes. "It all just got out of control. It just got nuts. They all went nuts."

"Did you try to stop them?" Turner asked.

Nance hung his head, whispered, "No."

"It was such a huge conspiracy," Fenwick said. "How did they expect everyone to keep quiet?"

Nance said, "You must take stupid pills. How long have they been robbing the dead? Years. Did you know about it? In all your investigating did you hear the slightest whisper about it?"

"Well, yeah, sort of," Fenwick said.

"But up until then, no. Not a word. They'd kept it to themselves for years. They thought they were invulnerable. They thought they were smarter than everybody else. That was Boyle to a T."

"If Boyle wanted to get rid of Belger, and he knew Belger was having sex with a kid, why didn't he use that?"

"But Belger still knew their secrets. No matter what crime they caught him on, he could turn on them. And because by that time, Callaghan was using the kid, too."

Turner said, "That is sick shit."

"It was out of control," Nance said. "I didn't know about their plan to kill him until just recently. I balked. I didn't want to go along. They made me do it. It was them."

"Why kill Belger and Scanlan at the party?"

"Pretty much what you'd expect. To have people think they died because they were gay or because gay people killed him. To get it blamed on the gay event. To get someone at the party involved or suspected. To divert suspicion."

"Did you tell Billy Dossett, the retired cop who contacted Molton, to try and get information from us?"

"We had to find out information. We reached out. Just like we all do, Boyle has contacts in the department everywhere. He knew Molton trusted Dossett, but even so Molton wasn't stupid and wouldn't tell Dossett anything, and you guys didn't tell him enough."

Fenwick asked, "Did Boyle know Callaghan and Belger had a sexual relationship?"

"I don't know. Boyle did know about Belger being on the website. That was enough for him. He knew he could leverage that against Belger. That kind of information was dangerous for Boyle to have. I think that's when he got the idea to kill Belger. The party happening was kind of a bonus."

"Where did you kill him?"

"I didn't kill him. It was them. It was in one of the speakeasy caverns. There's a secret entrance. It's down there."

"Who planned all this?" Turner asked.

"It was all Boyle. All Boyle."

He repeated the "it was all Boyle" defense ad nauseum.

Near the end, Turner asked, "What was the connection between the three of you? What was so important that kept you together? Why did Boyle protect Callaghan?"

Nance sighed his deepest sigh. He began with, "It was all Boyle. And Callaghan."

"What happened?"

"It started small. That theft ring when Belger and Callaghan were called to death scenes."

Fenwick interrupted him. "The theft is big enough to maybe justify murder, but I'm thinking something deeper. This must go way back. What happened?"

More deep sighs. They'd kept Nance supplied with brown paper towels from the washroom so he could wipe his sweat. He said, "You're right. What really turned their relationship into total criminal hell started years ago. A guy was pissing in an alley outside some bar. Callaghan was on his own. He decided to give the guy a hard time. But the guy got belligerent. Callaghan called for backup. Boyle and I were nearest. When we drove up, we saw Callaghan thumping the guy's head against a wall. He stopped when he saw us."

More sighs. More towels. The sweat poured off him. "I didn't do anything. I just watched. The guy wouldn't go down. Boyle got between him and Callaghan. I thought Boyle was going to put a stop to it, but the guy kept mouthing off and shoving at Boyle. Boyle hit him. Once. Jesus. God. Once. And the guy went down. He didn't move."

Turner asked, "They could cover up a murder?"

"You guys are so stupid. Do you read?" Nance asked. "You saw the series about the so-called cover up connected to the mayor's relative."

"Yeah, we know," Fenwick said.

Nance wiped more sweat and continued. "It's not that hard. This guy was just some out of town drunk. Nobody cared. Nobody got interested because he wasn't related to someone famous and his attacker was listed as unknown. Just a random mugging gone bad."

When they were done and as they were walking back to their desks, Fenwick said, "I feel dirty."

"Coming from you that's saying something about this mess."

"An underage kid?" Fenwick asked.

Turner said, "It's not the first time, gay or straight, that we've seen it. It won't be the last. We can only arrest the ones we catch."

An hour after the interrogations were done, Molton plunked his butt on Fenwick's desk. He asked, "How are you guys surviving?"

Fenwick said, "Just as much goddamn paperwork with this case as any other."

Molton said, "They arrested Vereski and Lensky."

"Good," Fenwick said.

Molton said, "Half the police department is looking for the room Boyle and company murdered Belger in. We'll find it. We'll get evidence from the scene no matter how well they tried to clean it up."

Turner asked, "How's headquarters taking this?"

Molton smiled, "Not well. But you guys solved it, and that means they'll get over it. Great work as always. Congratulations."

Turner gazed at him, "I don't think I feel as triumphant as I should."

Molton gazed at the detective. He said, "I know. It was a tough case. Tough on all of us. We survived this. We always do.

We endure. Maybe that's not enough for a party, but it's enough to feel good about yourself."

"Thanks," Turner said.

During the rest of the morning, arrests flew, paperwork happened, reporters breathlessly reported on television screens. Turner and Fenwick watched Zuyland get his air time. Neither of them felt the need to comment.

Forty-four

That Sunday night Paul Turner was in the living room, beer in one hand and gray boxer-brief clad butt on the couch. He'd slept much of the afternoon, then got up, showered and shaved.

They'd received text messages from both boys. Each reported they were having a great time at their respective camps.

A baseball game was on television. Wearing baggy white athletic shorts, Ben entered carrying another beer. The house was air-conditioned against the continuing brutal heat. Ben sat on the floor between Paul's legs. Paul encased his partners torso with his legs.

Ben used the tips of his fingers to caress the hair on Paul's legs. He said, "The kids are still gone."

"And we're not," Paul said.

Ben said, "I could change into something more leather, more butch."

Paul touched the back of Ben's head with one hand. He rubbed the stubble on his husband's chin with the other. "You're plenty butch enough for me just as you are. Although we could get rid of these." He reached for Ben's shorts.

Mark Zubro is the author of twenty-three mystery novels and five short stories. His book *A Simple Suburban Murder* won the Lambda Literary Award for Best Gay Men's mystery. He also wrote a thriller, *Foolproof*, with two other mystery writers, Jeanne Dams and Barb D'Amato. He taught eighth graders English and reading for thirty-four years. He was president of the teachers' union in his district from 1985 until 2006. He retired from teaching in 2006 and now spends his time reading, writing, napping, and eating chocolate. His newest book, *Black and Blue and Pretty Dead Too*, is his tenth book in the Paul Turner series which features a gay Chicago police detective. One of the keys in Zubro's mysteries is you do not want to be a person who is racist, sexist, homophobic, or a school administrator. If you are any of those, it is likely you are the corpse, or, at the least, it can be fairly well guaranteed that bad things will happen to you by the end. And if in Zubro's books you happen to be a Republican and/or against workers' rights, it would be far better if you did not make a habit of broadcasting this. If you did, you're quite likely to be a suspect, or worse.

Say Aloha to the Islands...
Kimo Style

Print ISBN # 978-1-60820-261-4
eBook ISBN #978-1-60820-262-1

Print ISBN # 978-1-60820-381-9
eBook ISBN #978-1-60820-301-7

Print ISBN # 978-1-60820-371-0
eBook ISBN #978-1-60820-302-4

Print ISBN # 978-1-60820-378-9
eBook ISBN #978-1-60820-379-6

Print ISBN # 978-1-60820-306-2
eBook ISBN #978-1-60820-307-9

Print ISBN # 978-1-60820-129-7
eBook ISBN #978-1-60820-130-3

MLRPress.com

CPSIA information can be obtained at www.ICGtesting.com
Printed in the USA
BVOW020111210212

283397BV00001BA/1/P